# THE AMERICAN STORY:
# THE BEST OF STORYQUARTERLY

# THE AMERICAN STORY

## The Best of StoryQuarterly

### Edited by
### Anne Brashler
### Melissa Pritchard
### Diane Williams

*CANE HILL PRESS*

ISBN No. 0-943433-05-3
LC No. 89-081157
Printed in the United States of America
First Edition

Published by Cane Hill Press
225 Varick Street
New York, NY 10014

Produced at The Print Center, 225 Varick Street,
New York, NY 10014, a non-profit facility for literary and
arts-related publications. (212) 206-8465

Cover: "The Deliverance of K.M., January 7, 1985, #2"
Artist: Melissa E. Weinman
Photography: Gamma One Conversations, Inc.

# CONTENTS

# DEDICATION

There are so many people to thank for their great efforts on behalf of this magazine, but some current thank-yous go to: Margaret Barrett, Jayne de la Huerga, J.D. Dolan, Donald Hoffman, Barbara Nodine, Robert Nelsen, Pamela Painter, and Audrey Reynolds.

We want to give special acknowledgment to the founding editors Tom Bracken, Pamela Painter, and Thalia Selz. We also thank Fran Katz, Janine Warsaw, and Dolores Weinberg for their many years of devoted work.

# THE AMERICAN STORY

## The Best of StoryQuarterly

# Way Down Harry I Go
## Donna Poydinecz

There's an architect on my mouth. And when I rub him I get three wishes. I know the trick. It's this: wish for more wishes. I say, "I wish a million wishes," three times, and way down Harry I go, until I go so far that we come to somewhere else entirely, and yet not so far that we go away in our heads and get alone. We can laugh real loud and we can look at each other in the eyes and on other places on us. There is something else I want you to know: Harry's bare arms in the air always achieve championship.

Enough of that.

Outside the truck I say, "Harry, get in," and he does and I drive until we come to everything all over again. Then Harry gets out and walks (he walks just great) and I stand still and watch this man travel my land, for hours, calm and aroused.

Let me tell you what Harry sees: water views, new-mown hay, millions of trees, trees of dreams, just like the best you see in the pictures, like the ones you hanker to climb. All seed catalogues say, "Buy this young, short tree and you, too, will have a tree that will look like this some day when you are too old to walk, unaided, outside." My trees are high right now, and I know what Harry is thinking. He is thinking, "How nice to have such trees when you are happy and in your thirties."

This man is a real appreciator of outstanding trees.

Harry likes sod. Better yet, Harry likes dirt. When Harry gets me down on the ground, things change forever. He presses my ear against the soil and says, "Calm down, relax, listen."

My God — the things I hear. I am amazed. I am amazed by what I hear and I am amazed because I see that Harry has done this before. Truth is, Harry has never not done this. Holes, how deep to dig them, the characteristics of various strata. Slate, shale, peat, and muck ... he hears it all. Harry belongs on the ground, and my belonging has never felt more huge, and before you can sing "Kentucky Bluestone" we head for the center of the earth and detonate a few hundred acres all over again.

All engine, this architect is. Harry's got an engine so big he can stick his eyes into mine and blast my heart to smithereens and still keep me standing, unscathed and smiling. When he gets that mouth of his on mine (his mouth so athletic there should be a contest) I shove my tongue against his teeth and open them up like a gate on a picket fence and slide down his throat like a wild thing racing along the path through the woods that leads straight to the house of the person it has been waiting to rest alongside of since it was old enough to think about everything all at once for only a moment and not get scared but be amazed. Are you listening? There's a brook there, a woodshed, a garden to sleep in. We are going completely home.

There is a house near no other and it is Harry's. Perhaps you can see it if you listen to me: Have you ever seen such a bed? Have you ever seen such a floor? Have you ever seen such a window, so pleasing and so well-made? Come over here and look at the plates; walk over there and examine the bricks. Watch Harry take a brick in his hand and turn it six ways and tell you, "This is a soldier, this is a sailor. Now watch this ... this is a bull stretcher," and so on. There is a bench and there are ten chairs. Some marble, six barrels, two globes (one lights up), and a horn. A row of boots, over there, forming a line on the floor. An assortment of tools, under stairs, in a pile. A robe, a hat, a length of leather, all on pegs. I say, "Harry, get rid of the robe," and sit down.

4

And Harry stands. Harry stands great. He stands just right. Every time he stands he starts from scratch and does it all over again. He never stands the same way twice. My God — Harry has invented everything. Even standing.

Harry cooks, too. And whenever Harry cooks, I cannot speak. He stands (just great) in his kitchen and says, "Sit here. You're hungry. Let me feed you." I die and stay alive as I watch Harry open up things: doors, jars, wrappers, drawers. I cannot speak. Harry takes one thing, adds it to another, then adds more of many things. Harry knows what he is doing. Then again, maybe he doesn't. It doesn't matter; he is doing it just great.

When he is done he says, "Well, come on, eat." Harry does not ask, "Do you like it?" If he were to ask I would say, "Yes, yes, I truly do." No, I would not say that. I would say, "Harry, I have been a fool. I have been all wrong about food. My God, Harry, you are so smart to have done it this way."

There is nothing quite like being fed well and often by someone you love and who loves you. It is a speechless thing.

Later on, we walk, and we go far. Harry has taught me world-class walking. Time was when I thought a good walk was all in the eyes, all meadows and forests and tender green hills rolling down to the sea. No longer. I will tell you something about Harry's way of walking: it unfills the mind and makes it clean again.

There is one more thing you should know about Harry. You should know that there is one sentence above all others of which Harry is fond, very fond. It is this: "Under all is the land." Under all is the land, indeed.

I say: Harry is the land. Harry is the sky. Harry is every apple tree, every rocking chair on every porch in Georgia, every song sung by mothers with laps to babies in summer under hot stars. Harry is so big the whole world could climb inside of him and sleep forever to the sound of his heart singing.

My God, Harry, aren't you swell!

4/81

# Frog Dances

## Stephen Dixon

He's passing a building in his neighborhood, looks into an apartment window on the second floor and sees a man around his age with a baby in his arms moving around the living room as if dancing to very beautiful music — a slow tragic movement from a Mahler symphony, for instance. The man seems so enraptured that Howard walks on, afraid if the man sees him looking at him his mood will be broken. He might feel self-conscious, embarrassed, leave the room or go over to the window with the baby to lower the shade or maybe even to stare back at Howard. Howard knows it can't always be like this between the man and his baby. That at times the man must slap the wall or curse out loud or something because the baby's screaming is keeping him from sleep or some work he has to do or wants to get done — but *still*. The man looked as happy as any man doing anything with anyone or alone. He wants to see it again. He goes back, looks to see that nobody's watching him, and looks into the window. The man's dancing, eyes closed now, cheek against the baby's head, arms wrapped around the baby. He kisses the baby's eyes and head as he sort of slides across the room. Howard thinks I must have a child. I've got to get married. At my age — even if I have the baby in a year — some people will still think I'm its grandfather. But I want to go through what this man's experiencing, dance with my baby like that. Kiss its head, smell its hair and skin — everything. And when the baby's asleep, dance with my wife or just hold her and kiss her something like that too. Someone to get up close to in bed every night for just about the rest of my life and to talk about the baby, and when it and perhaps its brother or sister are older, when they were babies, and every other thing. So: settled. He'll start on it tomorrow or the day after. He looks up at the window. Man's gone. "Tank you, sir, tank you," and walks to the laundromat he was going to to pick up his dried wash.

Next day he calls the three friends he thinks he can call about this. "Listen, maybe I've made a request something like this before, but this time I not only want to meet a woman and fall in love but I want to get married to her and have a child or two. So, do you know—and if you don't, please keep your ears and eyes open—someone you think very suitable for me and of course me for her too? I mean it. I had an experience last night—seeing a man holding what seemed like a one to three month old baby very close and dancing around with it as if he were in dreamland—and I felt I've been missing out, and in a few years will have completely missed out, on something very important, necessary—you name it—in my life."

A friend calls back a few days later with the name of a woman she knows at work who's also looking to find a mate, fall in love and marry. "She's not about to jump into anything, you know. She's too sensible for that and already did it once with disastrous results, but fortunately no children. Her situation is similar to yours. She's thirty-four and she doesn't want to wait much longer to start a family, which she wants very much. She's extremely bright, attractive, has a good job, makes a lot of money but is willing to give it up or just go freelance for a few years while she has her children. Besides that, she's a wonderful dear person. I think you two can hit it off. I told her about you and she'd like to meet you for coffee. Here's her office and home numbers."

He calls her and she says "Howard *who?*" "Howard Tetch. Freddy Gunn was supposed to have told you about me." "No, he didn't mention you that I can remember. Wait a second. Are you the fellow who saw a man dancing on the street with his baby and decided that you wanted to be that man?" "I didn't think she'd tell you that part, but yes, I am. It was through an apartment window I saw him. I was just walking. Anyway, I'm not much—I'm sure you're not also—for meeting someone blind like this, but Freddy seemed to think we've a lot in common and could have a good conversation. Would you care to meet for coffee one afternoon or night?" "Let's see, Howard. This week I'm tied up both at work and, in the few available non-work hours, in my social life. It just happens to be one of those rare weeks—I'm not putting you on. Or putting you off, is more like it. Would you mind calling me again next week—in the middle, let's say?" "No, sure, I'll call."

He calls the next week and she says "Howard Tetch?" "Yes, I called you last week. Freddy Gunn's friend. You said—" "Oh, right, Howard. It's awful of me—please, I apologize. I don't know how I could have forgotten your name a second time. Believe me, it's the work. Sixty hours, seventy. How are you?" "Fine," he says, "and I was wondering if there was some time this week, or even on the weekend, we could—" "I really couldn't this week or the weekend. What I was doing last week extended into this one, and maybe even worse. Not the socializing, but those sixty-seventy hours a week work. I'm not stringing you along, honestly. But I do have this profession that's very demanding sometimes—" "What is it you do?" "Whatever I do—and I wish I had the time to tell you, but I haven't. We'll talk it over when we meet. So you'll call me? I can easily understand why you wouldn't." "No, sure, next week then. I'll call."

He doesn't call back. A week later another friend calls and says he's giving a dinner party Saturday and "two very lovely and intelligent young women, both single, will be coming and I want you to meet them. Who can say? You might get interested in them both. Then you'll have a problem you wish never started by phoning around for possible brides and mothers for your future kids, right?" "Oh, I don't know," Howard says, "but sounds pretty good so far."

He goes to the party. One of these two women is physically beautiful, all right, but unattractive. Something about the way she's dressed — she's overdressed — and her perfume, makeup, self-important air or something, and she talks too much and too loudly. She also smokes — a lot — and every so often blows smoke on the person she's talking to, and both times she left her extinguished cigarette smoldering. He just knows — so he doesn't even approach her — he could never start seeing or not for too long a woman who smokes so much and so carelessly. The other woman — seems to be her friend — is pretty, has a nice figure, more simply dressed, no makeup or none he can make out, doesn't smoke or isn't smoking here, talks intelligently and has a pleasant voice. He introduces himself, they talk about different things, she tells him she recently got divorced and he says "I'm sorry, that can be very rough." "Just the opposite. We settled it quickly and friendly and since the day I left him I've never felt so free in my life. I love going out, or staying in when I want to, and partying late, meeting lots of people, but being unattached." She has a six-year-old son who lives with his father. "One child, that's all I ever wanted, and now I think even one was too many for me, much as I love him. Since his father wanted to take him, I thought 'Why not?' I see him every other weekend, or every weekend if that's what he wants, but he so far hasn't, and get him for a month in the summer. Lots of people disapprove, but they're not me. Many of them are hypocrites, for they're the same ones who feel so strongly that the husband — so why not the ex-husband who's the father of your child? — should take a much larger if not an equal role in the partnership. Well, it's still a partnership where our son's concerned, or at least till he's eighteen or twenty-one, isn't it? Do you disapprove too?" He says "No, if it works for you all and it's what you want and no one's hurt. Sure. Of course, there's got to be some sadness or remorse in a divorce where there's a child involved," and she says "Wrong again, with us. Two parents were just too confusing for Riner. He thinks it's great having only one at a time to answer to, and another to fall back on just in case."

He takes her phone number, calls, they have dinner, he sees

her to her apartment house after, shakes her hand in the lobby and says he'll call again if she doesn't mind, "for it was a nice evening: lively conversation, some laughs, many of them, in fact, and we seem to have several similar interests," and she says "So come on up. Even stay if you want; you don't seem like a masher." They go to bed and in the morning over coffee she says "I want to tell you something. I like you but don't want you getting any ideas about my being your one-and-only from now on. You should know from the start that I'm seeing several men, sleeping with three of them — they're all clean and straight, so don't worry. And you can be number four if you want, but I'm not for a long time getting seriously connected to anyone. You don't like the arrangement — no problem: here's my cheek to kiss and there's the door." He says he doesn't mind the arrangement for now, kisses her lips just before he leaves, but doesn't call again.

He sees a woman on the movie line waiting to go in. He's alone and she seems to be too. She's reading quite quickly a novel he liked a lot and never looks up from it at the people in front and behind her, at least while he's looking at her. Attractive, intelligent looking, he likes the casual way she's dressed, way her hair is, everything. He intentionally finds a seat two rows behind hers, watches her a lot and she never speaks to the person on either side of her. On the way out he does something he hasn't done in about twenty years. He gets alongside her and says "Pardon me, Miss, but did you like the movie?" She smiles and says "It was a big disappointment, and you?" "Didn't care for it much either. Listen, this is difficult to do — introducing myself to a woman I've never met — like this, I mean, and something I haven't done in God knows how many years. But would you — my name is Howard Tetch — like to have a cup of coffee someplace or a beer and talk about the movie? That book too — I read it and saw you reading. If you don't, then please, I'm sorry for stopping you — I already think you're going to say no, and why shouldn't you?" "No, let's have coffee, but for me, tea." "Tea, yes, much healthier for you — that's what

I'll have too."

They have tea, talk—the book, movie, difficulties of introducing yourself to strangers you want to meet, something she's wanted to do with a number of men—"I can admit it,"—but never had the courage for it. He sees her to a taxi, next day calls her at work, they meet for tea, meet again for lunch, another time for a movie, go to bed, soon he's at her place more than his own. She's thirty-three and also wants to get married and have a child, probably two. "With the right person, of course. That'll take, once I meet him, about six months to find out. Then once it's decided, I'd like to get married no more than a month after that, or at least begin trying to conceive." The more time he spends at her place, the bossier and pettier she gets with him. She doesn't like him hanging the underpants he washes on the shower curtain rod. He says "What about if I hang them on a hanger over the tub?" but she doesn't like that either. "It looks shabby, like something in a squalid boardinghouse. Put them in the dryer with the rest of our clothes." "The elastic waistband stretches. So does the crotch part to where after a few dryer dryings you can see my balls. That's why I hand-wash them and hang them up like that." Problem's never resolved. He wrings his underpants out and hangs them on a hanger, with a few newspaper sheets underneath, in the foot of closet space she's set aside for her clothes. A couple of times when he does this she says the drops from the hanging underpants might go through the paper and ruin the closet floor. He puts more newspapers down and that seems to assuage her. She thinks he should shave before he gets into bed, not when he rises. He says "But I've always shaved, maybe since I started shaving my entire face, in the morning. That's what I do." "Well try changing your habits a little. You're scratchy. It hurts our lovemaking. My skin's fair, much smoother than yours, and your face against it at night is an irritant." "An irritant?" "It irritates my face, all right?" "Then we'll make love in the morning after I shave." "We can do that too," she says, "but like most couples, most of our lovemaking is at night. Also, while I'm on the subject, I wish you wouldn't get back into bed after you exercise in the morning. Your armpits smell. You sweat up the bed. If you don't want to shower after, wash your arms down with a wet washrag. Your back and chest too." "I only exercise those early times in the morning when I can't sleep anymore, or am having trouble sleeping. So I feel, long as I'm up, I should either read or do something I'm going to do later in the day anyway, like exercising. But from now on I'll do as you say with the washrag whenever I do exercise very early and then, maybe because the exercising's relaxed or tired me, get back into bed." She also thinks he hogs too much of the covers; he should try keeping his legs straight in front of him in bed rather than laying them diagonally across her side; he could perhaps shampoo more often—"Your hair gets to the sticky level sometimes." And is that old thin belt really right for when he dresses up? "If anything, maybe you can redye it." And does he have to wear jeans with a hole in the knee, even if it is only to go to the corner store? "What about you?" he finally says. "You read the *Times* in bed before we make love at night or just go to sleep, and then don't wash the newsprint off your hands. That gets on me. Probably also gets on the sheets and pillowcases, but of course only on your side of the bed, and your sheets and pillowcases, so why should I be griping, right? And your blouses. I'm not the only one who sweats. And after you have into one of yours— Okay, you had a tough day at work and probably on the crowded subway to and from work and your body's reacted to it—that's natural. But you hang these blouses back up in the closet. On your side, that's fine with me, and I'm not saying the smell gets on my clothes. But it isn't exactly a great experience to get hit with it when I go into the closet for something. Anyway, I'm just saying." They complain like this some more, begin to quarrel, have a couple of fights where they don't speak to each other for an hour, a day, and soon agree they're not right for each other any more and should break up. When he's packing his things to take back to his apartment, she says "I'm obviously not ready to be with only one man as much as I thought. I'm certainly not ready for marriage yet. As to having a child—to perhaps have *two*? I should really get my head looked over to have thought of that." "Well, I'm still ready," he says, "though maybe all this time I've been mistaken there too."

He meets a woman at an opening at an art gallery. They both were invited by the artist. She says she's heard about him from the artist. "Nothing much. Just that you're not a madman, drunk, drug addict or lech like most of the men he knows." He says "Gary, for some odd reason I don't know why, never mentioned you. Maybe because he's seeing you. Is he?" "What are you talking about? He's gay." "Oh. He's only my colleague at school, so I don't know him that well. I know he's divorced and has three kids, but that's about it. May I be stupidly frank or just stupid and say I hope you're not that way too? Wouldn't mean I'd want to stop talking to you." "I can appreciate why you're asking that now. No, as mates, men are what I like exclusively. I didn't come here to meet one, but I've been in a receptive frame of mind for the last few months if something happens along." They separate at the drink table, eye each other a lot the next fifteen minutes, she waves for him to come over. "I have to go," she says. "The friend I came with has had her fill of this, and she's staying with me tonight. If you want to talk some more, I can call you tomorrow. You in the book?" "Hell, here's my number and best times to reach me," and he writes all this out and gives it to her.

She calls, they meet for a walk, have dinner the next night, she takes his hand as they leave the restaurant, kisses him outside, initiates a much deeper kiss along the street, he says "Lookit, why don't we go to my apartment—it's only a few blocks from here?" She says "Let's give it more time. I've had a lot of rushing from men lately. I'm not boasting, and I started some of it myself. It's simply that I know too fast from either of us is no good, so what do you say?" They see each other about three times a week for two weeks. At the end of that time he says he wants to stay at her place that night or have her to his, "but you know, for bed." She says "I still think it'd be rushing.

Let's just give the main number some more time?" Two weeks later he says "Listen, I've got to sleep with you. All this heavy petting is killing me. I've got to see you completely naked, be inside you—the works. We've given it plenty of time. We like each other very much. But I need to sleep with you to really be in love with you. That's how I am." She says "I don't know what's wrong. I like you in every way. I'm almost as frustrated as you are over it. But something in me says that having sex with you now still wouldn't be sensible. That we're not ready for it yet. That what we have, in the long run, would be much better—could even end up in whatever we want from it. Living together. More, if that's what we ultimately want—if we just hold out on this a while longer. It's partly an experiment on my part, coming after all my past involvement failures, but also partly what I most deeply feel will work, and so feel you have to respect that. So let's give it a little more time then, please?" He says "No. Call me if you not only want to see me again but want us to have sex together. From now on it has to be both. Not all the time, of course. But at least the next time if there's nothing—you know—physically, like a bad cold, wrong with one of us. I hate making conditions—it can't help the relationship—but feel I have to. If I saw you in one of our apartments alone again I think I'd tear your clothes off and jump on you no matter how hard and convincingly you said no. It's awful, but there it is." She says "Let me think about it. Either way, I'll call."

She calls the next week and says "I think we better stop seeing each other. Even if I don't believe you would, what you said about tearing off my clothes scared me." "That's not it," he says. "I don't know what it is, but that's not it. Okay. Goodbye."

He misses her, wants to call her, resume things on her terms, dials her number two nights in a row but both times hangs up after the first ring.

He's invited to give a lecture at a university out of town. His other duty that day is to read the manuscripts of ten students and see them in an office for fifteen minutes each to discuss their work. The man who invited him is a friend from years ago. He says "What'd you think of the papers I sent you? All pretty good, but one exceptional. Flora's, right? She thinks and writes like someone who picked up a couple of postdoctorates in three years and then went on to five years of serious journalism. Easy style, terrific insights, nothing left unturned, everything right and tight, sees things her teachers don't and registers these ideas better than most of them. She intimidates half the department, I'm telling you. They'd rather not have her in their classes, except to look at her. That's because she's brilliant. I can actually say that about two of my students in fourteen years and the other's now dean of a classy law school. But hear me, Howard. Keep your mitts off her. That doesn't mean mine are on her or want to be. Oh, she's a honey, all right, and I've fantasized about her for sure. But I don't want anyone I'm inviting for good money messing with her and possibly messing up her head and the teaching career I've planned for her. Let some pimpleface do the messing; she'll get over it sooner. I want her to get out of here with top grades and great GREs and without being screwed over and made crestfallen for the rest of the semester by some visiting horn. Any of the other girls you'll be conferencing you can have and all at once if they so desire." "Listen, they all have to be way too young for me and aren't what I've been interested in for a long time, so stop fretting."

He sees two students. Flora's next on the list. He opens the office door and says to some students sitting on the floor against the corridor wall "One of you Ms. Selenika?" She raises her hand, stands, was writing in a pad furiously, has glasses, gold ear studs, medium-length blond hair, quite frizzy, little backpack, clear frames, tall, rustically dressed, pens in both breast pockets, what seem like dancer's legs, posture, neck. "Come in." They shake hands, sit, he says "I guess we should get right to your paper. Of course, what else is there? I mean, I'm always interested in where students come from. Their native areas, countries, previous education, what they plan to do after graduation. You know, backgrounds and stuff; even what their parents

18

do. That can be very interesting. One student's father was police commissioner of New York. Probably the best one we had there in years. Another's mother was Mildred Kraigman. A comedian, now she's a character actress. Won an Academy Award? Well, she was once well known and you still see her name around, often for good causes. But those are my students where I teach. When I've time to digress, which I haven't with every student here. You all probably don't mind the fifteen minutes with me, but that's it. So, your paper. I don't know why I went into all of that, do you?" She shakes her head, holds back a giggle. "Funny, right? But you can see how it's possible for me to run on with my students. As for your paper, I've nothing but admiration for it. I'm not usually that reserved or so totally complimentary, but here, well—no corrections. Not even grammatical or punctuational ones. Even the dashes are typed right and everything's before or after the quote marks where it belongs. Honestly, nothing to nitpick, even. I just wish I had had your astuteness—facility—you know, to create such clear succinct premises and then to get right into it and with such writing and literary know-how and ease; had had your skills, intelligence and instincts when I was your age, I mean. Would have saved a lot of catching-up later on. Sure, we could go on for an hour about what you proposed in this and how you supported what you claimed, and so on. Let me just say that when I come across a student like you I just say 'Hands off; you're doing great without me so continue doing what you are on your own. If I see mistakes or anything I can add or direct you to, to possibly improve your work, I'll let you know.' And with someone like you I also say, which isn't so typical for me, 'If you see something you want to suggest about my work, or correct: be my guest.' In other words, I can only give you encouragement and treat you as my thinking equal and say 'More, more.' But your paper's perfect for what it is, which is a lot, and enlightened me on the subject enormously. But a subject which, if I didn't know anything about it before, I'd be very grateful to you after I read it for opening me up to it. You made it inter-

19

esting and intriguing. What better way, right? Enough, I've said too much, not that I think compliments would turn you."

He looks away. She says something but he doesn't catch it. Something like "I'm no different than anyone else." He actually feels his heart pounding, mouth's parched, fingers feel funny. Looks at her. She's looking at him so seriously, fist holding up her chin, trying to make him out? Thinks he's being too obvious? "I'm sorry, you said something just now?" he says. "Oh nothing. Silly. Commonplace. I also tend to mumble." "But what?" "That I can be turned too, that's all." Smiles, big beautiful bright teeth, cute nose. Button pinned to her jacket, children in flames, caption in Chinese or Japanese. Or Korean or Vietnamese. What does he know? And turned how? That an oblique invitation? He once read a novel where the literature teacher took his student on the office floor. She willingly participated. In fact, she might have come to his office to make love. It was their first time. The teacher was married. He always thought that scene exaggerated—the author usually exaggerated or got sloppy when he wrote about sex—but the feeling the narrator had is the same he has now. Her brains, looks, body, little knapsack. He'd love right now to hold her, kiss her, undress her right here—hell with his friend. Hell with the rest of the students. They'd do it quickly. She'd understand. Even if it was their first time. He doubts it'd take him two minutes. Another minute for them both to undress. He bets she likes that kind of spontaneity. "I have got to make love to you," he could whisper. "Let's do it right now." He'd lock the door if it has a lock from the inside—he looks. Hasn't and he doesn't have the key. Now this would be something: opening the door then push the lock-button with all those students in the hall waiting for him. Instead he could put a chair up against the doorknob. They'd be quiet; to save time, just take their pants and shoes off and make love on the floor. Carpet seems clean. He could put his coat down. He wonders what such a young strong body like that looks and feels like. He looks at her, tries to imagine her naked. She says "Thanks for reading my paper and everything, but now I must be wasting your time. It's a rigorous day for you: all those conferences and papers to read and your lecture later on." "You're not wasting it." She opens the door. "Oh, maybe you won't go for this, but another student and I — my housemate — would like to invite you to a student reading after dinner." "Listen, maybe I can even take you both to dinner before the reading." "You're eating at the club with Dr. Wiggens, aren't you?" "Right; that's a must. Sure, tell me where to be and when. I haven't been to a good student reading in years." "This might not be good." "Even more fun. I like to see what goes on at different campuses. And after it, you'll be my guests for food and beer." "If he wants to and we're up to it, fine."

She sits at the back of his room during the lecture, laughs at all the right lines, claps hard but doesn't come up after.

"So how'd everything go today?" Wiggens asks at dinner. "Great bunch of kids," Howard says. "Incredibly keen and bright. Wish I had some like them in my own classes." "None of the girls made a pass at you?" his wife says. "Nah, I let them know I don't come easy." Wiggens says "That's the best approach. Why get all messy in a day and possibly go home a father-to-be with a social disease?" "What nonsense," she says. "One-night stands with students is the safest sport in town." They drop him off at his hotel, he goes inside the lobby, waits till their car leaves the driveway and runs to the building of the reading. He's already pretty tight. He sleeps through most of the stories and poems and the three of them go to a pizza place later. The housemate downs a beer, puts on his coat and says to Flora, "Maybe I'll see you home." "Why'd he think you might not be home?" Howard says. "He meant for himself. He has a lover who occasionally kicks him out before dawn." They finish off the pitcher, have two brandies each, he says "This is not what I'm supposed to be doing here according to Wiggens, so don't let on to him, but may I invite you back to my room?" She says "I'm really too high to drive myself home and you're too high to drive me, so I guess I'll stay the night if you don't mind. You have twin beds?" "Sure, for twins. — No, okay," when she

shakes her head that his humor's bad, "anything you want."
When she takes off her clothes in his room he says "My good-
ness, your breasts. I had no idea they were so large. Why'd I
think that?" "It's the way I dress. I'm extremely self-conscious
about them. They've been a nuisance in every possible way."
"I love large breasts." "Please, no more about them or I'm going to bed in my clothes." They shut off the lights. He's almost
too drunk to do anything. In the morning he doesn't know if
they even did anything. He says he wants to stay another night.
"At my expense, in this same or a different hotel if you can't
or don't want to put me up in your house. Take you to lunch
and dinner and even a movie and where we'll start all over and
do the whole thing right. The heck with Wiggens and his
proscriptions." She says "My vagina hurts from last night. You
were too rough. I couldn't do it again for a day." "So we did
something? I was afraid I just passed out." "To be honest," she
says, "it was horrendous. Never again when I and the guy I'm
with are that stoned." "It'll be better. I can actually stay for two
more nights, get some work done in your school library simply
to keep busy and out of your hair all day, and we'll both stay
relatively sober throughout." "No, it isn't a good idea. Where's
it going to land us?" "Why, that you're way out here and I'm
in New York. I'll fly out once a month for a few days." "Once
a month." "Twice a month then. Every other week. And the
entire spring break. Or you can fly to New York. I'll pay your
fare each time. And in the summer, a long vacation together.
Rent a house on some coast. A trip to Europe if that's what
you want. I don't make that much, but I can come up with
it." "Let's talk about it again after you get to New York, but
you go this afternoon as scheduled."

He calls from New York and she says "No, everything's too
split apart. Not only where we live but the age and cultural
differences. You're as nice as they come—sweet, smart and
silly—but what you want for us is unattainable." "Think about
it some more." He calls again and she says he got her at a bad
moment. He writes twice and she doesn't answer. He calls again

and her housemate, after checking with her, says she doesn't want to come to the phone. Howard says "So that's it then. Tell her."

He's invited to a picnic in Riverside Park for about twelve people. He doesn't want to go but the friend who's arranged it says "Come on, get out of the house already, you're becoming a hopeless old recluse." He meets a woman at the picnic. They both brought potato salad. "It wasn't supposed to happen like this," he says. "I was told to bring the cole slaw. But I didn't want to make the trip to the store just to buy cabbage, had a whole bag of potatoes around, so I made this salad. Anyway, yours is much better. You can see by what people have done to our respective bowls." "They're virtually identical," Denise says. "Eggs, celery, sweet pickles, fresh dill, store-bought mayonnaise, maybe mustard in both of them, and our potatoes cooked to the same softness, but I used salt." She gives him her phone number and says she hopes he'll call. He says "I wouldn't have asked for it if I didn't intend to. Truly."

He was attracted to her at the picnic but after it he thinks she was too eager for him to call. Well, that could be good—that she wants him to call, is available—but there were some things about her looks he didn't especially like. More he thinks of them, less he likes them. Nice face, wasn't that. But she seemed wider in the hips, larger in the nose, than he likes. Were her teeth good? Something, but nothing he can remember seeing, tells him they weren't. She was friendly, intelligent, no airs, good sense of humor. But if she's wide in the hips now, she's going to get wider older she gets. And noses, he's heard, and can tell from his own, grow longer with age. Everything else though . . .

He doesn't call her that week. On the weekend he bumps into a friend on the street who's walking with a very pretty woman. She can't be his girlfriend. The friend's married, much in love with his wife. And he has two young sons he dotes on and he'd never do anything that could lead to his being separated from them, but then you never know. Howard and the woman are introduced, she has a nice voice, unusually beautiful skin, and the three of them talk for a while. Her smile to him when they shake hands goodbye seems to suggest she wouldn't mind him contacting her. He calls his friend the next day and says "This woman you were with — Francine. If she's not married or anything like that, what do you think of my calling her?" "Fine, if you like. She's a great person, stunning looking as you saw, cultured, unattached — what else? One hell of a capable lawyer." "Why didn't you tell me about her before?" "You mean you're still searching for that ideal lifemate? I thought you gave that up." "No, I'm still looking, though maybe not as hard as I did. Went out with several women — a couple you even met. Nearly moved in with one, but nothing materialized beyond that with any of them, which has sort of discouraged me a little. But if I haven't found someone marriageable after a year, that's okay too, right? I've still plenty of time." "Then call Francine. She's been divorced for two years, no children, and from what she's let on in certain unguarded moments, I think she's seriously shopping around for a new lifemate herself." "What do you mean 'unguarded'? Is she very secretive, uncommunicative, cool or distant — like that?" "Hardly. Just that some things about herself she keeps inside."

Howard calls her. They make a date to go out for beers. He feels she's not right for him the moment she opens her apartment door. Something overdone in the way she's dressed for just beers at a local place. Also her apartment, which is practically garish. The books on the shelves say she isn't much of a serious reader, and same with the music on the radio, records on the shelf, prints on the walls. During their walk to the bar and then in the bar he finds she's interested in a lot of things he isn't: money matters, big-time professional advancement, exercise classes, gossip about famous people, the trendy new restaurants, art exhibitions, movies, shows. They walk back to her building. She asks if he'd like to come up for a drink or tea. "No thanks, I've still plenty of work to do for tomorrow, but thank you." "If you'd like to phone me again, please do."

24

"No, really, I don't think it would work out, but thanks for suggesting it. It's been a nice evening." "Actually, I doubt it has been for you, nor in many ways for me either. We're a bit different, that's easy to see, but I thought after a few times together we'd find much in common. Something told me that. What do you think?" "I don't think so, honestly. It's all right to say that, isn't it?" "I suppose, but it's probably not something we should go too deeply into," and she goes inside. He's walking uptown to his apartment when he sees a pay phone. Call Denise, he thinks. It's been two weeks since he said he would. He'll give a good excuse if he feels from what she says that he ought to. That he's been so steeped in his work that he didn't want to call till now just to say he'd be calling again to go out with her once he's done with this work. Or that he simply lost track of time with all the work he's been doing and also some personal things which are now over. He puts the coin in, thinks no, don't start anything, she isn't right for him. Her looks. The teeth. Something. Plump. Not plump but wider in the hips and he thinks heavier in the thighs than he likes, and her nose. And so sweet. Almost too damn too—even meek. He doesn't like meek and overly sweet women either who let the man do most of the speaking and decision-making and so on. That's not what he wants. He wants something else. So he won't call her. He continues walking, passes another pay phone. Why not call her? Because he's a little afraid to. Already his stomach's getting butterflies. What would he say? Well, he'd say "Hello, it's Howard Tetch, and I know it's a bit presumptuous thinking you'd agree to this at the spur of something or another, but . . ." "But" what? Have a drink first. He goes into a bar, has a martini. After he drinks it he feels relaxed. One more. Then he should go home and, if he still wants to, call her tomorrow. He has another. Two, he tells himself, is his limit. Three and he's had it, not good for anything but sleep. But he doesn't want to be on the street with three. When he gets off the stool he feels high. He feels sexy when he gets to the street. He wants to have sex with someone tonight. He hasn't had sex with anyone since Flora and

25

that was around three months ago and what does he remember of it? Her large breasts, that's all, which was before they had sex. He thinks of the man in the window holding the baby. The baby must be a month or two past a year old. It was April, right after his mother's birthday, so it was almost twelve months ago. Today or some day this or last week might be the baby's first birthday. The man might still be dancing with it at night, but by now the baby's probably saying words. "Hi. Bye." The man might have slept with his wife three-hundred-fifty times since that night, made love with her about a hundred-fifty times. That would be about the number of times Howard thinks he'd make love to his wife in that time. But there is that period, maybe a month or two after the birth, maybe longer for some women if it was a particularly difficult delivery—a Caesarean, for instance—when you don't have sex, or not where the man penetrates her. So, a hundred, hundred twenty-five. The woman he ends up with will have to be receptive to sex. As much as he, in her own way, or almost. If more so, fine. And sometimes do it when he wants to and she doesn't especially. That isn't so bad. It isn't that difficult for a woman to sort of loan her body like that, turn over on her side with her back to him and let him do it without even any movement on her part, and he'll do as much for her if it comes to it. And if the baby was a month or two old when he saw it in the window, then the man and his wife might have just around that time started to make love again, and even, for the first time in months, that night. Call her. He goes through his wallet, thought the slip with her number on it was inside, can't find it, dials Information, dials the number he gets and she says hello. "Hello, it's Howard Tetch, from that picnic in the park, how are you?" and she says "I'm all right, and you?" "Fine, just fine. Thank you. Listen, I called—well, I wanted to long before this but something always came up —to suggest we get together tonight. But I now realize it's much too late to. I'm sorry. This is an awful way to call after two weeks, but tomorrow?" "Tomorrow?" "Yes, would it be possible for us to meet sometime tomorrow or any day soon

as we can? Evening? Late afternoon for a cup of something?"
"Excuse me, Howard. This certainly isn't what I wanted to speak
about first thing after enjoying your company at the picnic, but
am I wrong in assuming you've had a bit to drink tonight which
is influencing your speech and perhaps what you have to say?"
"No, you're right, I have, and right in saying it to me. I shouldn't
have called like this. But I was somewhat anxious about calling
you, and just in calling any woman for the first time I'm not
that . . . I get nervous, that's all. It's always awkward for me,
no matter how anxious I was in wanting to call you. So I thought
I needed a drink to brace me, you can say, and had two, at
a bar just now, but martinis. I'm calling from the street, by the
way." "I can hear." "What I meant by that is I have a home
phone but was on the street, saw a phone, wanted to call, so
called. Anyway, two martinis never hit me like this before. Never
drink three martinis and think you'll have your head also, I always say. What am I saying I always say it? I'm saying it now,
but probably have thought of it before. But I also had a drink
at my apartment before I went out, so it was accumulative.
Wine, gin. I'm not a problem drinker though." "I didn't say
or think you were." "Little here, there, but only rarely in intoxicating quantities. Just that I didn't want that to be the reason
you might not want us to meet." "All right. Call tomorrow if
you still want to. Around six. We'll take it from there, okay?"
"Yes." "Good. Goodnight."

He calls, they meet, have coffee, take a long walk after, the
conversation never lulls, lots of things in common, no forced
talk, good give and take, mutual interests, laughs, they touch
upon serious subjects. Her teeth are fine. Her whole body.
Everything's fine. Profile, full face. Some bumps, bulges, but
what was he going on so about her hips and nose and so on?
Scaring himself away maybe. They're right, all part of her, fit
in just fine. She's also very intelligent, not meek, weak, just very
peaceful, thoughtful, subdued, seemingly content with her life
for the most part. They take the same bus home, he gets off
first and says he'll call her soon, she says "That'll be nice," waves

to him from the bus as it passes. He doesn't call her the next week. First he thinks give it a day or two before you call; see what you think. Then: this could get serious and something tells him she's still not exactly right for him. She's a serious person and would never have anything to do with him in any other way and maybe playing-around is what he really wants right now. She might even be too intelligent for him, needing someone with larger ideas, deeper thoughts, better or differently read, a cleverer quicker way about him, smooth-spoken; she'd tire of him quickly.

He calls a woman he used to go out with but was never serious about more than a year ago and she says "Hello, Howard, what is it?" "Oops, doesn't sound good. Maybe I called at a wrong time." "Simply that you called is a surprise. How is everything?" "Thank you. Everything's fine. I thought you might want to get together. Been a while. What are you doing now, for instance?" "You're horny." "No I'm not." "You only used to call when you were horny. Call me when you're feeling like a normal human being. When you want to have dinner out, talk over whatever there's to talk over, but not to go to bed. I'm seeing someone. Even if I weren't. I could never again be around for you only when you have your hot pants on." "Of course. I didn't know you thought I was doing that. But I understand, will do as you say." The phone talk makes him horny. He goes out to buy a magazine with photos of nude women in it. He buys the raunchiest magazine he could find just from the cover photo and what the cover says is inside, sticks it under his arm inside his jacket, dumps it in a trash can a block away. He really doesn't like those magazines. Also something about having them in his apartment, and why not do something different with the rutty feeling he's got. A whorehouse. He buys a weekly at another newsstand that has articles on sex, graphic photos of couples, and in the back a couple of pages where they rate whorehouses, singles bars, porno flicks, peep shows and sex shops in the city. He goes home to read it. There's one on East 54th that sounds all right. "Knockout gals, free drink, private showers, classy &

tip-top." He goes outside and waits at a bus stop for a bus to take him to West 57th, where he'll catch the crosstown. He has enough cash on him even if they charge a little more than the fifty dollars the weekly said they did, plus another ten for a tip. He wants to do it that much. He gets off at 65th—butterflies again—will walk the rest of the way while he thinks if what he's doing is so smart. The woman could have a disease. One can always get rid of it with drugs. But some last longer than that. You have to experiment with several drugs before one works. And suppose there's one that can't be cured with drugs or not for years? No, those places—the expensive ones—are clean. They have to be or they'd lose their clients. He keeps walking to the house. Stops at a bar for a martini just to get back the sex feeling he had, has two, heads for the house again feeling good. No, this is ridiculous. His whoring days are over. They have been for about ten years. He'd feel embarrassed walking in and out of one; just saying what he's there for to the person at the front desk, if that's what they have, and then making small talk or no talk with the women inside, if they just sit around waiting for the men to choose them—even looking at the other men in the room would be embarrassing—and then with the woman he chooses. "What do you like, Howard?" or whatever name he gives. Howard. Why not? No last one. "You want me to do this or that or both or maybe you want to try something different?" It just isn't right besides. He still wants very much to have sex tonight—with a stranger, even—but not to pay for it. A singles bar? What are the chances? For him, nil, or near to it. He doesn't feel he has it in him anymore to approach women there or really anywhere. To even walk into one and find a free place at the bar would be difficult for him. Maybe Denise would see him this late. Try. If she doesn't want him up, she'll say so quickly enough. Or just say to her "You think it's too late to meet for a beer?" If she says something like "It's too late for me to go outside, why don't you come here," then he'll know she wants to have sex with him. She wouldn't have him up this late for any other reason. And if he comes up at this hour, she'll know what he's coming up for. If she can meet at a bar, then fine, he'll start his approach from there. Suppose she gets angry at him for calling so late and being so obvious in what he wants of her, especially after he said a week ago he'd call her soon? Then that's it with her then, since he doesn't feel there'll be anything very deep between them, so what he's really after is just sex. But don't call from a pay phone on the street. She might think he always walks the streets at night and get turned off by that.

He goes into a bar, buys a beer, tells himself to speak slowly and conscientiously and watch out for slurs and repeats, dials her number from a pay phone there. She says "Hello," doesn't seem tired, he says "It's Howard, how are you, I hope I'm not calling too late." "It's not that it's too late for me to receive a call, Howard, just that of the three to four calls from you so far, most have come this late. Makes me think . . . what? That your calls are mostly last-minute thoughts, emanating from some form of desperation perhaps. It doesn't make me feel good." "But they're not. And I'm sorry. I get impulsive sometimes. Not this time. You were on my mind — have been for days — and I thought about calling you tonight, then thought if it was getting too late to call you, but probably thought about it too long. Then, a little while before, thought 'Hell, call her, and I'll explain.' So some impulsiveness there after all." "All right. We have that down. So?" "So?" "So, you know, what is the reason you called?" "I wanted to know if you might like to meet at the Breakers for a drink, or maybe it's too late tonight for that too." "It probably is. Let me check the time. I don't have to. I know already. Way too late. If you want, why not come here?" "That's what I'd like much better, really. You mean now don't you?" "Not two hours from now, if you can help it." "Right. Is there anything I can pick up for you before I get there?" "Like what?" "Wine, beer? Anything you need? Milk?" "Just come, but without stopping for a drink along the way." "I already have. But so you won't get the wrong idea, it was because my phone wasn't working at home. Just tonight, which was a big surprise when I finally picked up the receiver to call you. So I went out to call from a public phone. But I didn't want to call from the street. Too noisy, and I also didn't want to give you the wrong idea that I'm always calling from the street. So I went into this bar I'm in to call but felt I should buy a beer from them first, even if I didn't drink it — though I did — rather than coming in only to use their phone. That's the way I am. I put all kinds of things in front of me." "Does seem so. Anyway, here's my address," and gives it and what street to get off if he takes the bus. "If you take the Broadway subway, get off at a hundred-sixteenth and ride the front of the train, but not the first car, so you'll be right by the stairs. The subways, or at least that station at this hour, can be dangerous, so maybe to be safer you should take the bus or a cab." "A cab. That's what I'll do." "Good. See you."

He subways to her station, runs to her building. If she asks, he'll say he took a cab. They say hello, he takes off his jacket, she holds out her hand for it, probably to put it in what must be the coat closet right there. He hands her it and says "I took the subway, by the way. Should have taken a cab, but I guess I'm still a little tight with money. I'm saving, from when I wasn't making much for years. I don't know why I mentioned that. It was a fast ride though — good connections — and I'm still pant-ing somewhat from running down the hill to your building," has moved closer to her, she says "I didn't notice — you ran down the hill here?" he bends his head down, she raises hers and they kiss. They kiss again and when they separate she says "Your jacket — excuse me. It's on the floor." "Don't bother with it." "Don't be silly — it's a jacket," and picks it up, brushes it off and hangs it in the closet. He comes behind her while she's separat-ing some of the coats, jackets and garment bags hanging in the closet, turns her around by her shoulders and they kiss. She says "Like a nightcap of some sort — tea?" "Really, nothing, thank you." "Then I don't know, I'm enjoying this but we should at least get out of this cramped utilitarian area. The next room. Or maybe, if we want, we should just go to bed." "Sure, if it's

all right with you." "I'll have to wash up first." "Same here."
"And I wouldn't mind, so long as you'd come with me, walking
my dog." "You've a dog?" "It'll be quick, and I won't have to
do it early in the morning?"

They walk the dog, make love. They see each other almost
every day for the next few weeks. Museums, movies, an opera,
eat out or she cooks for them in her apartment or he cooks
for them in his, a party given by friends of hers. They're walking
around the food table there putting food on their plates when
he says "I love you, you know that, right?" and she says "Me
too, to you." "You do? Great." That night he dreams he's being
carried high up in the sky by several party balloons, says "Good
Christ, before this was fun, but now they better hold," wakes
up, feels for her, holds her thigh and says to himself "This is
it, I don't want to lose her, she's the best yet, or ever. Incredible
that it really happened. Well, it could still go bust." He takes
her to meet his mother, has dinner at her parents' apartment.
He sublets his apartment, moves in with her. He can't get used
to the dog. Walking it, cleaning up after it, it smells, hair on
the couch and his clothes, the sudden loud barks which startle
him, the dog licking his own erection, and tells her that as much
as he knows she loves the dog, the city's really no place for it.
She says "Bobby came with me and with me he stays. Sweet-
heart, think of it as a package deal and that Bobby's already
pretty old." When his lease expires he gives up his apartment
to the couple he sublet it to. He begins insisting to Denise that
Bobby's long hair makes him sneeze and gives him shortness
of breath, which is keeping him up lots of nights, and that the
apartment's much too crowded with him. "If we ever have the
baby we've talked about maybe having, it would mean getting
an apartment with another bedroom at twice the rent we pay
now, which we couldn't afford, or disposing of the dog somehow and staying with the baby here." She gives Bobby to a friend
in the country. "If one day we do get a larger apartment," she
says, "and Bobby's still alive, then I don't care how sick and
feeble he might be then, he returns. Agreed?" "Agreed."

They marry a few months after that and a few months later she's pregnant. They planned it that way and it worked. They wanted to conceive the baby in February so they could spend most of the summer in Maine and have the baby in October, a mild month and where he'd be settled into the fall semester. He goes into the delivery room with her, does a lot of the things he learned in the birth classes they took over the summer, to help her get through the more painful labor contractions. When their daughter's about a month old he starts dancing with her at night just as that man did three years ago. He has two Mahler symphonies on record, buys three more and dances to the slow movements and to the last half of the second side of a recording of Sibelius's Fifth Symphony. Denise loves to see him dancing like this. Twice she's said "May I cut in?" and they held the baby and each other and danced around the living room. Dancing with the baby against his chest, he soon found out, also helps get rid of her gas and puts her to sleep. He usually keeps a light on while he dances so he won't bump into things and possibly trip. Sometimes he closes his eyes — in the middle of the room — and dances almost in place while he kisses the baby's neck, hair, even where there's cradle cap, back, ears, face. Their apartment's on the third floor and looks out on other apartments in a building across the backyard. He doesn't think it would stop him dancing if he saw someone looking at him through one of those windows. He doesn't even think he'd lower the blinds. Those apartments are too far away — a hundred feet or more — to make him self-conscious about his dancing. If his apartment was on the first or second floor and fronted on the sidewalk, he'd lower the living room blinds at night. He'd do it even if he didn't have a baby or wasn't dancing with it. He just doesn't like people looking in at night from the street.

# Atomic Facts

## Tom Grimes

Russell sat out the war and for a time was imprisoned as a dissenter. Wittgenstein served in the Austrian army, was captured shortly before the war ended, and spent the remainder of the war in a prison camp. In the trenches, he had composed his *Tractatus*.

— It has nothing to do with anything that matters, his companion Klein told him in Tarnev, near the front.

—That's what makes it important.

—Why?

— If it's said, we can get rid of it.

One morning, a bullet passed through Klein's liver. Wittgenstein cradled his companion's head in his arms, said nothing.

Wittgenstein may have hoped for a homosexual relationship with Russell, or he may not have, and everything else remains the same.

Russell received a letter from Wittgenstein during the first year of their acquaintance at Cambridge.—Your caring and encouragement I will always cherish when I recall them, but our temperaments and beliefs prevent our ever being friends.

Russell sought out Wittgenstein.— My temperament prevents my beliefs from ever being fixed. Don't destroy a friendship by taking the appearance of my beliefs as the reality of my beliefs. You, of all people, should understand that.

—What do you believe in?

—What I can figure out and write down. What do you believe in?

—Everything I can't.

—As philosophers, our work is important for what we say, not for what we don't say.

—Then we're either wrong or misunderstood.

After the war, Wittgenstein tried to have the *Tractatus* published.—Set in type, printed, distributed, I'll finally be free of it, he told his sister, Hermine.—I will finally be rid of logic, and then I can either be Ludwig Wittgenstein, or not be Ludwig Wittgenstein, and everything else will remain the same.

—Please make sense, Ludwig. You frighten me.

—I don't like who I am.

—And who is that?

—The one who knows that I don't like who I am.

Wittgenstein told his sister that he had found employment as a gardener's assistant at a monastery.

—You should be doing great things, Ludwig. I worry about you. What troubles you so?

—I can't stop thinking.

—Come home and talk with Daddy. That'll stop you.

Wittgenstein laughed.—Thank you.

—For what?

—A moment's peace.

Wittgenstein met with Russell in Holland, a year after the 1918 Armistice.

—What is happening with your work, Ludwig?

—It's distilling itself.

—Excellent. When can I see some?

—I don't know.

—Why not?

—I haven't written a word of it.

—Ah. But the course of the work is fixed in your mind.

—Some days I think it's finished as is.

—Ludwig.

—The general course is fixed, yes.

—And in what direction is it leading you?

—Toward silence.

— For you, naturally. But how do you intend to get there?

— By outlining the failure of logic.

Russell thought Wittgenstein was merely being ill-mannered and, for some reason, spiteful. Perhaps, Russell thought, because he had sat out the war Wittgenstein had fought in.

— Did you have to kill anyone?

—Yes.

—And what did you think?

— Any one fact can either be the case or not be the case, and everything else remains the same.

— Dear.

— Indeed.

Russell wrote to Lady Ottoline Morrell, shortly after he had met with Wittgenstein.— I was astonished to find that he had become a complete mystic. He reads people like Kierkegaard. I think (though he wouldn't agree) that what he likes best in mysticism is its power to make him stop thinking. Do you know what he reads besides his Tolstoy and Dostoevski? Detective novels. Do you know why? They allow him to stop thinking, he told me. Do you know *how* he reads them? Backwards. One goes from knowledge to ignorance that way, he said to me. Don't you believe that's the pattern and the point of our own work? I think our boy needs to get back into the real world.

Russell saw to it that the *Tractatus* was published. Wittgenstein wrote his publisher to mention that what he meant to say in the book's preface he had not said, that is— My work consists of two parts: the part I have written plus all that I have *not* written. And it is precisely this second part that is the important one.

The irate German publisher, Ficker, wrote back to Wittgenstein,— How would you like it if I only paid you for the second part.

But there was an introduction by Russell, whose name sold philosophy books. The unwritten portion of the *Tructatus* was published as it stood.

Wittgenstein did not like Russell's introduction. He wrote

him a final letter. —I told you, we cannot be friends.

Wittgenstein took a job teaching schoolchildren in a poor Austrian village. He taught them how to build engines, and asked them to draw pictures of what it was he was trying to teach them. His sister Hermine visited him.—You've taught them to make useful things, Ludwig, like the sewing machine. Remember? Wittgenstein had once built his sister a sewing machine out of wood. And it worked.—Then I've taught them something in exchange for all they've taught me.
    —Which is what?
    —That I do not know what I do not know.
    —A child said that to you?
    —If one had, I would not have listened. I asked them to tell me what God had to say to man. One boy handed in a blank page.
    —He may have just been lazy.
    —And everything else remains the same.

Russell had been moving away from the logic he had produced in the *Principia*. In 1921 he published *Analysis of the Mind*. He postulated a doctrine which he called "neutral monism." There are not two worlds, he said, one subjective, the other objective. There is only one. It can be viewed alternately, depending on how we construct it. We construct it from "neutral" constituents, and these we find in the data our senses provide for us. He sought out Wittgenstein one last time, for Russell felt that he had always learned more from Wittgenstein than he had taught him.
    —Mathematics ceased to interest me when I came to see it as one immense tautology.
    —That's God's explanation of his relation to man, Wittgenstein said. —There is your proof of his existence.
    —Nonsense.
    —If you can't accept that, then it is not that mathematics does not interest you, it is that you do not exist.

—Word games.

—You taught me.

Wittgenstein spent two years building a house in Vienna for his sister. Then he was recalled to Cambridge in 1929. Before he left, his sister asked him if he felt strong enough to live with his depressions alone.

—Yes. My life has meaning.

—What is it?

— I couldn't say.

— I do not want to see a fourth brother commit suicide, Ludwig. I am speaking to you frankly, and I am telling you that the difference between that being the case, or not, will not leave everything else the same for me.

— I'm fine.

—Truth.

— My hand to God.

Wittgenstein returned to Cambridge. He refused to wear a tie, sleep on anything but an army cot, or dine with the other dons.

—Why? his colleague, John Wisdom, asked him.

—Their conversation is neither of the heart nor of the head.

—You won't have many friends.

— I had one, once.

—What happened to him?

— A bullet passed through his liver.

— But everything else remains the same.

— Not for me. Or for him.

Wittgenstein worked on his second and final piece of philosophy. He chose to express it in "ordinary" language.— I do not want to fall prey to the bewitchment of my mind by language. Philosophy must leave the world as it is.

In 1940, Wittgenstein's sister gave him a copy of Chandler's *The Big Sleep* for Christmas.— I rank this book with Kierkegaard and Dostoevski, he told her.

—Ludwig, it's a mystery.

—Indeed. I've read it backwards and forwards sixteen times, yet I still can't accept the story on anything but faith. Who did what is never solved. Reading it, one moves from ignorance through knowledge to bafflement.

—It's his first novel.

—To have gotten it right the first time.


Wittgenstein continued to write his ellipses around the zone of silence he had left hanging at the end of the *Tractatus*. He continued to read detective novels. He decided to call his work *Philosophical Investigations*. He finished the work in 1945. He did not allow it to pass from his hands until he died in 1951.

—What belief would we give up last if we were compelled to, he asked himself.

He decided that, for him, it was that he had no more not to say.

—If I could no longer believe that my work pointed beyond the world, I could no longer live in the world, he said the last time he spoke with his sister.

—Ludwig, why were you always unhappy?

—I have always been happy.

—Then what tormented you so?

—I simply wanted to know why.

—Why what?

—Exactly. Why anything, instead of not anything.

—And in either case, everything else remains the same, no?

—I wonder.


*Several statements attributed to Wittgenstein and Russell in "Atomic Facts" are taken from the book* The Illusion of Technique *by William Barrett. Copyright © 1967, 1975, 1976 by the American Jewish Committee. Published by Doubleday & Co., Inc.*

5) Teachers
5) Photographers
5) Marriage problems

4/83

# Late Summer: Driving North
## Ann Beattie

It was easy to open the window from outside, so that was the way he got the cat into the house. David knelt and clicked his tongue softly, to lure Lucifer into his arms. Then he walked to the side of the house, put the fingertips of his left hand on the window and pushed up; with the other hand he placed Lucifer inside and quickly closed the window. The cat stared at him through the screen, realizing that it had been tricked. If David had looked back, he would still have seen the surprised look, several seconds later. But he bowed his head and walked to the car, sure that Mary would be crying. He was surprised that she was not. Her face was even fixed in a pleasant expression. If he had looked several seconds later, he would have seen the expression fade first from her eyes, then from her mouth, and perhaps a minute or two after that the first tear. But he had the excuse of looking at the road as he drove, so he didn't have to see it. As they turned the corner toward the highway David smiled — the poor cat had really been tricked. He looked over at Mary, to tell her about the dirty trick he had played on Lucifer. She had stopped crying by then, and although the pleasant expression had not returned, she no longer looked miserable. He had been going to tell her the story about the cat — he really had — and was as surprised as she to hear himself saying bitterly, "Okay, Mary. I hope that now you're happy."

They had spent the past three years in a town in the South. A nice town with magnolia trees — sophisticated enough to have a French restaurant, so old-fashioned that there was a cobblestoned Main Street they had strolled down hand in hand the summer they arrived, before he began teaching. They had lived in a rented house outside of town — a larger, lovelier house than they could ever have afforded to buy. Conveniently, the lease was up at the same time he was denied renewal. Conveniently, the camellias, her favorite flowers, although the front lawn was dotted with clumps of odd, beautiful flowers, had stopped blooming. The day they drove down the driveway for the last time they passed strawberry plants that had not yet begun to grow berries, daisies, the flowering quince. The furniture was being sent to Vermont, where they would put it in a spare room. They were going to spend the rest of the summer, and all winter, at her brother's house while he was in Italy. That had fallen conveniently into place too — that Lawrence was going to be away for a year, and needed someone to watch his house. "If they try to snowmobile on the land in spite of the signs, shoot the gun into the air," he had told them. He had meant it. He did it himself. When he said that it was late spring, and hard to think of the snowy winter in Vermont.

David was bitter about not being kept on at the University. When he found out, he had been tempted to take a rifle and blast them. All of his thoughts had been violent and childish. He had sulked. He had made no further efforts to be a good teacher, going into his classroom and lecturing to the back wall for the rest of the term, marking papers harshly, deliberately ignoring raised hands. He had not kept office hours and had stopped talking to all his students in the hallway, before class, except one. With that student he would often stroll across the campus when class was over to the bar across the street and stand there having beer after beer, although after only a few sips of one beer his head would begin to swim. Several times during the week he got the bad news he had come home drunk. Mary became bitter that he was bitter and accused him of turning inward as he always did when he had a problem. He felt the accusation was unfair because usually when he got home she was not even there — she was in the woods, taking pictures. Endless pictures. She could not go out for a simple walk without the camera. In the winter there had been summer pictures hung in the house; the summer, scenes of squirrels on snowy logs, the white curve of the driveway, cumulus clouds in a pale grey sky at the end of the field. She was like her brother Lawrence in always thinking ahead. She had been shocked, too, when he was denied promotion. She had thought ahead, and she had envisioned buying a house. She had envisioned going into partnership with another woman to open a small studio, where they would give photography lessons. She had even thought about having a baby.

Instead, the day they left the rented house they had only a gerbil in a cage. The gerbil, her cameras, tripod, lenses, photographic supplies, two suitcases full of clothes, and odd last-minute things — a bottle of wine left unpacked but undrunk, an earring she found glittering in a corner as they were making a last check of the house.

"It doesn't feel like I'm really leaving it," she had said, standing in the empty house after the moving van pulled away.

"You aren't, until tomorrow," he said.

That night they had slept stretched on the floor, on a faded sheet they did not intend to take with them, the box full of plants on the hearth. It would have been logical, she had argued, to go to Vermont immediately and spend a day or so with Lawrence before he left the country, but David had held out for staying one night longer in the rented house. Lawrence irritated him. He knew that Lawrence was being generous in offering his house, and he even half-liked Lawrence, but he was in a bad mood and he wanted his way. He had not gotten his way about the job, and he had not gotten his way about moving to New York and taking any sort of work he could find, so finally he had put his foot down and insisted that he was not going to spend time hearing Lawrence's plans for a glorious year abroad, or Lawrence raving on about new advances in computer technology. In fact, he had also wanted to release the gerbil into the woods, and she had refused to do that.

As they rode down the driveway the little animal rushed back and forth in its cage. He could see it in the rear-view mirror. That, and the house. The daisies blooming. The bright pink-orange of the quince bush.

Before they could get started they had to drive into town, with a box of plants for Alice. He had said the obvious about that; that he thought it perverse.

"What other people do I know to give them to?" she said.

"Leave the God damn things here. People will probably move in right away and water them."

"And let the gerbil loose in the woods. Let it fend for itself when it never has. Let it die. Let everything go to hell. Good idea."

"Are you going to be this pleasant all the way to Vermont?"

"My feeling," she said, "is that I did not start the unpleasantness."

"My feeling is that if you never intend to forgive me, you might have said so, so I could have gone to New York instead of escorting you into the wilderness."

"To tell you the truth," she said, "I was reluctant to part from my only friend."

He hated it when she pretended no one else liked her.

"Sheila is your friend."

"Sheila was interested in making money. I hardly heard from Sheila when I backed out of teaching photography."

"You'd have more friends if you'd be sociable. You had a good time at Alice's garden party. All you're going to meet in the woods is Mr. Squirrel. And you're not going to meet anybody at all in a darkroom."

"Stop ridiculing me for being a photographer."

"Stop blaming me for what happened with Alice."

"I'm not going to hold this tangle of plants on my lap all the way to Vermont, David."

They were already halfway to Alice's house. He pushed whatever tape was in the tape deck into the machine, and turned down the volume. They rode listening to a quiet chaos of saxophones.

Alice was not there, of course. She had gone to the Hudson Valley a week before, after giving herself what Jack Zaran reported was a lavish send-off: a lantern-lit backyard party—a "garden party" was what Zaran called it, falling into Alice's way of talking about things. They had gone to a party on the small plot of grass in back of Alice's house the last week she was in town, but earlier in the week. They had not gone to her send-off party. Alice's neighbor was feeding the cat. The neighbor would also water the plants until Alice returned. Alice had told everyone she would be gone a month, but he suspected—and knew everyone else did, too—that she would return soon after he and Mary left.

They had had an affair for almost a year. He had first met her when he gave Jack Zaran, the student he sometimes had drinks with after class, a ride to her house when Zaran's car wouldn't start. Students as well as faculty went to Alice's house. She had been looking out her window for Jack, because he was late, and when David's car pulled up and Jack jumped out, she had thrown open the door and motioned David in, too. Her hospitality was legendary. Of course, David knew who she was. She was, the former wife of the head of his department, now divorced and completing psychiatric training. He had heard about her from people on the faculty who had gone to parties at the home of Alice and Daniel Vreeland when they were still married. And the first week he was in town he had seen her on Main Street, in the used bookstore, laughing with the owner. He remembered where he had seen her the minute he walked into her house that cold December afternoon. The bookstore owner had stroked his beard and remarked that she was a very special lady after she left the store, and he had asked who she was. She and Daniel had lived in the town for fifteen years, and most everyone knew her. No one ever had anything bad to say about her. When she left her husband, she asked for no alimony. She voluntarily moved out of the big house on Foxhall Drive and into the small four room house closer to the center of town. She sold their house in Maine, which had been bought with money her mother left her when she died, and lived on the money from the sale. Since she did not have a great deal of money to entertain, she served jug wine and passed out pita bread stuffed with cheese instead of having exotic dinners. Everyone liked to go to her house better than to the fashionable formal dinners that were always being given. When the French restaurant opened, they even recruited her as weekend bread maker, saying that maybe if she had some part in the restaurant people would eat there rather than waiting for an invitation to her house. She did it, and picked up a little money, but mostly she did it because she was flattered to be asked. She was often given compliments, but never seemed to expect them. She reacted like a child, half delighted and half embarrassed. When David told her she was childish, she hung her head, but came up smiling.

"Can you help me with something?" she had said to him on the phone a few weeks after he first met her.

He had been surprised, after having met her once and not having seen her for nearly a month, that she would call him at his office and ask him to come to her house. But he had been thinking about her — about the pleasant hour he had spent with her and Jack Zaran, warm in her house, comfortable on her huge pillow-banked sofa, having a drink and winding down — and he said that when his office hours were over, he would be glad to help. He phoned Mary and told her that there was still a line of students to see him, so not to expect him by five, then left the office early and walked through the empty corridors, out of the building and to the stadium, where his car was parked. It was the worst winter since he had moved South two years ago; it had snowed again a day ago on sidewalks already so caked with ice that he walked through the trickle of muddy water in the gutter rather than trying to balance on the sidewalk.

When he got to Alice's house, she handed a glass of hot mulled wine out the door.

"I want you to dig out my car," she said.

50

"What do you mean? I spent yesterday digging out my own car."

"Now you can do mine," she said. "Will you? I'll shovel with you. I just couldn't bear to tackle it myself."

He looked at the old black Chevrolet in the driveway. She knew she was being girlish, and he never liked it when women acted that way. Mary's seriousness, and her lack of dependence, had been what first attracted him to her. Yet he could see that Alice was uncomfortable in the little-girl role, and thought that maybe if she would put on the act in the first place that she was desperate for help. Although the other day he had come to her house she had proudly shown off the table she had made, the top inlaid with tiles from a trip to France, it was clear to him that she worked very hard at being competent. Her small hands had been badly scratched, with Bandaids wrapped around the knuckles of several fingers. She was embarrassed about her hands and kept them hidden when she could. So he looked at the big car, snow banked around it, and shook his head and took a shovel from her front porch and walked toward it. As she said she would, she came to help, purple wool stocking hat pulled low, bright yellow scarf wound around the hat, the collar of her parka pulled high around her throat. In the cold, wrapped in all the layers of wool, she looked older. He had asked Jack Zaran how old she was, and he said he imagined she was in her mid-forties. They had nodded in agreement over that. He knew that he had spoken of her more times to Jack than would have been usual; but then, Jack was clearly infatuated, too.

When he got home that night, breathless (but only from shoveling snow) the story he told Mary was that a plow had pushed snow against his car while he was teaching. Even though it was not the truth, it was close to it.

It had been an odd winter for him. In class he would find himself drifting away in mid-sentence, lose his train of thought completely, rap the side of his head with an apologetic smile and take up the lecture in another place. The students liked

him, so the only real tension it caused was in his mind. Severa
things, at least, were wrong: his grandmother, to whom he wa;
very close, was making slow progress from a stroke, and he fel{
guilty that he had flown only once to see her when she wa;
hospitalized; whether or not he would get re-hired kept bothering
him—particularly since other people on the faculty had corrobo-
rated Jack's opinion that they fired any teacher who was liked
excessively by all the students. And it bothered him, too, that
Mary wanted to be so isolated. They had agreed when they
married that she should not be compelled to go to social gather-
ings with people who bored her, but when people phoned and
he said his wife could not come, the invitation was not extended
to him alone, and soon most people stopped calling. He still
loved Mary—his feelings had not changed about that—but it
bothered him that she spent so much time apart from him, and
he began to resent the sight of her Nikon, which always seemed
to be in whatever room he went into, on a piece of furniture,
pointing up. One night he had gone into the bedroom and put
on the light, and she had been enraged—angrier than he could
ever remember seeing her—because she had been in the dark,
under the covers, winding exposed film onto rolls for process-
ing. "I told you not to come into the bedroom," she screamed
at him. And she had—at least, he knew that she had called
something to him which he did not hear very well because he
had been in his study, typing the next day's lecture.

"Is it ruined?" he had asked, horrified. "Was it something
special?"

"Oh, just *pictures*," she said. "Pictures I spent all day shoot-
ing. Nothing important at all." She had thrown the thin streamer
of film out of the covers and onto the floor, and although it
fell soundlessly to the rug, he heard it hit.

When she was still angry two days later, he asked what the
real trouble was.

"I'm tired of being stuck away in the country while you work
and socialize with Jack Zaran all the time. I'm tired of putting
your interests first."

"You wanted this house," he said. "You liked it."

"I didn't realize I'd never see anyone. Or I didn't realize that I'd never see anyone civil. If I try to make conversation with the woman at the post office, she just purses her mouth. Everyone is so unfriendly, because we don't have ancestors who were born and died here. They call us 'the rentals,' did you know that? They think we're just phantoms passing through."

He nodded. He had feared, all along, that that might be the truth. He had always had the feeling that he would not be kept on, even though people in the department were pleasant to him, even though he was well-liked by his students. It was the sort of place where people were pleasant, and it meant nothing—just good, Southern manners. He sympathized with Mary for not wanting to spend evenings at dinner parties—the few he had gone to alone he had not much enjoyed. When he had been a graduate student, things had been so much more relaxed. One of the things that appealed to him most about Alice was her lack of pretense: she would hand him a hunk of cheese, pour cheap wine into a water glass for him. He thought that Mary would like to meet her, and after he had seen her twice without Mary, he asked the next time Alice phoned him at work if it would be all right to bring his wife. "Of course—that's great," she had replied. At the time, he had not doubted that she meant it.

At the end of the week they had gone to Alice's house. He had told Mary that he had met Alice when he dropped Jack Zaran at her house. He did not mention the late afternoon of digging out Alice's car, when they spent as much time throwing snowballs as digging, and hoped that Alice would not allude to it either. He could not think why she would, so it seemed safe not to mention it.

After a few awkward moments, it was clear that Mary liked Alice. And when the whole visit passed without Alice's asking Mary what she did (Mary hated the condescending attitude she thought academics took toward people who did not teach), he was sure that his wife had found a friend. That made him both happy and a little uncomfortable. He was probably a little jealous. He would have liked Alice for a confidante, but Mary needed her more.

"Yes, I liked her a lot," Mary said, in the car. "She's an unusual woman. Do you think she'll call me, if I don't call her?"

"Sure," he said. "She liked you. Why are you so cynical?"

When Alice did not call for a week, he called her. He did not know exactly what he meant to say, but he had some vague idea of asking her if she would call his wife, who was lonely in this academic community and who had liked her very much. By amazing coincidence, when he reached Alice she had run into Mary downtown, and had invited the two of them for drinks on Friday.

"Great," he said. "I look forward to it."

There was a pause, and then Alice asked: "Why did you call?"

"I wondered if Jack was there," he said.

"No," she said.

"I didn't really think so," he stumbled on, "but I thought I'd call and check."

"You worry too much," she said. "See you Friday."

She was making it easy for him to hang up. He silently thanked her, and put the phone down. Walking to his car, he counted the days until Friday. What would she be doing for the next three days? Was that the first night she was free?

They saw her through the winter and spring—either at her house, where they were often invited for drinks, sometimes with Jack Zaran or the O'Haras, sometimes alone, or at their house for dinner, to which Mary invited no one else. The three of them bought old postcards of the South at an antique show in Richmond, and another time they went to a horse show, and several times they went to the late night movies. He was a little embarrassed that inevitably, when Alice called late Saturday night to try to rouse them for the midnight movies, they were home, and alone. The one time Lawrence visited them, David made it a point to have the three of them stop by her house, using as a pretext that she had asked him the next time he and

Mary visited if he would hold the ladder for her so she could climb into the attic to search for a painting she thought she had stored there. The three of them had braced the ladder as Alice climbed.

The day they held the ladder it was the first of May, and he had slept with her twice. You could not tell it from the way she acted; in fact, she was so cool—she still saw Mary for lunch, asked the two of them for drinks—that he began to be afraid that she slept with other men, and was equally cool about her relationships with them. But even if she did have other lovers, he had no right to say anything. He knew that, and it made him angry. As she backed down the ladder, he was seized with the desire to step away, to let her fall, sure that he was not her only lover. But even if he had, the other two stood there, holding the ladder steady.

The picture she found in the attic was lovely; an oval *trompe l'oeil* painting of a pretty woman with a pink gardenia in her hair. Before they left, Lawrence drove a nail into the wall, and David lowered the picture into place—in the bedroom, facing the bed in which they had slept.

As time went on, he confessed to her that he was bothered by thoughts that she had other lovers. If she did, he said, he did not want to know about them. If the thoughts bothered him, the reality would be unbearable. She looked at him across the table (both were sitting on the thick brown fur rug spread underneath her tiled table) solemnly, and nodded.

"Jesus!" he said. "You do!"

"What have I done?" she said. "I only nodded."

"Then tell me—do you?"

"You said you didn't want to know."

"Don't play games with me. I want you to tell me. If you do, there's nothing I can do about it, but I want to know."

"You don't want to know. You started the conversation by saying you didn't."

"I do, God damn it. I want you to tell me."

"I don't," she said.

"If you don't, then it's not because other men haven't tried. They've asked and you've said no, isn't that right?"

"How flattered do you want to be? Would you like it if I said that I was so unattractive that *of course* no one else has been interested — ever? Do you need me to see myself as undesirable?"

He shook his head, confused. "What?" he said.

She moved over beside him and took a drink from his glass and laughed into his arm, clutching him around the elbow.

"I don't know," she said. "I got confused in the middle of what I was saying."

He told her, then, about how his own thoughts evaporated during his lectures.

"Because you're in love," she said.

He smiled, but said nothing — letting her flatter herself that that was the reason. In spite of her always seeming in control, she had confessed to him that life alone was difficult and at times frightening, having been married for so many years. She had told him, patting the table, that she only showed off her successes. He understood what she was saying, but he still thought she was extraordinary. In spite of her competence with photographs, his own wife would not try to hang a plant from the window or even change the bag on the vacuum.

"Mary's never been scared into having to do things," she said. "If she got scared, she'd do it."

They rarely talked about Mary, and the few times they did, Alice had only kind things to say.

"She's lucky she's not scared," Alice said.

And the two of them sat side by side in front of the table, the ivory painted wall across from them, acknowledging silently that they were both afraid.

He was afraid that he would tell Mary everything and leave her. He was afraid that if he did, Alice would not have him, because she would think him cowardly for doing that. Or he was afraid that Alice would simply send him back — and that Mary would take him — that the two women would force him into his former position, and that his having spoken would mean only the loss of Alice. He knew that Alice really liked Mary, and that the feeling was reciprocated. For as long as he had known Mary she had never given away her photographs, let alone mount and sign them. Four pictures hung in Alice's living room, above the mantel. They were springtime pictures, and it was spring. This month the committee would decide whether he would be rehired. He had thought for a long time that he should not let the committee's decision decide for him what he did about Alice. If he continued to stay in limbo, married to Mary and being Alice's lover, or if he broke it off, or if he left Mary, it should not be because he had lost his job and had to leave town. Alice already made it clear that she loved the town in spite of its faults, and would never leave. If she had ever left, she said, it would have been after the divorce, so she would not have had to endure explaining to people. If she had intended to leave, she would have gone long ago, at the time of the separation, to the house in Maine.

He also began to wonder, in the spring, if his wife knew, or suspected. She talked to him more than she usually did — often about silly things, or things she remembered from her childhood. One night as he was drifting off to sleep, she had asked him in a quiet voice if he ever played the game Who Do You Love when he was a child. He had not caught all of her question, and had turned to face her in the dark, wide-eyed, thinking she was asking about Alice. But she took his surprised silence as a negative answer, and began to explain the game: how a ring of children would surround another child on the playground and circle around and around, making the child shout out who she loved. Then the child would be teased about it. "I'd never say," she said. "I'd cry and they'd run away, or I'd just silently stand in the circle."

"Who do you love?" he said, hugging her.

"You," she said.

"Do you? You really do?"

He hugged her closer, wondering why her declaration had

not made him surer of what his decision would be.

She found out because she stopped by Alice's house one afternoon when he was there. Seeing him, she probably would have thought nothing. In fact, when she came to the door, he and Alice were dressed and in the kitchen holding hands and having coffee. He heard a noise that sounded like Mary's car (the muffler was bad, and Mary refused to take it to the shop for repair and he had not yet found the time), and watched it pull into the drive. Alice got up to answer the door, and he panicked. He pulled her to him, whispered for her not to go to the door. Of course it was ridiculous, and the worst way to have handled the situation. His car had been parked in Alice's driveway. When he held Alice and frantically whispered for her not to go to the door, Alice gave in and stood with him, frozen in the kitchen, until the knocking stopped and finally Mary left the front porch and went to her car and drove away. Later, he would think that he had handled the situation so badly because subconsciously he wanted her to know.

"I don't understand," Alice said, her voice still a whisper, though Mary had driven away. "Why couldn't I go to the door?"

"You could have, you could have," he said, confused. He was thinking to himself, aloud.

"Then—"

"I don't know," he said. "I just got frightened. I thought she knew, and that she had come here on purpose."

"She doesn't know," Alice said.

"She does. She knows now. What could she think?"

"Tell her we weren't here. Tell her our cars were here, but that we'd gone somewhere."

"Where? Where could we go? And I phoned her, saying I was going to the gym with Jack."

"Tell her you changed your mind. That you came here and that we—"

He had walked out of the room before she finished the sentence; that was the sort of lying he had never done, and that

58

he did not want to do.

"I'm going to tell her," he said.

"Then you're telling her because you want to."

"She knows, Alice. She isn't stupid."

"I'm not stupid either," Alice said, coming up behind him. "Why did I do what you said? Why the hell didn't I go answer my own door?"

Alice was angry at him because he had made her lose faith in herself. And he was angry, too—at the University, at his betrayal of Mary, at his betrayal of Alice, even at Jack Zaran, because if only Jack Zaran hadn't been going to Washington to visit his girlfriend, he would have been at the gym, playing handball with him when Mary came to Alice's door.

"I should have known," Mary said. She had gotten home enough before him to have downed half of a drink when he came in. Or perhaps it was her second drink. Or her third. He was so upset that he could not judge her sobriety.

"But how could you do that?" she said. "How could you coerce her into being my friend?"

"I didn't. She likes you."

"Did this start after you weren't rehired, or before?"

"Before."

"I wish you had lied about that," she said.

She left the room. He did not want to follow her. He stayed in the living room, his car keys in his fist and cutting his palm. He went to the table and picked up her drink and drained it. What he had assumed was her favorite drink—sherry on ice— was bourbon. He went after her.

She was leaning against the wall in the hallway. When he turned the corner, he collided with her.

"Why didn't you make up some story to tell me? Couldn't you have gotten your clothes on and made up some lie?"

"We had our clothes on. I didn't—I thought you should know."

"But you didn't think you should tell me, you thought that if I happened to—"

"I didn't think anything. I don't know what I thought. When you came to the door I thought you should know, but I didn't have the courage to open the door."

"If you had opened the door I wouldn't have known."

"I thought it would be insulting to tell you right there, in front of Alice."

"I think the first thing you said was correct: you didn't think anything."

"I did. I didn't mean that. I would have been embarrassed not only for me, but for you."

Mary walked into the bedroom and sat on the bed, her forehead pressed into the bedpost. Her camera was on the bed, and a balled-up red sweater. They had been there since she dropped them on the bed after she returned from Alice's. He could tell that looking at them — that they had been thrown there.

"I really liked her," Mary said. "I liked her comfortable house and the way her only clock was the tiny one on the stove that was always slow. I liked it that she made me sandwiches and soup, like I was an invalid."

He sat beside her. He nodded slowly. She lifted her head and looked at him, her expression no longer sad, but blazing.

"What did you like?" she said, sarcastically. She stared at him, full face, pretending to expect him to talk about it. Then she got up and slammed through the house. He listened as she threw back doors, kicked things. He heard something shatter, then the front door slam. He wanted to go after her, but he just could not. He sat there as her car started and as she backed up quickly. He turned his head and saw the car go out of the driveway backwards, then move forward. He saw her driving away. He sat on the bed, in his clothes, until past midnight. Then he took his clothes off, lifted the camera and sweater to her dresser, and went back to the bed and got under the covers. He had left the light on and once he was stretched out he was afraid to move again. When he awoke in the morning she was still gone, and all the next day and night she was gone. The day after that he came home from taking a walk and found her there, in the living room, reading the mail that had piled up in her absence.

That night, they went to the French restaurant for dinner. She drove and he sat in the passenger seat. She drove too fast, but when he made conversation with her, she answered. They got all the way to town before he realized that her car was so different to ride in because she had gotten the muffler fixed.

They ran into Alice on the street, the week before they were to leave for Vermont. Alice looked embarrassed, and they were both sorry that they had run into her, but both cared for her too much not to at least stop and speak.

"Forgive me," Alice said. "Come to my garden party tonight. Are you doing anything? The O'Haras are coming, and Jack Zaran and his girl from Washington, and Mike Touley and some friend of his from Arizona."

"What do you say?" David asked Mary, putting the burden on her.

"Sure," Mary said. "Might as well meet these people before we take off."

"Good," Alice said, and took both their hands for an instant. "I hope you do come," she said, "even though I know you won't."

He was surprised when Mary called after her: "What time?"

"Seven," Alice called back. "Come early if you want."

At seven-thirty they went to her house, walking around to the back because they had seen some people standing there as they drove down the street. Holding hands, they stepped over a row of newly planted rose bushes, none higher than ten inches, and into the group of people. Marty Fagan was there — a tall, rotund man who had gone on record as being appalled that David's contract had not been renewed. With him was his wife — Japanese, a war bride — and their teenage son, who was sitting in the corner feigning interest in a Siamese cat. Jack Zaran was the first to notice them, though, and ran over to say hello, seeming nervous that they were there. David had told the whole story to Jack during the time that Mary was gone, and Jack had been in favor of calling the police to try to get them to find her. Jack brought over his girlfriend, Rachel, and introduced her. She looked as if she was very interested to meet them. They were talking to Rachel about the Kennedy Center, where she worked, when Alice came out the back door and down the steps, followed by the O'Haras carrying jugs of wine and trays of cheese and pita bread. Alice smiled in the second her eyes met David's, then looked at the steps and walked down them carefully, although before their eyes met she had not been watching her footing.

The few moments that he spent alone with Alice—shortly before they left the party—she was friendly and pleasant, talking the same way she had the day they met, when he gave Jack Zaran a ride to her house. He was sorry that the gathering was taking place outside, because he had wanted to see the inside of her house one more time: the fur rug rolled and put away, replaced by the mat with tiny yellow stars woven through it; the broken mantel clock that was painted with cherubs carrying wreaths of roses and that stood on feet of golden orchids—a family heirloom Alice thought was hilarious. But instead they stood outside the living room window, and she talked to him about the garden she had put in, saying that she intended to harvest a crop of vegetables, even though there was so little room. They stood side by side, looking down at a patch of soil about three feet wide and five feet long, already sprouting small bits of green. At each end of the plot were larger plants: flowers, she said, that would bloom at night, so the back yard would always smell delightful for garden parties. He nodded enthusiastically, but was surprised at what she had said; delightful flowers and garden parties were something the other Southern hostesses would preside over. The plants he admired, though only about four inches high and not yet flowering, were called Night Blooming Cereus, she told him. O'Hara joined them and after another moment of praising her garden, Alice excused herself and went into the kitchen, leaving him to talk to O'Hara.

He wanted to leave the party, but Mary was still talking to Jack Zaran's girlfriend, and anyway they could not leave without saying goodbye to Alice, who was spending most of her time in the house. He wanted to go in and say goodbye to her, but of course he could not. No matter how involved in conversation Mary seemed, he knew she was actually keeping track of him. As he listened to O'Hara rattle on about a discovery he had made in *Ada*, he caught sight of Alice coming down the stairs. He nodded along with whatever O'Hara was saying, then went briefly to Alice's side as she put a fresh plate of crackers on the table. He said goodbye.

"Goodbye," she said, and gave him one of her familiar barrel hugs. It was a nice hug, and would have been very convincing, if he had not known that when she was serious her embrace was tender, light, much more lingering than the hugs she usually seized people in. She hugged Mary, too, going over to put her arms around her (which was the first Mary knew they were leaving the party). It was easy to leave without saying goodbye to everybody else because the party had been going on a while, and they were all pretty drunk and involved in whatever they were talking about.

"I want to take her my plants," Mary said, when they settled into the car. "The woman with the long blonde hair is her neighbor, and she said that while Alice was out of town she was going to watch the cat and the house, and that she'd water the plants until Alice got back."

She was letting him drive, reclining in the passenger seat. "Alice always liked my plants," she said.

He looked at her, to see if she was drunk. She seemed okay.

"What cat?" he said.

"Didn't you see the Siamese cat the boy was playing with? That's Alice's. She got a cat."

"She got a cat?" he said dumbly.

"She got a cat. What's so miraculous about that? Anyway — the neighbor said she'd take care of the plants. I'm not telling Alice. I'm just letting it be a surprise."

"Where is Alice going?" he said.

"To the Hudson Valley. To her aunt's house."

Long ago, in the winter, they had talked about their old relatives and about how fond of them they were. Neither he nor Alice had good relationships with their parents (her mother, of course, was dead), but she was fond of her aunt and he was fond of his grandmother. Her aunt lived in Annandale-on-Hudson, his grandmother lived in Connecticut. "The nice people are all up North," she had said to him one time when they had been talking about the two old ladies. "Sometimes I think I'd like to go up to those gorgeous old trees and rip off the magnolia blossoms and kick them like footballs."

So this, he thought, crouching, was her cat. It was more kitten than cat, you could tell when you came close, although since it was rather large he had taken it at first glance for a full grown cat. And when Mary lowered her plants in the big box to the front porch and carefully unpacked them, the kitten stood back and watched. When Mary had removed them all, and turned over the box and put them on top, just back from the edge of the open porch but far enough into where the sun shone for them to get light, the kitten made its first approach. It sniffed one of the plants, then began to bat it.

"Get away," Mary said, putting her hand under its belly and lifting it back.

The kitten circled and, as they were leaving the porch, came back to bat at a leaf.

"I can't leave them if the cat is going to destroy them," Mary said.

"They'll be all right."

"Look!" she said. "It's going to ruin them."

"Get away, kitten," he said, this time lifting it himself.

When they were halfway down the lawn, she turned to see the kitten approaching the box.

"Make it stop," she said, her voice quivering.

"Go sit in the car," he said.

"I'm not going to leave them to be destroyed."

He saw that she was close to tears. "I'll go back and see if there's not some way I can put the kitten in the house," he said. "Then it won't get the plants."

"But when the neighbor lets it out it will."

"Go get in the car. When the neighbor lets the kitten out you'll be in Vermont."

"Whether I'm here or not, it's still happening."

The kitten hopped down a step, coming toward them.

"I'm going to put it in the house," he said. "If you will go sit in the car."

"Put the plants inside," she said. "I can get the key from the neighbor and put them in and the cat can stay out. It's probably outside most of the time."

"God damn it," he said. "Go sit in the car."

She glared at him and turned, going to the car and yanking open the door and slamming it shut. He knelt and lured the kitten to him. This was his replacement. She had even let him see what it was. He reached out and scooped up the kitten and went to the side window, which he knew could be opened from outside. He had told Alice to get it fixed, after he opened it with no effort to let her crawl in the house the time she lost her keys. He could easily have fixed the window, but he knew she liked to do things herself. He put his fingertips on the window and pushed up; with the other hand he placed the kitten (Mary had even told him its name; Alice had named it Lucifer) inside and quickly closed the window. Though he wanted to, he did not stand there and look a final time into the house. He focused, instead, on the surprised look on the kitten's face. He could have looked past it, through the screen, but he did not, choosing instead to look at what was closest. He remembered Mary complaining, when she first started studying photography, about the difficulty of getting a sharp, even picture. If you focused on a close object, the background was hazy; and if you focused on something in the distance, what was closest tended to blur.

Realizing how little he had ever expected to spend a winter in the snow of Vermont, he drove down the street without looking to either side, only vaguely conscious of the haze of magnolia trees, until he came to the highway, and on the highway began to accelerate.

# Knowledge
## Gordon Lish

She said, You want me to kiss it and make it well? Come sit and I will kiss it and make it well. Come let me see it and I will kiss it and make it well, just take your hand away from it and let me just look. I promise you, I am just going to look. Oh, grow up, could looking make it worse? Do us both a favor and let me look. I swear, all I am going to do is to look. So is that it? Are you telling me that's it? That can't be it. Are you sure that's it? You're not really telling me that that is what all of this fuss is about. Is that what all of this fuss is about? I cannot believe that that is what all of this fuss is about. Is that what you have been making such a fuss about? Don't tell me that that is what you have been making all of this fuss about. You call that something? That's not something. That's nothing. You know what that is? I want to tell you what that is. That is nothing. Does it hurt? It doesn't hurt. It couldn't hurt. Why do you say it hurts? How could you say it hurts? You really want me to believe it hurts? Is that what you are telling me, you are telling me that it hurts? Because I cannot believe that that is what you are really telling me, that you are really telling me that a thing like that could hurt. A little thing like that could not conceivably hurt. Do us both a favor and don't tell me it hurts. So when I do this, does it hurt? What makes you say it hurts? Are you sure it hurts? How could it hurt? Give me one good reason why it should hurt. I should show you something that really hurts. I am going to give you some advice. You want some advice? Count your lucky stars you don't have something that really hurts. You know what you are doing? Let

69

me tell you what you are doing. I want you to sit here and hear me tell you exactly what you are doing. Because guess what. You are making something out of nothing. You want me to tell you what you are doing? Because that is what you are doing, you are making something out of nothing. So don't act like you didn't know. You know what? You're not doing yourself any good when you put on such an act. I am amazed at you, putting on such an act. So how come you never figured this out for yourself? You should have figured this out for yourself. Why should you, of all persons, not be the one to figure this out for yourself? I want you to promise me something—next time try to figure things out for yourself.

Forget it.

I do not need anybody to promise me anything.

Let me ask you something.

No, definitely again you better skip it.

The answer would make me sick.

Listen, you know what is wrong with you? Because there is something very, very, very wrong with you. I guarantee you, I promise you, a person's mother knows.

# Extra Days
## Janet Burroway

Eventually, his breathing slowed and she could free her arm. She knew he was overtired and had had too much sun and that in the morning he'd go on about nothing but whether she'd got the new Alligator Point patch sewed on his patch jacket and he couldn't find any socks and was there crackerjacks for his break; she knew all that. The fundamental source of sanity is the knowledge that grief won't last. If that gives you your suspicions about joy, too bad for you. It's the price of sanity; you don't expect the price of anything to go down, do you? Nevertheless, she thought ten years was young to have an actual suicide plan.

She shook the sand off his things into the shower and picked up the conch, the plastic bag of clam shells and periwinkles, and the horseshoe crab. (A find, that — amber, translucent, only an inch-and-a-half across — usually the little ones broke as they washed up.) Still smaller, the fiddler crab crouched in the sand pail and, when her shadow fell across it, put up its claws like a boxer in mismatched gloves. Come'n get me. How do you convey your kind intentions to minor crustacea?

She picked up the pail as well, in the crook of her little finger, and juggling his wet things and the fruits of their scavenging, watched Michael for a moment to make sure. Salt over salt, the tears had left streaks in the fine-powdered seacrust around his ears. His freckles hid in the fever flush; the new-bleached hair was scattered from his thrashing and a shock of it fell across his lashes. He was beautiful, all right. Which was a fact to take out and acknowledge only incidentally, in the moments, say, between shaking sand into the shower and setting a belligerent fiddler crab outside. Because there's nothing special about the beauty of a sleeping child. Because she would not give him a memory, not one, to drag on into adulthood, like the memories she dragged, ruffled and smothered and cooed over, "Booful dolly! Baby girl!" Also, because she wanted to live in Garth's perspective, and to Garth, Michael must be just another boy, unchosen, set more or less by chance in continuing proximity. Yes, and because apart from that, out of some letter or other from her erstwhile husband, was a phrase her anger still snagged over: *You owe it to the beauty that is Michael.* What it was she owed she couldn't now recall. Something to do with money, probably, or preserving the family, or keeping him in the True Church. *The beauty that is Michael.* You don't love a child unless you'll wipe its nose.

She closed the door as quietly as she could with her few free fingers and went to make space on the living room shelves among the driftwood, shells, skulls, and stones already crowded there. She passed Garth cleaning snapper at the sink as she headed for the back porch.

"He asleep?"

"Mn-hmmm."

"I heard you. You were terrific with him."

"Was I? Thanks."

She spread his things on the line between the old pillars and turned to the fiddler crab. Alarmed, no doubt, from its roller coaster ride, it huddled now against the piece of moss, claws clenched back into its body and the body minutely jerking back and forth with watchfulness. The sand was dry, but they'd found it on dry sand. She didn't know whether she should wet the sand. She didn't know whether she should set it in the shade or where the morning sun would hit it. She didn't know what it ate. So she did nothing except reach to stroke its back with her index finger, and because she knew perfectly well this wouldn't be allowed, scarcely flinched when it took a grab of the toughened skin beside her nail. She lifted her hand and the crab clung, held, persisted till it was tipped up on the edge of its shell, then lunged for a better hold and fell, scurrying bellicose around the rim. Come'n get me. Okay, now *you* go to sleep.

In the kitchen, she poured the Clorox out of the butter tubs and rinsed the three bleached sand dollars they'd chosen of their bucketful. At the Point this time of year they were so plentiful that anywhere you dug your fingers half-an-inch below the sea bottom you'd encounter one, little hairs waving like a round brown meadow and the mouth at the center of its star slowly pulsing. It was as if the sea was paved with them, Garth said, and said every inch of the water was invisibly alive like that.

And said, "Is there room in the freezer? We've got snapper for a month."

"We can take some to Merri and Doug."

He was nearly done, and into his rhythm: the point of the fishknife at the anus, a single clean slit through the white belly flesh, his thumb pushing up from the bottom while the knife arched toward the spine, and the guts plopped out in a lump on the slimy newsprint. He tossed it aside and took another. Point, slit, push, plop. The offhand competence of Garth's gestures always stirred her. Shifting gears, or building a fire. As if the idea of work itself was caught in his easy hands, though you do not tell a man you love him because he can tie his shoes, or that watching him gut a fish makes you want to go to bed. And yet when it came to that it was not necessarily more grotesque than the fact that, now, she was going to light a candle and a stick of incense to sit by while she hemstitched a souvenir on a jacket. It doesn't do to focus too hard on your incongruities, because that leads to selfweariness, which leads to depression, which leads . . .

"You look upset." Although he'd scarcely broken his rhythm to glance between fish and fish.

"Of course I'm upset. You said you heard."

"Just part of it."

She turned off the tap and dried the sand dollars in paper towels, thumbing off the hardened hairs that clung underneath.

"He says he sits in school feeling as if his insides were being scraped, and if he knew how to go on scraping he'd kill himself that way. He said he tried to drown himself this afternoon."

"That's bullshit. He was having a great time till we got ready to go."

"It doesn't matter if it's true, Garth. It's true to the way he was feeling then."

"He'll be over it in the morning."

She took the sand dollars to the living room and lit the incense angrily. Why is it that being told what you know amounts to accusation? And why, being accused, do you seem to deny the thing you know? She was pinning the alligator on Michael's cuff when he followed her in, wiping his hands.

"I just think," he said, "it's about time he ought to be able to see me put my hand on your ass without pulling the Hamlet routine."

"Okay, I agree with you. So what am I supposed to do, since I'm so terrific?"

Carefully, he wiped a few flecks of fish dirt from his tee shirt, his belt, his jeans. "Do you want to get married?" He flipped the hair out of his eyes, new-bleached, if not as blond as Michael's then blond enough to be Michael's father's. Come'n get me.

"I don't see what good that would do. He doesn't believe in second marriages."

"Believe! Did he tell you that?"

"He told me that a week or two ago. He thinks marriage is a sacred rite, and you only get one chance. If you flunk it, that's it."

"Where does he get that stuff?"

"God knows. Maybe Catholicism is hereditary."

"Well, to tell you the truth I don't feel bound to live by his moral code."

She shoved the needle through a section of alligator tail and caught it through the loop, pulling it tight before she asked, "What about you? D'you want to get married?"

76

"I'm perfectly satisfied the way things are."

"Well, so am I." Conscious of her mother's voice in her own — why is triumph *prim?*—"So to tell you the truth, I don't feel bound to get married just to spite him."

At which he laughed and went to get his book; as easy as shifting gears.

Whereas she, as usual after one of Michael's overarticulate tantrums, sat ragged in the yellow light from the old globe, jumpy as the candle flame, not done with it. You couldn't say Michael didn't come by his tendencies honestly. His paternal grandfather had damned himself in the old style, shotgun in the mouth, on the 28th floor of an office building in Stamford, Connecticut, on a Friday night. And his father had called hysterical once a week for six months after they left, fifteen-hundred miles down the eastern seaboard, to say the gas was on, the pills were in his hand, if they found him at the bottom of a cliff it'd be her fault, until finally her fist-clenched nights and haggard mornings erupted in the right phrase, "Well, for God's sake, do it then, so I can get some sleep!" And he'd stopped calling and bought himself an MGB and married an editorial assistant out of Boston. And she herself, twice before she was thirty, had gone so far . . .

She knew that Garth was deep in Cambodia with Malraux, and that reading brought a fishing weekend to closure for him, like coffee after dinner or a cigarette after sex. She knew that if she brought it up again he'd have no choice but to turn sensible and soothing on her, as she had with Michael. He reads too many war comics. Television. It's the way kids are. And that she would then have no choice but to thrash out, like Michael: I won't be soothed! Having reasoned this through, she said, "All the same, ten years old seems early to have an actual plan."

He looked up, leaving a finger on his sentence. "He's got a plan?"

"A beauty. You know those Vietnamese spear traps you told him about?"

"Pungee sticks."

"That's it. He's saving up for a boy scout knife, and he's going to whittle a stick to a point and smear it with dog shit, then plant it in the ground and fall on it. If the spear doesn't kill him, the poison will. He told me it was 'very inventive' of the Vietnamese."

He let his finger slide from the page and leaned back to look at her. "You blame me?"

"Oh, Garth, don't be dim. He'd've picked up some other idea somewhere else. I just think it's a pretty ugly obsession for a ten-year-old."

He granted, "Pretty heavy." And then, almost visibly shouldering the role she'd cast him in, "But, you know, when he gets his boy scout knife he's going to take up soap carving."

"I know."

"I always liked the ant-torture myself when I was a kid. You know, where the Indians tie you down and smear honey in your eyes and ears?"

"I know, Garth."

"Hey." He laid the book aside and made as if to come to her, and then—maybe she looked more stubborn than distressed—set his mouth and leaned back again. "You told me you stole sleeping pills yourself a time or two. And here you are. Just waiting for me to finish this chapter so I can take you in there and throw ya' everywhichway."

"Actually, I'm sewing."

He went back to his book. She sewed, eyes sun-sore in the inadequate light, but not wanting any more light. Such sounds as there were attested to absolute domesticity—a tap somewhere, his page turning, the old beams sighing from the temperature drop. It was not that she thought Michael was going to kill himself, or at least not on a pungee stick, and not for forty or fifty years. It was precisely that she, herself, was still here, and knew what it had cost her, in mistakes and hate and self-contempt, before the night she reached up into Myrtle Clifford's gilt medicine cabinet and pocketed two amber plastic vials of Nembutal; and then before the night she finally, keening and rocking on the bathroom rug, flushed them down the toilet with her vomit. She wished her son survival, but she couldn't easily wish it at such a price. It hurt her, tired her, to foresee what years he was going to go through, and that she had no more weapon against it than "being terrific with him."

"It's not as if death isn't real!" she blurted, not to be answered, and was not. Just because he's a child and I've turned childish; there's evidence enough, God knows . . . And looking around the dim room for it, found, suddenly, more evidence than she bargained for. The dog skull's sockets flickered. The parched driftwood was hung with seahorse skeletons and dried crabs. Her own chair was a felled tree, the floors and walls dozens of others. Bound and hung with jute, skins, hide. She wasn't sentimental about causing death — slitting fish or bleaching sand dollars. But we *decorate* with corpses. Peacock feathers. Cattails. Grass. The candle is consuming tallow melted out of animal flesh. There are jars and jars of shells that are the bodies of creatures once alive; the jars themselves are melted sand, which is nothing but crushed shells, which are the bodies of dead sea things. The life cycle is not the point; the point is that death *accumulates*. If matter stays, and the earth recreates out of the dead, then every atom carries in every incarnation another death upon its back, and every live and dead thing in this room has died over and over again. Pollution is only a cosmic joke to lay the blame on us; in any case, everything would eventually be so dragged down by death that the cells would fail to hold, the hair would slide from its follicles, sap would puddle at the roots, the sea would go sluggish with the weight of it while we sat ignorant with oysters in our ears, stupefied with alligators on our feet, staring at pulp logs consumed in oozing flame in the center of the grate.

Perversely — she know she was perverse — this terror partly stilled her. When he clapped the book shut at the same instant she bit her thread, they laughed at the felicity of their timing and became more or less mutually aware — that their muscles were comfortably overextended and the skin burn-stretched no more than they could take, this time of year. In bed they came together, easily, smelling the sea again.

Which would have brought them out of another weekend in the black if he had not, as if to illustrate her point, to make the briefest possible interlude of fecundity, fallen asleep just as she turned to tell him what she'd seen, and so left her alone awake, damp with however many million poisoned sperm and fingering the blanket binding, which was in fact acrylic (crushed and burned from coal; nothing is synthetic, it's only dead), but had been deliberately devised to resemble the unwound cocoons of a Japanese vat's worth of steamed worms.

When she finally slept, she found herself at the butcher counter of the old Cochran Grocery on Seventh Street, where she had brought her mother's body to be trussed. It was already skinned, and had so little flesh on it that she did not know what animal she could say it was that Mr. Cochran would find credible. The teeth, particularly, stripped of the softening skin, protruded forward like a rodent's jaw. Also, her handbag was overflowing with capsules of Nembutal, which squirmed out through the orifices and dropped to the floor, where they crawled away. She kicked sawdust over them, as inconspicuously as possible. The black-haired woman beside her said pleasantly, "How do you fix that? With garlic plugs?" "Yes, I do," she said. I take the point of a fishknife and make however many million slits ... "I use tarragon," she said. "Rosemary." Mr. Cochran put an apple in the corpse's mouth.

So that, by morning, she was caught in the ineluctable superiority of the neurotic. She could not eat, but cooked an elaborate breakfast, to make this the more evident. The bacon bubbling made her nauseous and the nausea panicked her; the last time she had stood for an hour at a time at the supermarket meat counter, unable to choose, unable to remember what it was she did to meat. Michael knelt on the back porch in his pyjamas dragging a twig in front of the fiddler crab, laughing when it lunged. She said he was not to tease it. He said he wasn't teasing it, it was his. She said that was lousy logic and to get himself dressed right now, he'd be late to school. Which he didn't until she yelled like a fishwife: This minute! So when she showed him the jacket he grumbled a begrudging "Ummph," and when Garth asked was he feeling better this morning, Michael defied him, "No!" and, sly-eyed, threatened to buy a boy scout knife. To which Garth replied that he'd better make sure it had a nail file because he badly needed one. To which she said, "For Christ's sweet sake," and they left by various doors in settled mutual hostility.

Day chastened her. Indulging her vision, she had worn it out by noon. Pig's feet and lettuce leaves in the supermarket, tomatoes she picked herself, newspapers she burned, ammonia with which she expunged the overripe germs on the sink drain, spray against aphis, fake sponge, real chamois, bleach . . . once aware of the omnipresence of death and her steady domestic murders, it became so obvious that it lost any saving dimension of discovery. But like someone condemned to see the road passing under the car all night, she registered this food, that cloth, the other disinfectant, until she was shaking with the boredom particular to anguish, ready to repent, as if she might stand before the interrogator, pigeon-toed, pleading, "I *will* be normal."

Or maybe day chastened all of them, or simply rounded to its balance. When she went to pick Michael up, he came swinging his lunch pail down the hill, stopping to engage in intense negotiation with a pale girl in a scarlet undershirt and the boneless stance of incipient sexuality. Merchandise changed hands. He crashed and slopped himself into the front seat crowing, "That dumbhead traded me four motorcycle cards for a crackerjack ring!"

She mother-feigned interest in his motorcycle cards. But he caught, perhaps, something controlled about her, because he studied her sideways, looked away and mumbled, "I'm sorry about last night."

"That's okay, Mike. Sometimes it's good to get it out."

This minimal absolution left him uneasily shuffling his cards. Thinking perhaps it was the wrong thing to do — she didn't want to reward him for a tantrum—but reasoning recklessly that if she took it for a gesture of trust then he would, too, she drove to the shopping center and advanced him a dollar-and-a-half on his allowance toward the knife. Then she bought him a dozen blocks of blunt balsa wood and sat on the back porch steps with him, assuring herself that he knew how to hold it. He had never owned a knife, but he knew perfectly well. He notched and whittled skillfully which—had he been Garth's son it would have come as no surprise—startled and delighted her; the delight registered as genuine, and it was all right. Half-an-hour later he was raking flat the sand in a sandbox he hadn't bothered with for years, and she, relieved and wry, supposed he wouldn't even get around to soap.

But she misjudged his attention span. The next time she looked, he had upturned the fiddler crab's pail into the sandbox, and by the time Garth got home he had constructed a whole subdivision of balsa buildings, bungalows and towers, with a lake in the middle and a faintly oriental bridge of whittled popsicle sticks.

"Right. Now," said Garth. He hadn't got his jacket off. They went to the woods and, with the biggest blade, sliced out plugs of damp earth around pine sprouts three or four inches high. They dug holes in the sandbox and banked wet sod around them. Michael found a cypress sapling which they planted by the bridge so it overhung the lake. The balsa buildings were solid, fake, so they made a mutual decision to sacrifice the sand pail and sliced a door in it, over which they hung a wood sign: CRAB. They disagreed about the fence, but Garth stood firm on his superior experience in favor of palm bark over popsicle sticks, and he carved the chips while Michael poked them in a square around the pail. Their air of solemn enterprise left her very much on the sidelines until it occurred to her to go in for a jar of shells. She edged a path with periwinkles from the sand pail to the break in the fence.

"That's it. And around the lake," Michael said.

The object of these attentions cowered for the most part in the shade of the corner brace, and though they talked to it (praising the lake view, the solid construction, the high tone of the neighborhood) only twitched occasionally—a fat client, suspicious of a hard sell. When they returned from the woods with a taller pine sprout for the front yard, it had disappeared. Mike cried out in disappointment, but Garth searched around the box, pointing—"There"—to a little mound of sifted sand; and within a few minutes the crab emerged on the other side of a balsa hut, scuttling upward big-claw-first and racing a foot or so sideways before stopping to take up its pugnacious stance again. "Digging the cellar," Garth explained. After that, out of some obscure amphibian instinct impossible not to take for enthusiasm, it stayed on the surface dashing in short spurts back and forth, streaking a maze of paths around its property.

They left Michael weaving string between the fence posts, brought out the snapper and lit the grill. While it burned down they lay in the grass, using his jacket for a pillow. He'd shrugged it off on the ground at some point and it was so stained she'd have to take it to the cleaner's anyway, where they'd remove the evidence of crushed grass and sterilize out such invisible organisms as it had picked up off the ground. . . .

Okay. Day was dying too, and the sky decorated with it, blue-black behind them and yellow in the west, the pines shifting, soughing in the air and throwing thin shadows over them, over the one sharp point of light where the coals died down. Mike humming absently. She hoped Garth wouldn't find it necessary to say I told you so.

"You had a bad day over him," he said.

"And a night. It's strange to me to think . . . that sometime or other he'll dream about my corpse."

He took a heavy handful of her hair and pulled her toward him. "I close up because I don't know how to help."

"You do all right."

He stretched against her and leaned up on one elbow, tracing the hump of her hip with his palm. She let herself roll into him and gave in altogether to gravity, sagging into the corner formed by his body and the grass, feeling the unstable gusts, the surer cadence of his hand, the individual blades of grass against shoulder and thigh where her body didn't fit the ground.

Michael's shriek split them apart. She stumbled up guiltily, caught only a glance of him by the sandbox before her hair, trapped under Garth's elbow, jerked her back. Garth moved, she pushed up to one knee and stood awkwardly, already taking up the weight of it, collecting the slim resources for another day. Two nights in a row is hardly fair, it's about time he ought to be able to see me put my hand on your ass, it's not as if death isn't oysters in our ears, however many million poisoned I'm sorry about last night . . .

"I killed him!" Michael shrieked. He stood by the sandbox shaking, one hand extended, splayed. It took her a moment to understand because, teeth bare and eyebrows meeting, his face so clearly seemed to fling out accusation.

"He pinched me and I broke him! I killed him!"

The hand hysterically fended them off. If they touched him he would fight. The crushed crab lay against the sandbox where he had flung it, bloodless, instantly inert, a piece of trash.

"I didn't mean to!" Michael screamed, and began to howl. The hand went limp and he ran toward her, she put her arms out, no, past her, to throw himself on Garth.

"I didn't mean to . . . he pinched me and I just . . . !"

In one motion Garth swung him up and sat down with him, huddled him on his lap where he clutched at Garth's back and butted his head into the collarbone.

"I didn't *mean!*"

"Of course you didn't, of course you didn't," Garth repeated again and again against the rhythm of the butting head until it subsided into mere rocking and the howls diminished to sobs.

"Look, he'd've been dead on the road by last night if we hadn't found him, Mike. You probably gave him an extra day."

Garth sat holding him like a child of two, stroking his back and the hair out of his eyes, forming the sentences whose meaning is in their tone, while Michael cried, insisting now and again, "I killed him," but meaning by it, "Hold me," and clutching up for reassurance with his arms, his eyes, to Garth.

To Garth, because Garth was the fixer, the doer, the one for whom the sea was alive. She, herself, was not at all reassured; not reconciled. She was only, standing at a little distance from their private enterprise, flooded with unabashed pity for her son, because he was her son and her son, for whom the longest thing to learn and the hardest to remember, for whom the decision of every day, never finally made nor wholly understood, would be how willing he was, after all, to live.

# Calculus

## Art Winslow

She is like me in that way, trying to be happy but somehow unable, and with me it is just me, something I grew into, like my shoe size, that is there for good and I pay it no mind, but with her it was something done to her once, I know or think I know, though I'd never ask and she has never volunteered, but in the earnestness of my pursuit I am saying "Don't worry, it won't happen with me," though how I can make any such guarantee, having changed lovers so many times myself, is preposterous, and the real thrust of my statement is "Fuck what you think, listen to me," which is no great feat, since people do it with regularity, though not with me, specifically, they still do it, whether it involves adultery or not, and it is all a form of adultery anyway. Yes, her husband is my friend, if you employ that term with a certain laxity and forget that maybe Damon and Pythias did exist and the rest of us are too ashamed to admit we have no friends, or that maybe it's like prospecting and only a few lucky ones will strike it rich; but whichever is the case, that term and her husband are irrelevant to the question at hand, which is really do you take thrill as you find it and consider it providence, dumb luck, or do you pinch it off according to spec.

Seeing her this way and gloating in its special thrill has come to mean something, and that this something could be removed or dissolved somehow soon and irrevocably is what tempts me to mail her husband an anonymous letter detailing his own affairs and counseling him that the wisdom of the ages is "ignorance is bliss," and while his friend may be a blackguard and his wife rife with infidelity, that he has been as base, and pots don't call kettles black. Though such a letter would no doubt reveal its authorship, I would rather have her than him; in truth, I would rather have her than anyone, at this moment, and at this moment the existence of any other moment is also preposterous, though in other moments I am married, too, and carry through them a shame from this that my lovers often cast as noble, when the only nobility, and this in small measure, lies in the absolute affront of the act itself, not its aftermath.

Aftermaths are the messy parts anyway, though joining in a knot on the sheets is such a sweet ticket to ten minutes of childhood that the only way to approximate it, and this by a considerable inferior distance, is to mount a swing, pump high, and wait for the forward spill of your crotch, though there is no aftermath to that, and mess is what life is all about, the more you create the more that fact becomes indelible and is transmuted from observation to motivation, a means to beat back the torpor that will surely drown us eventually, and perhaps if I can get her to accept this she will relax and manage to come next time, in which case I can forget about the natural advantage of being male and having something that does not lie, either works or doesn't, and almost always does.

There is a certain pall that one's own bedroom can draw over relaxation, I admit, though what magnitude, precisely, the violation of this room has assumed in her mind I can only guess, the conversation being of such minimal scope that I watch the black swath of her pubic hair, which I have parted with my hands and tongue and own pubic hair not just this Wednesday but for the fourth Wednesday in a row, and wonder why, when I am accepting of all I have said, and was truly thrilled when I came, those acts have failed to satisfy me.

Some residue of satisfaction must grace this bed for more than an instant, for Jeannette, the second wife of my friend Vern and the particular focus of my Wednesday attentions, begins Mondays now with exploratory calls to my extension at the office, though she will marshal such glee to report that Vern had called but the line was occupied by us that I begin to feel contrition, not for what we are doing but for loosing a malevolence that seems to be growing of its own accord, quite irrespective of any parameter I could erect to keep it in check, which as a friend to Vern I naturally do, such as the cautionary mention to her that switchboard operators in any company are among the first to know who is clinched on the springs with whom.

But it may not be malicious, as I have inferred; this is Jeannette's first time flouting the marital premise, and, that being the equivalent of a virgin these days, perhaps it is merely the hard try for happy that she is giving full rein by demonstrating her abandon to me, and further, while Vern has no right to expect any more than the rest of us do from the thin soil of our marriages, that there is no contempt of him inherent in her acts, that it is in fact the natural arc of an emotive pendulum, inertia and gravity at work, and were I to interfere unduly with this, it would constitute an unnatural act.

I am, for obvious reasons, mindful that some would call the union of Jeannette and me unnatural, Vern and my wife coming most immediately to the fore, and while I would view their reasoning with considerable disdain and argue that they fail to comprehend the vicissitudes of life, I don't hazard that either of them or either of us could explain the petulance of Jeannette's face when she insists that I watch her masturbate, or just what it is she is probing, the gentle teeter of her hips and crimp of fingers in her flesh arousing in me not only thrill but the tandem desires to hurt her and avenge Vern of a debasement that seems beyond call.

Submission is never distant in these affairs, after all, for I have often found that those most pliant with me claim to be running from domination at home, the fugitive taint of our contact by some alchemy convincing them that they have chosen, they are free, and it being neither my task nor to my advantage or even liking to illuminate for them the preposterous mess their thoughts would make were they to be set on a page. Not that

I regard my motives as selfless; on the contrary, in the present instance, a strict veracity would probably unduly complicate my midweek labors and poison the whole affair before its time, an eventuality which will certainly occur, though it will doubtless take Jeannette, possessed as she seems to be by the undertaking, considerable time to recognize that what she says it is about me isn't there, and our prospects will fade, though my cognizance of this throughout will not diminish my excitement. I can focus on other things: the random strew of objects, for instance — socks on the floor, Vern's shirt on a chair — to act as a goad in contrast with the utter calculation of our act.

5) Mothers and daughters

5) Swimming

4187

# Up Late

**Linda Svendsen**

We were going for a moonlight swim. It was just us. She parked by Trout Lake and said take off your pedal-pushers, panties will be O.K. Who will see? Her dress was over her head and gone. She wore girdle, garters, a white bra with fat straps. She rolled the windows down, turned the radio on, up, and the song said *you say potato and I say potahto.* I kept my sneakers; between us and water were rocks and evergreen needles, and then in the lake, invisible nipping fish. My mother took my hand. She said, "Come on, small fry."

That lake had no bottom. Every summer a boy fishing fell backward out of a canoe and it was curtains. None were found. I didn't think about drowning: I was six, could kick and float, held Mum's hand, would never die until God needed a new angel. We followed the flashlight beam until the moon took over—down the little hill to the dock. Then she remembered the emergency. She had parked on an incline and the car might roll down the hill to sink in the lake. We would have to sleep on the dock until sunup or the lifeguard. People—my father, who was dead—would wonder. She headed back to the road.

I climbed the big water slide and sat up top. No breeze. Across the lake were houses with sundecks, porch lights, wind chimes and pools, and I could hear people living a late August life, and the ruckus of grasshoppers rubbing themselves, and the radio host in our car say, "Speak up, you're on the air."

I was forbidden to slide in the dark, in the deep part. I stayed still and sang "Kookaburra," and when the door hadn't slammed, and I didn't see her light, "Policeman, policeman, do your duty,

95

here comes Adele, the bathing beauty, she can do the rumba, she can do the splits," etc., and then stuck in my mother's name, June, and then her middle name, Ruth.

I was the baby and Mum had taken me with her to the Elks Club. This was how she kept steak in our mouths, barrettes in my hair. I usually sat at the staff table with my coloring book and crayons and soft drink, guarding everybody's smokes. This time I had waited in the coat check. It was empty in hot weather. In the heat all the women were bare shoulders and napes and loud splashed cologne. A cocktail waitress named Cindy brought me a big glass of ice cubes with a pink straw and let me look at the photos in her wallet and read the backs. I wanted her for my sister.

When my mother touched the piano, the crowd shut up. They squeezed each other and slowed down. The men stood tall and swayed a little this way, a little that. Ladies closed their eyes and just didn't care. It was *"Que será, será."* Lights went off. I was lying on the cold linoleum under hundreds of thin wire coat hangers. This was where we were before the lake.

She walked back to the dock keeping the beam barely ahead of her next step. I saw a face in her knee. Without clothes on, my mother looked like somebody else and I didn't know who. She put towels down by the slide and raised her arms. I let myself into them. "Ready, mermaid?" she said. Behind her the lake loomed like a trick. Light glinted off safety pins fastened below.

She clung to the rope ladder and lowered her body bit by bit. She said it burned. She was only waist-deep when I jumped. I liked getting things over with. I could hold my breath for seconds. My mother couldn't even swim. She hated getting her hair wet and losing her style. She wouldn't even duck her head underwater to see what was what. She found a warm spot and didn't budge.

When I asked, she spread her legs wide to let me swim between. The first time I couldn't find her. The lake was ink. Once

I got the knack I couldn't get tired of this. I made it harder. If my hand brushed, if I bumped into, if the smooth rubber sole of my sneaker nicked, she would die. She would die before Christmas. I touched her. I changed the rule. She would die after I skipped grade two, before 1961, whenever I wanted. I kept touching. She stayed living. Her life stretched long, longer than mine. It was up to me. She was goosebumps. She was just a shadow I passed through to get to the other side.

She heard it first, of course. I was diving. I was beneath her. I was being pickled by the lake. I thought it was a speedboat — a fisherman trolling for breakfast with a bright hook. The motor was rude; it was a lawn mower chopping away at the water. Whether to stay under, I wasn't sure. If I came up, someone might see my no top, our hardly anything on. A little later, and I didn't hear it anymore.

After that I lost track: lost track of how long I'd skimmed bottom, of when she would be kaput, lost track of fun and was I good. I was more water than girl. I was on your mark, get set, go, keep going or else. The lake spilled up my nose. My mother was still my arch. This may have taken one sheer minute.

Her face wasn't like an ice cube, a crack, the flame of a match, or the moon. It didn't keep you looking. Sometimes the hook of her nose scared me and I could not hug her. I had to glance behind, around her waist, as if somebody surprising us had just walked in a door. Then she would turn around, turn back and say, "What did you see?" and forget we were going to touch.

We were lying on towels on the dock and I was looking at her. She was looking up at the night. I shut off my flashlight and twinned her. I bent my knees, making my legs steep hills. I crossed myself. I tried to think about everything she could think of and this was too easy so I tried to look like I was thinking. I put her soft voice in mine and said *Look both ways* and *Did you have enough? There's more.*

"Who are you whispering to?" She rolled over. "Do you have a secret friend?"

The stars were still out. Each star was part of a family picture, each family of light had a name. It all fit. People said stars told stories if you shared. I did this for a long time, different times, and I could not see a spoon spilling cough syrup or the dog lifting a hind leg or an arrow aimed at us. When I looked, each star was already gone. I was only seeing old light left behind. This was science. I stared at the space between two stars then shut my eyes to see which was darkest. It was darkest inside. I heard her go by, each plank making a new noise under her foot. "Where are you going?" I said.

"I don't know." She stopped by the ladder of the slide and grabbed the bars. "I don't want to go home yet," she said. She leaned back letting her arms do the work, hold her, and then climbed up. She looked down on me from the top of the slide. "I think you took a nap," she said.

I shook my head. I never slept, I was never not awake, I had never had a dream. In the middle of the night, if she woke thirsty, she was out of bed after me, after water ran cool and hit the glass bottom. When my father was sick, I sat big and close by his side and watched the life drip clear into him. He could not die if I was watching. We both knew it.

"I'm going to let go," she said. "I'm letting go."

I slid the switch on the flashlight and buttered her in its cone. Her arms surrendered over her head. Her legs were crooked, straight when she slipped in. She was here, then gone. Her whoop, mouth wide open, was eaten by the lake. The splash— noisy, tall, a surprise, a lily shaking—made stars leap out of the lake and gleam where she had hung.

The night did not stop being hot. It kept getting warmer. Across the lake, the people in those houses were lying on top of beds listening to fans like big bugs. The trees were slack and bored, and the ones wearing leaves gave some up. They rode the water. When my mother tried to float, her face stayed above

98

the water and the rest of her sank. She did not believe me when I told her. I had done breath bobs beside her. "You're sinking," I said and she said, "I am not."

I left. I could tell when she wanted to be alone. I leaned forward onto the lap of the water and kicked once. I didn't need her; I kept my chin down in the water and turned into a crocodile: all eyes, silence, might.

I looked up when the man walked out of the bush and onto the dock. He saw us and kept coming. He sat on the edge of the dock and undid his sandals. The moon lit us all. He looked older than her. He was seeing her in her brassiere. She saw him seeing and ran a hand through her hair, then hung onto a strand and twisted. He looked at me. Without blinking I looked back. He eased off a sandal, a black sock, and tucked the sock under the sandal straps, watching me. He did the same to the other foot. The socks weren't all black. There were stripes of lightning on the sides. He stood up and started taking off his shirt.

My mother glanced back where our car was parked like she had a kink in her neck or had to be somewhere by a certain time. The radio in our car gave the report. It would be the same again tomorrow and that was hot. Her face said she had lost something. I wondered where he had come from and when he would go. I wondered if he would be naked soon. "Guess what I am," I said to her. I spun in the lake. My sneakers slapped and raised mud. I tapped her. "Guess." "Not now," she said and tried to take my hand. "Swizzlestick," I said. "In a drink." He folded his shirt. I kept whirling. I refused to let go and be dizzy. I looked at the dock, her, the dark yards on the other side, the tongue of the slide, the dock, to keep my bearings. I wondered if he lived in a cave in the woods. "Guess now. Guess what I am now," I said. "You're very loud," she whispered. "Do you want to wake up the fish?" He was pulling down his pants. I could see the shiny rim of swim trunks. "I'm a swizzlestick in Orange Crush," I said. I was exhausted. They were both tilting.

The man looked down on us. He was so strong, he looked

like he could throw me high up in the air and catch me and keep doing it. He nodded at her, then me, and said, "Ladies." His hands made a prayer. He fixed upon a point and then sprang off the dock and flew over me. For a moment he made another kind of night, pale, closer to day. For a second I smelled his hair and under his arms and breath. He smiled back at me. I wasn't afraid. He entered the lake like a stone thrown sideways, skimming, and broke into a crawl. He swam without a splash, his stroke and kick caught no light. I watched until she clapped. "Out," she said. "It's late. It's time to go."

We got out and she wrapped me in a damp towel. I lost my balance and almost fell back in; she made me lie down and pulled me across and over her legs like a cape. Before Dad died, he could not hold me on his knees. I was too heavy. "Keep your head down," she said. "Close these," she said and kissed above my eyes. Her garter biting into my cheek would make a mark gone by morning.

I felt much better. When I asked who he was, in her story voice she said she didn't know. Maybe his wife read long books in bed and kept the light burning. Maybe he was on a team and had to practice to beat everybody. Maybe he was a man who could never fall asleep in August, or after midnight. Maybe he was king of the lake. She said he could have been anybody.

In my mother's arms, I looked for him. I couldn't tell if he was coming or going. He was a tear, a tiny rip in the white scarf tossed down by that moon. He could have been an angel.

# Living With Snakes
**Daniel Curley**

*Death is in the garden*
*Waiting til you pass*
*For the cobra's in the drain pipe*
*And the krait is in the grass.*

Kipling

When Peter Watts moved into Indiana Price's house, the ground rules were explicit. He would have a room in the house, a Federal house near a village out the river road. He would be a presence in the house for her young son while she was travelling. She travelled a lot. She consulted. She moved and she shook. A son—after all, well, you don't exactly like to leave him at the vet's. And there would be no sex. She wanted the arrangement to last. She had theories about that. Statistics bore her out. Her own experience bore her out; there are some things you just don't try to mix. Living arrangements and sex for example. She wanted someone who would stay. Someone her son could get used to. Someone he might even watch and learn from. Male role models—Peter winced at that—were hard to come by but very necessary, especially about twelve—John had just turned twelve.

Peter's heart went out to this boy he had not yet seen. If there was one thing he knew, that was what it was like to be a chicken with no chance to peck up gravel for his crop, nothing to chew with. Of course, never having had models himself, having always seen power in the hands of women, he felt like a fraud in this new light. Shall the blind lead the blind? But perhaps he and the boy could teach each other. The whole thing terrified him, but he thought he would try it. After all, he deserved no better.

And he was glad he did try it. With the situation clear between them, it was as if they had gone through sex and come out the other side. As if they were waking up together in the morning and it was time to begin to tell her who he was. To pour it all out to her. To account for all the years they had not been together.

He felt this from the first moment they sat together in the room she assigned him. It was a lovely room, the room he had chosen secretly but had been afraid to request. Its windows opened on fields that ran down to the river. Inside, it had the look of a study with desk and bookcases and best of all a fireplace. She had built a fire that first day, and they sat in front of it and drank herb tea and ratified the terms.

He reached far back beyond the things he had told his wife when they were first married, beyond the things his mother knew, to things he had never told anybody, stretching and reaching for things he didn't even know himself, striving for something to offer her, something absolutely pure and untouched. Something just for her, just from him. It was truly that moment of openness that usually comes in bed the first time after sex is safely behind, that moment of desire for perfect sharing, before the sediment of doubt and evasion silts it all up. He thought they would go on from vision to dazzling vision. He was beside himself with delight.

And then, almost at once, he began to despair of the contract he had so gladly assumed. For one thing, he saw little of the boy except at meals. He was a studious boy and kept to his room, doing his homework and reading books about the Bermuda Triangle, UFO's, and the lives of inventors. Sometimes late at night when the house had gone all still, Peter would hear the boy's radio, which was never turned off, playing softly upstairs. At first he thought John had a woman in his room — by that hour of the night Peter was usually over-tired and not strictly accountable for his impressions. And if the mother had her lovers in, why shouldn't the twelve-year-old son? The mother was very big on openness, on equality, on the personness of all persons.

It was on the night the lovers came that Peter heard the radio, that he lay awake and tried to cry to relieve the pressure in his throat. Sometimes he slipped out of the house and took long walks along the dike. Sometimes he planned to smash the radio. Sometimes he was able to cry. It was quite clear that he had not got beyond sex at all. Sleep, however, knit it all up, and there was only another day with Indiana — or without her if she was off again. In some ways it was better when she was off.

The next surprise was that Indiana suddenly went against her own dictum and let a lover move into the house, mixing sex and living arrangements. During this time Peter repeatedly left the house in the night with the intention of never coming back. But once he had walked himself into a stagger and finally into a standstill, he turned around. Where was he going anyway?

It would still be winter dark when he let himself back into the house, but all along the valley he had seen lights coming on in bedrooms and kitchens and barns, and he had heard clear from across the river the sound of tractors starting, the warning clang of heavy equipment creeping backwards through the dark. Then he slept, slept far into the day. The fiction was that he had been writing late.

The lover's name was Francis Moreton. He was called Fran, and he had very long hair and a very long beard and very dirty feet. Of course he went barefoot all the time, so his feet were bound to get dirty. But they not only got dirty, they stayed dirty as long as anyone knew him. He was also a very young man. Younger, of course, than Peter, younger even than Indiana. Not so much older than John when you came right down to it. Peter wondered, in fact, how a man so young could have such a long beard. He must have begun growing it in his cradle, must have been dedicated, like Samson, never to know scissors or razor, a Nazarite before the Lord, destined to mangle monsters and strangle snakes. Or was that Hercules? Or did it matter?

And Fran Moreton had snakes. He had cages and cages of snakes. He had boa constrictors. He had rat snakes. He had milk snakes. He had king snakes. He seemed to have all the snakes that ever were. He stacked the cages in a little room upstairs, an old sewing room. Peter was never able to determine if Indiana knew about the snakes in advance.

A Dutch woman from Java once told Peter that when she was a child, cobras lived under the veranda. It was bad luck to kill them. He shuddered and supposed it was even worse luck not to. A man he knew used to kill garter snakes in his garden, apologetically, but he didn't want his children to be frightened when they got into the house, and they would get into the house. He himself had once dealt with — or failed to deal with — a large brown and white snake in the attic of the place in Maine. He was about to put his hand on a patch of mottled attic light as he came up the stairs. The patch flickered, writhed, and vanished under the eaves. He never told anyone. It would catch mice, he assured himself. Surely, he said, it was less dangerous than the bees in the chimney, honey oozing down the walls. Less dangerous than the wasps in the outhouse. But the truth is that he was afraid. It was a mystery, and he was afraid of sacrilege. That was just what it was. And at the end of *Pather Panchali*, a snake crawls in across the threshold of the now deserted house.

"But," Peter said, "you said —"

"I know," Indiana said. "It's against what I've always said, but it feels right."

Having lived all his life up to that time in the grip of principles, Peter was but newly turned on to feelings. To be sure he had always been one to quote Cummings' "Since feeling is first, who pays any attention to the syntax of things will never wholly kiss you." So when Indiana said it felt right, Peter said, Yea, verily, although he didn't have the least idea what she meant. His old accustomed systems were flashing SELF INDUL-GENCE SELF INDULGENCE. But he was determined to pay no attention to them. There was a new way—whatever it was—of seeing things, of feeling them. Verily, he said, and amen.

"Is this where I say 'right on'?" Peter said.

"That's not your style," Indiana said.

"Thank you," Peter said. "I couldn't have said it anyway."

"Just say what you think," she said.

"Well," he said in the face of this wholly novel idea, "I assume you know what you're doing." He was really thinking that—among a great many other things.

"Thank you," she said. "I think I do—on some instinctive level. I mean it feels right."

Peter had an inkling then of what it meant to feel something. He didn't trust it of course, because he was so unused to regarding feelings. But it seemed to him that something was telling him that what Indiana felt was right was, in fact, very wrong.

"Fantastic," Indiana said when Fran moved the cages in.

"How come so many snakes?" Peter said, trying to think of something not too stupid to say.

"I dig snakes," Fran said.

That first night, Fran held an indoctrination meeting. He let them handle the snakes. John was tentative at first but became more confident as he went on. Indiana was enthusiastic from the beginning. Mind over matter, Peter repeated to himself, but he let the others go first, and he quickly faded out of the receiving line.

Then Fran fed one of the boa constrictors. He took a white mouse out of his pocket and put it into the snake's cage. The snake was not particularly interested. The mouse smoothed its fur. "My mother always believed," Peter said, "in wearing good underwear in case she got run over by a streetcar."

The others looked at him oddly.

Then the snake began to stir itself. Peter drifted into the background. He got heads between himself and the cage. This was a very different matter from an optical illusion in the attic devouring imaginary mice. The others leaned into the cage like bubbles at the edge of the vortex in the bathtub drain.

"Fascinating," Indiana said. Or at least Peter supposed it was Indiana. John's voice, however, was very unreliable at about that time.

After that night, Fran Moreton was seldom seen in the house. He had the room next to the snake room, and he stayed there all the time. He never came to meals, so he never shared in the cooking rotation. He seemed to live on Pepsi Cola and potato chips. "He goes out for pizza sometimes," Indiana said. "Of course he's a night person." She seemed to think that explained everything and conferred some great, though vague, distinction.

Peter preferred to make his own observations and deductions. He heard quart Pepsi Cola bottles rumble across the floor sometimes. He found pizza boxes in the trash. Sometimes Fran's door was mysteriously ajar. The floor was littered with gaudy paperbacks, perhaps a dirty foot showed at the end of the unmade bed. Once when Peter had to check Fran's room for a leak—where was Fran that day?—he saw that the paperbacks were covered with space ships and monsters. Galaxies and mystic symbols. Books slipped beneath his feet. Bottles clinked and jostled. In the night sometimes Peter heard Fran's bare feet slithering in the halls and on the stairs, pervading the house, passing all the doors.

Silent as Fran normally was, however, he was a very noisy lover. He groaned and he bellowed. "Shit, piss, fuck," he shouted. Not a sound from Indiana. "Say it," he shouted. "Say it. Tell it like it is." Not a sound. "Cunt," he said.

Peter, lying rigid in his bed, thought of John lying rigid upstairs over him. Perhaps he slept through it, though. Perhaps he was safe.

John wasn't safe, of course, but it wasn't the love cries that threatened him. At least Peter could see no sign of that. No, it was something very different, and it began quite simply.

"Fran hasn't fed the snakes lately," John said. "It's way past time."

"Really?" Peter said.

"I've been reading up on it," John said. "I've asked at the

pet shop."

"I'm sure he knows what he's doing," Peter said, and he let it go.

"I suppose he does," John said. "He ought to anyway."

That night, however, when Peter heard Fran slide out of the house, stalking a pizza no doubt, he went cautiously into the snake room. He looked at each of the snakes, but he could tell nothing. They behaved very much like snakes. They were either completely still or they rolled slowly over their own coils. Their steady eyes watched him. Their nervous tongues tested his air.

He lay awake for a long time waiting for Fran to come back. He would sleep, he thought, when the last flame of his fire flickered out. But he didn't sleep. When the checkered log finally went black. When the blackened log at last broke and fell from the andirons, he woke with a start and lay rigid as Fran's feet hissed past his door, past Indiana's door, up the stairs, past John's door. A door shut firmly. Clicked shut. A bottle rolled. And all was quiet. It occurred to Peter then that it had been a long time since he had heard Fran shrieking the obscenities of love, since he had himself lain awake alternately listening and putting his hands over his ears, straining to hear and dreading to hear, angry, indignant, despairing. At least this was better for John, he thought or thought he thought.

Two days later, John said, "He still hasn't fed them. I don't know what to do. Perhaps I could buy some mice myself. I have a little money—"

"I'll speak to him," Peter said. Now he would have to do it. He was very unhappy, for once a little displeased with John.

Nevertheless, that night he settled into the kitchen to make bread. Fran would have to pass him to get out, but it was very late before he heard Fran's stealthy rustle on the hall matting.

"Oh, hello," Peter said, looking up from his book. "I decided to make some bread."

"Hello," Fran said. He never ceased to flow toward the door.

"Smells good, doesn't it?" Peter said.

"Uh," Fran said as if bread was not at all among his interests — but then what was?

"Anything wrong with the snakes?" Peter said. "John says you haven't fed them."

"It's OK," Fran said. And he slipped out the door.

"What about Fran?" Peter said to Indiana in the morning as they set up their day.

"What about him?" Indiana said. "He's a very odd young man." She sounded as if Fran were someone she barely knew, a crackpot of dubious reputation.

"He's not feeding the snakes," Peter said. "John and I are worried. We think maybe we'd better buy some mice. John knows what to do."

"We can't interfere," Indiana said.

"He's crazy," Peter said.

"We mustn't interfere," Indiana said. "They're his snakes."

"But he's killing them," Peter said.

"There's nothing we can do."

But John insisted that there was everything they could do, and Peter for once sided against Indiana. He bought mice at the pet shop and secretly brought them home.

"He's put a lock on the door," John said. "Why is he doing this?"

"I don't know," Peter said. Having committed himself to an action against all his habits, he felt the more bitterly frustrated. He was ready to assert himself. And he was very simply prevented. The unaccustomed exertion was nearly proving too much for him.

Still, the next day, Peter waited until he was alone in the house — or thought he was alone. It was more and more difficult to know where Fran was. He had gone very quiet in his room. If he ever left it at all, it must have been when they were all away. He must have lain there straining to hear, listening for doors, for cars starting. He must have tried to piece together scraps of overheard plans — Peter knew all about that. He was totally silent. He was totally invisible.

Peter went out into the yard and climbed the big old maple on that side of the house. Even as a boy, tree-climbing had terrified him, and now he climbed in thorough terror and in anger. He could see into the snake room. The snakes were quiet in their cages. What had he expected? No big branch went close to the house. If he was going to try the window at all, he would have to use a ladder.

He shifted his gaze to Fran's window. Fran was watching him. His hair and beard were wild as a prophet's. He stood in the attitude of denunciation. His lips moved silently. Peter clung to the tree for dear life and then, slowly, trembling, made his way to the ground.

"You've got to tell him he can't do this," Peter said to Indiana.

"There's nothing I can do about it," Indiana said.

"You've got to tell him he can't do this in your house," Peter said.

It's crazy, he said to himself. He knew he should have said it to her, and he was ashamed. You can't do this to John, he should have said. You can't do this to us. You can't do this to me. To me. To me. And I've got to do what I've got to do, he should have said. But he had no idea what that was.

When he woke up in the morning, however, a voice in his head was saying, I shall get a ladder. I shall break the window. I shall have a box of mice. If he tries to stop me, I shall kill him.

Peter was used to these voices. He had had them all his life off and on. They spoke to him in the morning usually, when he was still not quite awake. Lately there had been an aged Indian, a blind prophet of his people. The Indian spoke to him morning after morning about the spells and incantations he sang for his people. Spells for buffalo and spells for fish. Rain spells. And spells against a hard winter. I am an old man, the Indian sang, I live in my daughter's house. Droplets of life seep under my door. I take them up on blotting paper and sniff them while I lie awake. The Indian was a sweet old man, and Peter was making a book of his sayings.

It was not, of course, the Indian who spoke to Peter that

morning, although the Indian had often enough referred to stealing the strength of men he had killed. This was a new voice, an alarming voice, a dangerous voice, a voice that threatened and promised at the same time, the two sides of a coin that could be spent only once. I'll kill him, Peter said in his own voice and sprang out of bed.

"Don't tell me about it," Indiana said.

"All right," Peter said. "I won't."

"I can feel it," Indiana said. "You radiate it. It's all wrong and I want no part of it."

"You shall have no part of it," Peter said. He felt like a rock in a frost, solid and hard but full of water ready to explode him.

"It's an invasion of privacy," Indiana said. "It's a violation of integrity."

"It's puking up sick," Peter said, "and it's gone on long enough."

"I can't stand it," Indiana said. And she walked away.

Peter was astonished. It was natural law with him that Indiana could stand anything. All the water in his rock froze at once, and he was as dust. But he was left with a box of mice in his room, with a ladder laid ready, with a hatchet to break the pane near the window lock, with heavy gloves to reach through the jagged hole. It was this same hatchet he would use to kill Fran Moreton when he burst into the room.

For days now Peter had worked on his plan. He had waked up with full resolution to carry it out. And now he collapsed. Even in defying Indiana he had counted on her equal resolution. He had exulted in his decision. Now that she proved as fragile as he, he was at a loss. He had never expected this.

It happened, however, that the plan had a life of its own. Just sitting in the kitchen, drinking coffee and sending John off to school and Indiana off to work had always been the first step.

"Have a good day," he said to Indiana. "Good luck on your test," he said to John. "Hope you make the team." John wanted to play basketball. Peter really wanted him to play. He wanted to watch him and gloat. But at the same time he knew it was a step apart. He saw John with less time for walks and talks. He saw, say, a coach touching John's mind, touching, shifting, diverting. He saw John moving away, opening out, and he saw himself never again going anywhere.

He began his morning routine as soon as the others had left. He pulled on his heavy gloves to carry up the wood for the fireplaces, and he used his little hatchet to split some kindling. He laid Indiana's fire carefully and then his own — he had built up the kitchen fire before anyone else was up. But then with the gloves and the hatchet to hand, he was so far into the imagined plan that he went on without really willing it.

The aluminum ladder was light and easy. He looked out carefully for electric wires near the window, although he had scouted the area a dozen times in advance. The mouse box went into a pack he strapped tightly to his back. He went up the ladder slowly with his hatchet in his hand. It must have been like this when his Indian scaled the palisades at Deerfield. He tapped the glass with the back of the hatchet and reached in for the lock. It was all so easy.

Then he was in the room waiting. There was no sound from the next room. There was no sound in this room. The snakes lay still in their cages. They were very like snakes. But they were dead. It was only then that he became aware of the smell. He put his head out the window and threw up.

He tossed the hatchet out the window. It split the earth without a sound. He crept down the ladder even more slowly than he had gone up. Retrieved the hatchet. Passed through the kitchen. Through the hall. Past Indiana's door and past his own. His eyes felt red and fierce. He was completely noiseless on the stairs. Even the steps that always groaned were now silent. His blood was thudding in the back of his skull — unless it was Fran's blood, bleeping and listening, bleeping and listening.

Fran's door latch was silent, the same latch Peter listened for in the night, its small shriek, its snap on its secret. And the door eased open on an empty room.

The floor was covered with empty potato chip bags, an old

trick Peter knew. He had read of it and even practiced it himself when he stopped in dubious hotels. No one could have taken a step in that room without an uproar of paper or a clatter of bottles. A barrier reef of paperbacks in toppled piles outlined the bed. The bed itself was unmade, the sheets grey. Fran had somehow slipped out and vanished.

Peter faced the door of the snake room. He smashed at the lock with the back of the hatchet. The sharp click echoed through the house. It echoed through Peter and released the force for a greater blow. He had never smashed at anything like that before except wood. The lock sprang open. He turned aside. He was not yet ready to open that door.

He went down the stairs. Every tread now groaned as it knew how to do. He must find a shovel and dig a hole, a deep hole in the garden, down into the winter earth, black loam on his boots, among old roots of things and sleeping bulbs, memorabilia, and the silt of ten thousand floods.

# My Father's Roses

**Glyn Hughes**

In one of my most enduring images of my father, he is coming home from his work as a ticket inspector on the buses and he is riding my mother's bicycle. He rides her bike rather than buy one of his own because she does not like his doing it, and he feels that he has to get his own back on her for something: for something that makes him ache. He is a small, chubby, gentle, superficially unimpressive man who, however, inspires an extraordinary love and admiration from his workmates. He is forty, the age that I am now, and he has begun to put on weight, especially (like myself) around the face. His movements are often hesitant and awkward, yet on his bicycle he claims the crown of the road. This is because he is a socialist. His head is full of confusions. He has felt the power and originality of his own imagination and he reads books, especially H. G. Wells, Bernard Shaw, and George Orwell; stretched before the fire and 'wasting coal' (so my mother puts it) he reads them through the night until dawn, rather than go to bed. He cannot understand why life has trapped him where he is. But he soars out of it through dreams which his wife, and her sister-in-law upon whom my mother depends for consolation, bluntly call 'lies,' whilst expressions of hurt, hatred or bafflement contort their faces.

This is the time of the Second World War. He has not been called up because, so he tells my mother and me, his work at the bus depot is more important. In the event of a German invasion he is to operate a 'contingency plan': his fleet of buses will evacuate the population into the nearby Cheshire countryside. This plan was personally explained to him, he told us, by General Patton, stationed then at nearby Knutsford. Years later I was still having pointed out to me the house — half-secret amongst orchard, horse-littered paddock, and shrubberies — to which my father was summoned for this meeting.

Before he reaches the council-house estate where we live, he pedals through a suburb of Victorian mansions that were originally built for Manchester cotton merchants. Those palaces — outdoing one another in bizarre Gothic, Eastern or Italianate spires, turrets and fancy bricks or tiles — are hidden in deep layers of lawn or shrubbery with double or treble wrappings of mossy yew, beech or privet hedge, in the same way the rich Victorian bodies were hidden in layers of skirts and petticoats. Besides cotton merchants, they had been inhabited by at least ten times the number of servants. Where had they melted to, the thousands of maids, cooks, and gardeners who had worked in the fastnesses of those evergreen shrubberies? They had sunk away like ghosts. With their world covered by moss and haunted by dry rot, one or two were left at some houses. Here an old person reigned alone and aloof in a vast kitchen; there a girl, usually Irish or Jewish, still dressed up as a maid. Mostly the places were now served by a regiment of "dailies": one of whom was my mother.

In this overgrown jungle, muffling all sound, moss underfoot and up the sides of walls and trees, my father would pause, overcome by a glimpse of beauty — a yellow leaf catching the sunlight, or a blackbird's notes like hammer blows in the heart of a shrubbery — and engrossed in the mystery of life's meaning and purpose. A motor car would hoot at his aggressive refusal to move from the crown of the road, and father would calmly wave it on, the way he did to buses at the depot, his socialist — egalitarian — pacifist dreams a furnace raging inside him.

Engels, as my father knew, had lived hereabouts: a rich businessman who had inspired and fed Karl Marx.

The mansions are on a hill, whilst our housing estate, a place bare of all but a few damaged trees, is on the flat land below it. The council houses bisect the plain. In one direction Cheshire is private, consisting of one aristocratic park after another, the neat tenanted farms hedged between. In the other direction it stretches to Lancashire and Manchester, where almost nightly the flares and bombs flowered so prettily—or so it seemed to my childish imagination. On this part was everything that no one wanted on their doorsteps, and so those who were power-less and vulnerable had to put up with the sewage works, the prisoner-of-war camp, the crematorium where my father and my mother have now disappeared, factories for light industries, and some scrappy market gardening; at the limit of my child-hood explorations in that direction, I found ocean-going ships drifting through fields of wheat, potatoes and celery, as they went along the Manchester Ship Canal. The division of the plain still represents a division in my mind. On one side, a calm ele-gant landscape governed by cultured aesthetics, which I asso-ciate with gentility, but also more deeply with femininity. In the other direction was industrial spoliation, a world of suffer-ing history, the origins of socialism, and, it seemed, male.

People from these two realms mingled in the housing estate, but remained distinctively either Cheshire or Manchester. The latter were recognised by the beaten earth and weeds of their gardens, their gappy undernourished privet hedges, their bat-tered doors and threadbare curtains. My mother believed, as firmly and as vaguely as she believed in Jesus Christ our Lord, that Manchester folk kept coal in the bath. She, you see, was that other sort of person, the kind driven out of the genteel villages by the erosion of servants from country houses and farms. As soon as these left, their world of half-timbered cottages became 'stockbroker belt'. When their homes were sold by land-lords for unimaginable sums, rather than feel a grievance, these people instead felt glad to move closer to Manchester, with shorter bus-rides in to buy post-war utility tat. Gladly my poor mother broke up and burnt inherited antiques in the back garden, or she paid out money, that she earned from cleaning houses, to have them taken away. Mad with a post-war hubris, such as she let their heirlooms and cultural possessions be taken

119

from them. They absolutely closed the door on the values of their country ancestors, whom I only know from one or two sepia photographs that have faded to a charred look as if they have survived a fire.

What did persist into the housing estate was the art of gardening. You could distinguish the homes of such as my parents by the rows of vegetables growing, the flowers, the neat thick hedges and even topiary work. A sometimes absurd richness, as if they were trying to scale down Chatsworth or nearby Tatton Park to the dimensions of a council-house garden.

My father was a wonderful, a passionate gardener. But when his marriage went wrong, when it became my mother's constant complaint that he 'never did anything,' that he 'lied,' and 'let things go to rack and ruin,' he did indeed allow all the plants to grow wild, seed themselves, and fight out their survival in the jungle of our garden that dangled above my head exotic flowers and leaves, together with the stings of startling insects, and the moths that I loved to disturb out of the grass and herbage.

When my father married and moved in, he celebrated his joy and his optimism by planting climber roses. He chose exactly the right variety for the soil and position. The flowers were large, deliciously scented, and pink. They were a naughty dream of petticoats; they were symbols of the desire that could blot out all other consciousness from a virgin male. I have never seen since such flourishing roses. After he became disheartened, his dream of roses went on to lead an even richer life on its own. When he ceased to prune them or nail them back, they clambered greedily over the whole house-front and flowered densely even over the roof and up to the eaves. They tapped and threatened with their amazing beauty at the windows and doors. Visitors even *complained*. Visitors were my aunt, who came full of suspicion and accusation on excursions from the country, some school-friends of mine, and the men who collected sixpenceworth of insurance premium weekly, or who came to talk my mother into hire-purchase agreements. It was especially the latter who persuaded my mother into throwing out her piano and her Welsh dresser to make way for a 'utility' three-piece suite, and who complained about getting scratched at the door by my father's wild and extravagant blooms. These men represented the god, *Gentility,* so my mother was thrown in a panic at offending them: maybe they would never visit again, maybe she would never receive Grace again. But my father would not 'cut them back a bit,' nor do anything else that she wanted. And my mother was from then onwards on at me (often at the same time obliquely threatening my father) for her and me together to attend to the roses. Still my father at home positively refused to do anything, anything at all. He spread himself on a sofa across the fire, reading H. G. Wells, smoking, dozing until his book clattered to the floor, waking up and calling for a cup of tea (which my mother, quivering with bitterness, nevertheless always brought to him), picking up his book again and perhaps saying excitedly to me, "Sit down, son, I want to talk to you . . ." and reading out the heady socialist passages. He heaped too much coal on the fire, and in the stuffy room there was a smell of the hot serge of his ticket-inspector's trousers and of the foam-rubber hire-purchased furniture getting so hot you could barely touch it. An atmosphere that seemed threatened with spontaneous combustion. He realized that our nerves were on edge and that we hated him.

What was it made him behave thus? Then, I never questioned after the reason. Now I understand, because I connect it with another experience, occurring on many nights, when I would be awoken by his coaxing of my mother. It was a soft ever-repeated note; as was her equally often-repeated refusal. It would descend into a moan, so that I would anxiously rise, stand in the passageway or go into the bathroom, fearful that one or other was ill with a sickness that I didn't understand, and in summer I glimpsed the great pink florid roses, turned blue with the light of night-time, around the window frame and I breathed their heavy scent. During my teens, the mystery, and the quarrelsome evenings, so set me on edge that I took to leaving the house and wandering the countryside for days on end.

But earlier, when I was about nine years of age, he himself took me on prowls around the countryside. It began with his buying me a bicycle for Christmas and teaching me to ride it, by walking at my side and holding the saddle. He did this patiently for miles and miles. It was as soon as I could balance by myself that he started to borrow my mother's bike, and she could hardly refuse him; although she tried, often putting it away in the larder and padlocking it when she went out, so that there were rows, which Dad, loving any chance to talk, always won.

We were suddenly able to penetrate into Cheshire together and thus I first discovered my native countryside. It filled me with ecstasy. Odd little things penetrated my imagination so that they still will not leave me. The way that the light pierced a hawthorn bush loaded with berries and small golden leaves, on a particular autumn evening when everywhere was still, there was a smell of earth, and curtain after curtain of bird-song reached into a far distance. Oh, I can hardly explain such ec-stasies as these! The countryside was wild and tantalising, the shrine of my holy grail.

Whereas my father in the house talked socialism, in the countryside he often spoke about God, or combined these two themes in ideas which I don't think he'd read about: they were an oral tradition surviving underground in Cheshire villages from the time of seventeenth-century Ranters. He told me, for instance, that God was the spirit of flowers and trees and that all God's creatures were equal. An ancestor had sheltered on a common listening to the wandering disciples of Winstanley or Abiezer Coppe, and had passed on what he heard to my father, who keyed it all into his reading from Gollancz 'yellow books' of socialism for the working man.

So we cycled, philosophically, slowly along the lanes, shar-ing in our inadequate embarrassed language the beauty of meadow, park and sky. Or he talked to me bitterly about the past. He believed — and had learnt it from his own experience —

that the ruling class continually strangled or tamed the creative genius of the working people; but also that each historical
event had opened the door of freedom for the latter whilst being a crisis for their masters. For instance, the First World War,
which had been intended, he thought, to massacre working men
in the trenches, had accidentally liberated women. Thus the
world inevitably, crisis by crisis, grew better and better.

Or it would do if everyone was like my Dad. He himself
wanted these freedoms in order to gain education and understanding. He envied the rich man, not for his money, but for
his opportunities to go to Oxford, to speak French and Greek.
But he also understood the men with whom he worked (and
as a trade unionist to some extent led) at the bus depot: had
the working class stormed the breach of history in order to es-
tablish the kingdom of their own creativity, he wondered, or
had they merely looted? Grabbed the profit and run?

My father was the busmen's first union organiser and he was
instigator of their first strike, poetically convening a meeting
on the romantic site of Peterloo in Manchester. I remember
him poring with painful difficulty over a handbook of committee procedure. His unionism, just as much as anyone else's, was
created out of abstract anger, but there was also a strong element
of deeply felt passion and compassion. He seized the chance
of one action, at least, which I consider to be heroic — and said
not a word to me about it, so that I heard about it only from
the lips of his brother at my father's funeral. During the Depression my father got a job as a bakery delivery boy. He used to
leave free loaves, stolen from the bakery, on the doorsteps of
the unemployed, and then vanish — knowing how they hated
the whiff of charity. This risky, generous action from a boy of
seventeen or so — about which he was so modest all his life —
makes me weep to think of it.

Eventually, his union voted him their delegate to Transport
House, and in response the bus company offered him promotion from conductor to ticket inspector — security and super-
annuation on condition that he was not a member of the union.

Such things, I have learnt since, happened many times, deliberately, to tempt the best people of his class and so weaken it. My mother persuaded him into accepting company promotion, and he, to secure his marriage, became a ticket inspector. Jack Jones, I have been told, took that first job which my father rejected.

At that time we used on our cycle rides to come across German or Italian prisoners of war working in the fields, often unsupervised and generally quite relaxed. Not one seemed interested in walking off and assassinating General Patton, though he was only five to ten miles away. My father would stop, offer a cigarette, talk firstly about the weather and the crops, offer two or three more cigarettes, then the whole packet, and finally move into the subjects that most interested him: socialism and pacifism. Once or twice he found a German prisoner who in good English gave a lecture, over a hoe stuck into a row of potatoes or turnips, on Bernard Shaw, Kant, Bertrand Russell, or Thomas Mann. This was in fact the education that my father had longed for all his life. Meanwhile I fidgeted restlessly with my bike or with the grasses in the hedgerow. I saw no connection between these gentle, intelligent Germans and the bestial Krauts of the cinema. And my father always said that if the conduct of wars was left to the people who fought them, there would always be peace treaties immediately.

On cycling home, my father's excitement would be dampened as we realised that the time had come for us both to slot back again into our bitter domestic roles, and a silence descended upon us. My mother had been out at work cleaning someone else's house, and I felt that I had to side with her resentment. By going out with my father, I had betrayed her. Yet in guiltily switching to her side when back in the house, I felt that I was deserting my father. It was awful. Dad understood and tried to smother all the anxiety with chatter. But it never worked. This was a different war, one more difficult to fight than his country's struggle with Germany! He relapsed into his slovenly habits. My mother, too, showed the worst of herself indoors.

She hardly spoke, except to utter something pessimistic — one of her 'bad luck' sayings, such as, it was unlucky to bring green into the house, or to drop a glove and if by chance she said anything hopeful, she 'touched wood.' None of us was happy when we met indoors.

But when I cycled in the countryside with her, whilst he was at work, she was more excitedly child-like even than I was, and a Cheshire different to my father's revealed itself. She had no unhappy memories, but only nostalgia. She longed for the return of what made my father bitter. My father told me angrily of the vicar who begged money for his church from parishioners who often could not afford to buy food, and himself left a fortune of ninety thousand pounds, not one penny of it to the church. My mother on the other hand recounted sweetly how she first went into 'service,' at the age of fifteen, to the house of the manager of the tinned-milk factory. On the bank of this brown river, creeping stickily under alder and willow, was where she sat whilst her father was fishing. In the grounds of this sandstone church, slowly crumbling back into the red earth out of which it had been made, my grandfather had tended the graves and paths. It was now, like our council-house back garden, a jungle of brambles and nettles. I think it seemed to mother that all of nature's violent ugly passions were released after she left her father.

Grandfather seemed a man who could keep threats and dangers at bay. Old photographs, as well as my mother's stories, show a well-balanced kindly man with a firm jaw and stiff moustache. A person of great self-control. He was a groom at the manor-house. A man with gentle and persuasive hands. Animals were bewitched by them and for miles around he was sought out as a 'poor man's vet.' With those hands, he coaxed his wife into bearing seven children. She was a maidservant at the same manor, and she had the beautiful name Harriet Scattergood. The only surviving heirloom in our family is her bible, which was a gift from her mistress when she went into service: 'To Harriet Scattergood with Mrs. Hall 1870' it says.

Oh, Mrs. Hall, what a gift, the only written history of my ancestors, you gave to me! For after Harriet's marriage, my grandfather took over the management of the bible (as of everything else), and on the flyleaf he listed the births of each of their children, in handwriting as firm as the control he exercised everywhere over his family. His last entry, however, is large and shaking, and reads 'My darling wife died, 1909.' The later entries are by my Uncle Billy, and then, yes, finally by myself.

The bible, black and square with sides of gold leaf, is battered and stained from being read close to candles and paraffin lamps and from being transported through the attics of her mistress's addresses. The manor-house is now swallowed into a landscape that has been exploited by the chemical industry, and which is now as scorched, stained, burnt and brown as my grandmother's bible. There is hardly a cottage in the countryside that has kept its organic relationship with the original landscape, that is not spoiled by crude 'conversion.' Nonetheless, and although I possess nothing of it, when I travel those lanes now I cannot help a secret proud feeling that it was my ancestors who moulded this landscape out of the woods and marshes.

My mother when 'in service' knew that this finely evolved gentility was impossible without her, and it gave her the bearing of a queen. To help the War Effort she was persuaded to work in a factory for a short time, but she hated it. When with the other working women she daily left the housing estate, she now had to go in the other direction, towards the industrial plain, and it was as if a bird's migrating instinct had gone wonky—as if only she out of the whole flock was going astray. So she soon started to do housework again. At eight o'clock every morning she pedalled to the foot of the hill, walked up it with a gang of similar women, in their wrap-around overalls and with scarfs bundling their hair, and all parted to their individual 'places' at the top.

My mother's, hiding in its shroud of rhododendrons and laurels, their leaves shining as if polished, didn't know whether it was a Tudor mansion or a Turkish mosque. The lady for whom she worked was like Dorothy Lamour. I found in her — in her different scent and confident walk — a tantalising sense of freedom and daring. There is an instinct which brings together those who need one another and my mother stayed at this house until she was seventy. Twenty-five years. She was satisfied to be paid five pounds a week, she never missed a day, her only bonuses were a box of chocolates (always the same chocolates) each Christmas, and a postcard from the South of France every summer, which she received with the most magnanimous gratitude. But from the day she retired she gave 'Dorothy Lamour' no more thought than one gives to a dead cat.

In the school holidays, and on those evenings when she was paid the equivalent of 50p to wait on and wash up at a dinner party, she took me with her. She had a bath for the occasion, wore a black dress, did her nails, and sometimes hesitatingly applied a mild dash of cheap scent. As we climbed together out of the housing estate, she probably looked to everyone else a nondescript, shabby, crouched little woman, hidden in her old coat and carrying an empty bag for the leftovers. But I was aware of what lay underneath: not only the bathed and scented skin of my mother, but also the anticipation of adventure and joy which clouded us both. By all this my senses were magically increased, as we plunged under the dark chestnut or beech trees that overhung the scented gardens, and I felt for nature as intensely as I have ever been able to feel in my life.

With her own key she let herself in through the back door, hid her shabby coat and bag in a broom cupboard, went to a drawer and took out a beautifully ironed white apron bought for her from the Army & Navy Stores. I can still recall its design. It was folded to make vertical panels, the centre one being the largest: a design found on sideboards, radios, cinema-fronts and tube stations of the period. My mother took the greatest pride in this gift, and as she adjusted herself before a mirror she seemed to grow much younger, all her dissatisfied council-house self being shed. I saw what it was that caused men sometimes to stop their cars for her and make her blush.

As a child of seven, eight, or nine, I then helped my mother and her employer to lay out a table with silver, with candles, and with flowers. It was my first experience of being close to sheath dresses, the bare tops of breasts and thighs, nylons, jewelry, scent, and thus I became a slave to the world of women. Before long the doorbell was ringing and my mother was caring for coats, furs and wraps. The house, beyond the door and serving-hatch of the kitchen where I was now confined, was full of the buzz of invisible speakers, and of cigar smoke. Soon dirty dishes started coming in and my mother and I washed up, side by side. I peered into the sink to watch her raw red hands, her swollen finger ends that cracked each winter with the frost, skimming through the dishes like livid anemones. Eventually Dorothy Lamour, tired and less elegant but even more magical because of the evening's disarray, tottered in with my mother's money. She removed her apron, put it in the washing, filled her bag, and once again we were our original shabby selves ready to go home, if we were lucky, in a taxi. (These were the only times I ever saw a taxi until I went to college.)

Back home, my father attacked from his front-line position in the class war. The anticipation of it knotted our stomachs. My mother knew that she had no answer for him and that she could not excuse the contentment and feeling of security that she had received. How could she explain that she would have been happy without the chaos and agonies of marriage, child-rearing, and the rawness of life as she found it outside 'service'? A spinster's life in comfortable service spelled magic for her, the acquiescence brought a sense of belonging. How could she explain when, I suspect, she only divined the truth about herself in glimpses? The tension made her wring her hands. It would begin in the taxi or on the streets of the housing estate. I have never seen such wringing of hands. They were like two hawks locked together at the claws. From time to time she would unfasten one and make a savage, scything gesture. When facing my father, her lips trembled with the words she could not quite form: or if she could shape them, dared not utter. She could eventually only answer his elaborated sentences about 'exploitation' and so on, with savage little reproaches of her own, about 'our house,' 'our garden,' and the mess of the neglected roses.

One autumn day, when my father was at work, and when the countryside was bathed in calm chrome-yellow sunlight, the air so still that you could hear thrushes and robins singing in the far-away shrubberies on the hill, and when I had nothing to do except to get under my mother's feet whilst she was going on about those roses, she persuaded me to go out with her and 'prune' them. My mother, with her angry energies roused, could do things with reckless savagery, and we cut them down to the roots. In a frenzy, we pulled the vast growth off the walls. We tugged it free of the nails with which, by leaning out of the bedroom window, it had once been fixed to the mortar, and it snaked down to curl up slowly in the wrecked, abandoned garden.

The roses were a little way past full blossoming, and petals, winged, flesh-soft, sensual, butterflied over neighbouring gardens as my mother tore (for it was her right!) at what filled my father with pleasure and desire. The growth would not all pull from the walls, and months later the remaining briars, hacked through at ground level, withered, and were like strands of tobacco twisting in the wind. The house-front became a mess of nails, tatty bits of leather, and crumbling mortar. Hurrying, to stop ourselves thinking, and black with dust, we lugged all the cuttings round to the back garden, ready for a bonfire. My father's roses never grew again.

# Ball and Socket

**Yannick Murphy**

At first I thought it was safe to dance with my father, he would not push his leg between mine, but then I realized it was dangerous and that I would show him anything, I would show him how my breasts shook as I danced and I would check to see if he was watching mine or somebody else's.

He said turning left or right was always a sure thing when I sat on the handlebars; fifty pounds made it hard to make a false move. You are my Buddha, he said, my small kid fitting in between my arms whose belly I can reach up and touch at every red light.

I saw him cry from joy when he hugged my brother at my brother's wedding. Then my brother cried also. But I knew it was false and not a sure thing, no one cries from joy, a person cries because he is losing someone, or because he did not spend enough time with someone.

In cold weather, the mist I breathed out he swallowed in his mouth and said something like that would keep him going till noon.

Bad luck, he said, felt like when his small Buddha got down from the handlebars, to him lightness never felt good.

At home, he let me stand on his feet and we walked to the kitchen and back, he said he could teach me to dance that way. I told him the box step was easy, I could have learned it on my own two feet, not standing on his. He taught me how to play the piano, but that was hard, when he pulled his fingers out from under mine, I could not follow his rhythm.

One day he said I had grown too big for the bicycle. My

feet touched the ground and he said turning left or right was a chore. I told him the bigger the Buddha, the better the luck. He laughed, he said he did not deserve all my luck and that he wanted to ride alone. In a way, he said, I want to get hit, and I fear for your life, or my life in taking yours. If we stopped short he would let one hand go and use it to hold back my chest. I thought his hand stayed there awhile, even after we had been safe for some time.

I would lift up my shirt and show him the places on my back that itched so he would scratch them, and when I was sick, I told him the only thing that helped my belly was to lie across his.

When I rode with him all I saw were my feet near the fast turning spokes and the sides of his arms, hairy with spots that I thought the smell of him came out of.

When fishing, he planted me before him and showed me how to cast, he said we will catch Buddhafish who sit at the bottom, but I did not think of the Buddhafish, I thought of how my shoulder fit neatly between his legs as we swung back the rod, it was a ball-and-socket motion that made the line fly.

He told me his mother taught him to fall asleep with his arms crossed over his chest so if he died in his sleep he would be ready for the coffin.

I rode our big dog like he was a horse, my father bent down close to my ear, he said what he would not give to be little again, a baby Buddha holding onto the scruff of the neck of our dog.

I watched him watch other women's breasts all the time.

I grew long hair, I asked him to brush it, he said cut it short. He was the one who cut my hair. I heard him say to my mother, I know the shape of her head better than you do, this kid's head is flat in the back, he said, you hang a picture there, it will lie like it's on the wall. When he did my bangs, he pulled my head back toward his belly and said it did not feel like a head, he said it felt like the palm of my hand was there.

When he pushed his leg in between mine I moved back. He

said I should have stayed there, though, he said he was falling and then he asked if that is what I wanted, for him to fall down at his only son's wedding.

I showed my father that my brother looked at me when I danced. I showed my father that the bride looked too, she looked at my breasts. She watched my brother watch me wanting to be watched by my father, who was looking at another woman, maybe my brother's bride. Then nothing was safe. Maybe his leg in between mine was safe, for a moment, before he fell to the floor. His leg let me think about how old he was and that putting his leg in between mine was as far as his body would go.

He lost the hair on top of his head when he was sixteen. He said all that is passed on through the mother but I cannot believe it, not when I can see the scabs on his bald head from hitting low doorways. He is the living proof, after all.

I brushed the hair that was leftover, the hair on the sides of his head. I used the soft brush that was made for a man. It had no handle, it was meant to fit in the palm of your hand. He said he could not feel it go through his hair, he asked me to use my fingers instead.

He rode me in the rain. Those days he used one rain poncho to cover us both. He wore the part over his head that you can see out of, but I rode in the dark. I heard him tell people on the street, who asked him, that I was his Siamese twin. In the dark, I held onto the handlebars with tight fists, I thought I would lose my balance because all that I could smell was him under the poncho. Riding in the rain, it was cold. His warmth held the smell. It stayed on my back and my neck after I had gotten off the bicycle. I took his smell to school every day that it rained and I was afraid that my teacher would think I was wearing my father's shirt, and only the poor kids wore their father's shirts.

Because I could not see what he said to people I imagined he frowned a lot. I did not hear people laugh when he told them I was his Siamese twin. They must have seen pain in his face. Because they could not see me, I thought then neither could he. I thought, if his bald head had hair, I would not blame him for passing on baldness. What you can see always makes for a sure thing.

When we flew birdy he put his feet up high on my chest, saying my belly he dare not harm, round perfection he hated to push out oblong. He had my baby nipples between his toes. Facing him was hard, he pushed, with his feet, his heaviness into me. I could not breathe. I was flying in the room. He made me touch my nose to the bedside table and my toes to the sheets. I had thought heaviness could only come down, it came up though, from him, and I was scared, I did not want my ribs to meet my backbone. I did not want him to have to reach inside me and pull them apart.

My knees smelled of pavement. It was an iron smell, like blood. It was a hard smell, my knees hurt. My father helped me up off the curb. He looked at me as if wanting to know why I fell off the handlebars, didn't I know that good luck Buddhas had to be strong? They did not fall down for no reason. I had a reason, I was looking up. I had never looked up the entire ride to school before. I had been fighting not to look at the spots on his arms. I thought looking up would be good, who would dare make a little girl fall off the handlebars of a bicycle while looking up at the sky at the same time? It was my pose of looking heavenward that I thought would save me. It did not save me, I thought, because at the time I was not thinking of God, I was thinking of how to make my father stop riding me to school so that we could turn back for home. I had just learned to drink tea. I wanted to go home and drink tea with him. I wanted to make the tea for him. He knew about cave men. I thought he could tell me again about life in a cave and life without fire.

We did turn around, he told someone we did not know on the street that it was not a day for school, not when his Buddha fell from the handlebars, when just at rest, waiting for a light to change. He said he would not be caught dead without me if that is how the day began.

At home, he drew a cave-man scene on my palm for me. The feeling of his pen drawing on my palm shot through to my bellybutton, then down to where it made me want to pee. I wondered if that was the way to learn, not to hold the pen with him, but to let him draw on me. Later on in the day, I tested it out, I tried to draw, but my skill was not any better than it was before. I wore out the drawing on my palm by stamping my hand against the bathroom walls but the image was reversed and because it was false and not the real thing, I did not feel guilty about signing my name to it.

Then he danced with the bride. He cut in on her dance with her father, he walked up to her, he must have thought this is what he waited his whole life, as a father, to be able to do at his son's wedding. He crossed lines that were complicated. The bride and her father looked alike. Her father must have looked at my father's face, hoping to find that my father did not look like his daughter, my brother's bride. Then her father looked over at me, he must have seen that I do not look like my father, maybe he also thought that he looked a little like me, to get back at my father. I thought to myself, I do not want to dance with that man also. People would get confused, they would want to know who the father of the bride was. I had to tell them. I cut in on the bride and my father, I thought to myself, I am doing this woman a favor, this man puts his leg between yours and everyone will think he is your father.

As my teeth grew in, he put his finger in my mouth to feel them. He checked the baby teeth for looseness. He showed me how to check them myself, then both of our fingers were in my mouth at the same time. My saliva on his finger he did not wipe on his shirt or his pants, instead he used his hand to smooth down my hair.

He told me to let the dog lick my cuts, he thought what was in dogs' saliva had a natural cure. One day, I did not tell my father, but I let the dog lick a cloth, then I went to my father and patted the scabs on his bald head with the cloth while he slept with his arms crossed.

137

Some nights I went to his bedside and thought about uncrossing his arms for him, I thought that if I uncrossed them, he would never die, because he would never be ready for the coffin. I did not do it, because in his sleep his arms looked heavier and if I touched them I might find that he was already dead and I was keeping his body from going to Heaven.

He said he did not wish for me to be as light as a rabbit's foot and that it was good I liked being picked up all the time.

Before the bicycle, he carried me on his shoulders, and asked me to look out for low doorways. He told people one of the reasons he had had me was so that he could carry me on his shoulders and so that I would put my hands on his bald head as he walked.

Then, at the wedding, I thought, He wants to marry me. Maybe, I thought, he thinks that it would be like marrying the half of him that is a girl, or the half of his life that he did not live, or the half that takes the leg between hers and knows what it's like for the other half also.

The day I grew too big for his shoulders was a winter day. I blamed it on the hat that he wore. I was jealous that it was on his head, closer than my hands could be and better than I could cover his baldness. Then I blamed it on the cold and that was useless. The cold came every year, it was not something he chose or wished for to happen, except maybe in the heat of summer when he told me that although there was no breeze, me standing in the doorway made him hotter.

He also said that I made the fish go away. He said they've got ears and that they hear my humming when I'm sitting on the rock while he demonstrates casting. He said me standing in front of him and the two of us casting together did not work, that we both had too much swing and that the trees took advantage of our strength and caught our lines like they were the hungry fish on dry land.

After he cried, he turned to me at the wedding. I thought I saw him wanting me to be little again, fifty pounds of good luck to prop on his shoulders and walk through the guests;

138

holding onto my thin ankles where his hands would make two warm spots against my skin.

Then he smiled, to him it was simple and not dangerous, a father and a daughter courting until death made them part, a pact in the night to leave his arms crossed was the only vow, silently, that I ever made. He made no vows to me. If he could, maybe he would have promised to keep me little his whole life, a good luck Buddha whose belly he reached up and touched at every red light.

# Sleep

## Kathleen Spivack

Whan Jack came into her life she was so grateful. She could have wept with gratitude. And did. Which bewildered him no end. But he held her nevertheless. "It's okay," he said. "It's okay." He kept saying this over and over and patting her, dumbly, she thought. But still she cried. And could not tell him how lonely she had been. How she had missed him. Or maybe not *him*, but a large male animal of similar size and comforting bulk. Who drank beer occasionally and opened the refrigerator at intervals and got in and out of her bed.

Finally, Ruth felt, she could sleep after all these years. All these years of keeping her tattered household together, feeding, raising, and comforting the children. Finding the money somehow. Holding the children together so carefully and constantly she never gave a thought to herself. So tired. So tired.

"I want to sleep with you," he said. And she took his meaning literally.

But of course she could not. Sleep that is. She lay beside him at night, listening for sounds of the children. She tingled; she wished she were alone. Carefully she stretched out beside him, unable to make contact with any part of him. He reached for her. "Let me hold you," he said. But she had grown entirely used to sleeping alone. "Mmmm," she said, and that was all, moving away from him and his embrace in the dark. "Maybe you should check the children," he suggested helpfully. For he was graceful and understanding and he sensed her concern in the dark. So she did, padding around her house in bare feet, forcing herself not to put on her robe, not to go down to the

143

kitchen to make herself hot cocoa and read, blessedly alone under the glaring light over the kitchen table, reading and reading until dawn came. She forced herself to remember the large kind man in her bed, and merely for politeness' sake she remembered she would return to him.

But nevertheless, there she was, at one o'clock in the morning, unable to sleep, prowling around her own house in the dark, doing everything to avoid her bedroom. She looked in on her children, who woke for a moment the moment she looked at them. Her older boy swam a few slow strokes across his bed, muttered something, thrashed a bit and fell asleep again. The younger boy reached for her in his sleep, breathing his sweet clover breath against her cheek. He was her truest lover.

And the house creaked and called her. The kitchen, with its old stove and tin pot and the box on the shelf marked "Cocoa." And that junky magazine she had been saving for herself. And the way dark looked through the kitchen window, and dawn came up, the windows growing lighter and lighter, a faint seashell pink coming in and enclosing her, and the whole world swimming both away and toward her as she sat reading, early into the morning, when they were all asleep.

She wished the man were asleep. Maybe he was. Maybe if she stayed away long enough he would forget about her and fall asleep, his arms enclosing a dream. And she tiptoed downstairs and looked at her plants, growing dimly in the dark. And by now she was wondering why she had ever agreed to let this man into her life. She had been doing just fine by herself.

Ruth had successfully kept men away for nearly three years now, repairing her shattered life, her pride. Yes, of course she had been with men during that time, but never at her house, never in her bed, which had become once again her virginal white bed of her girlhood, where she lay with her secret dreams and loneliness, her books and her thoughts, and her retreat from day. She remembered the bedroom of her girlhood, her own sweet bed, and her own thoughts of boys and love and life. How she had looked at herself in the mirror and whispered, "You are beautiful, Ruthie," pretending that she were a man whispering to her reflection, imagining what it would be like to have a man love her and whisper to her, preferably in a foreign accent. And, indeed in that whisper she felt herself truly beautiful. Misunderstood, of course, by her parents and endless brothers and sisters, who did not realize her true exquisite nature. Misunderstood by her classmates, for to them she was of course ordinary, if not a total outcast. But there, alone and in her bedroom, she dreamed and thought. And wept and read. And now, in divorce, in single motherhood she had had a second chance. She had even managed to achieve a measure of contentment.

For of course, the pattern of children was ordinary and in the end happiness-making. And so too was the pattern of supporting those children. She felt strong, successful, and above all virtuous, as she got them off to school in the morning, went to work, returned from work, fixed supper with them, underwent the usual frustration over homework, sat and rested as they struggled with elementary arithmetic. For her day truly ended after supper. There, in the circle of the kitchen, with the radio playing, dishes somehow getting done, or not, and the children sitting around with their homework, and their jokes and squabbles, she felt complete. More complete, to be honest, than she had ever felt in the years of her marriage. For the husband, who had loved her, at least for a while, was impatient with the children and the noise and the flurry and the laughter. He worked hard, and wanted to be extremely serious. He wanted her to himself.

And, after they had their children, he had left and found someone else to have completely to himself. So that, in the end, was that.

And then eventually, after Ruth had tried and tried to understand and she had tried and tried to change and he had tried and tried to change her and make her see that really everyone should have lots of sex and lots of mates and "open marriage" was the catchword of their times as well as "mid-life crisis"— his, that is: well, finally he had gone off with the young single woman who had all the time in the world for him and Ruthie had stayed with the children. So both, you might say, were in the end somewhat satisfied. Though of course each would have preferred to have it all.

And her husband of course had his side of the story but since this is Ruth's story and she is living it this is the one that is getting in print.

And so now she, Ruthie, was sitting downstairs, in her own kitchen with a strange—well, not so strange—large man upstairs in her bed whom she was trying to avoid. When only two hours ago she had been weeping and yearning for him, and even agreeing to share her bed with him.

"But wait until the children are asleep," she had asked him. And he had agreed, waiting patiently through dinner, sitting with the boys over their homework, even helping with the dishes. He did not display impatience even when she lingered tucking them in, elaborately kissing each one. And they, of course, took twice as long to go to bed as usual, sensing as they did that she wanted them out of the way. "I want a drink of water." "Don't forget I need lunch money tomorrow." "Kiss my Snoopy goodnight." A chorus of needs and reminders followed her as she left their rooms and went downstairs into the kitchen where the man still awaited her—no, he hadn't gotten up and gone away during the bedtime interval—seemingly still sitting patiently in the kitchen, her dishes done, and even the pots dried and stacked neatly. "A household jewel," she said to herself somewhat cynically, as she noticed his kitchen work. And then she repeated it to him, snuggling against him as he sat there. "A household jewel." "Think so?" Jack answered, tousling her hair. And then he cradled her breast. He looked at her significantly. She thought, "Oh dear," but aloud she said, "I need to wait a bit longer until the children are asleep." "I understand," he answered. But he didn't.

And in her bedroom he undressed too quickly, immediately tossing off his clothes and getting into her bed. It was too fast . . . it was not seemly, that large naked body. But after all, they had known each other a bit, they had spent evenings together, he had spent weekend afternoons with her and the children. She liked him. She almost trusted him. She felt perhaps she could love him. Oh, it might take a couple of years — that was her mental timetable for getting seriously involved again with a man. But he was kind and smart and lovable and attractive to her and good to the kids. Why not?

"I'm waiting for you," he said from under the covers, as she left her bedroom to go check on the children one more time. Oh, she thought, this is too much! She was in a panic. Here he was, in her bed, not waiting at all. And in her side of the bed! For years, ever since her husband left, she had stayed on the same side of the bed, letting the rest of it gasp clean and white beneath her. And now this stranger had jumped right in and taken her side: "Move over," she told him trying to prod him gently on to the other side of the bed. "I can only sleep on this side." "Okay," he said, rolling over. She had to restrain her panic and impatience.

Just once before, she had tried this, letting someone sleep with her in her bed. And since that man was smaller than she, she had, in her sleep, thrashed and kicked him so much he had ended up on the floor. And by unspoken agreement, that had been the end of that relationship.

By now you are probably wondering whether Ruthie will ever end up with anyone. Me too. And Ruth is wondering this also, sitting in despair downstairs at her kitchen table, where she has somehow drifted. For all the old virtues, like Compromise, and Love and Caring, and Woman Sacrificing Herself, et cetera, have been washed out of her in the struggle to support her children. "I'd like to help you with that," Jack has said. But she has already refused, so proud is she of her strength. And anyway, the husband — sorry, the *Ex*-husband — has decided he wants to become an artist, and has no desire to help her or the children at all. And Ruthie, in her pride at going it alone, will now accept help from no man. She knows what the price of accepting help might be.

And without the ex-husband, the father of her children, Ruth has determined in some stubborn part of her to accept no substitutes. She is fine without a man and so are her children. And anyway, they do see their father. And they love him, and he them. So in that way they are complete. And Ruth too has become complete. Half-man, half-woman, she is managing.

Sitting here alone, in the middle of the night, Ruth has forgotten about things like loneliness. Need. Those many evenings when she hasn't even had the strength to put the children to bed. How she falls into bed with or before them. And sleeps and sleeps. And how, for two years after the ex-husband left she would wake in the middle of the night, reaching across the void from where she lay on "her side" and weep and think she would die of loneliness.

Somehow, Jack coming into her life has made her think of all this when he takes her hand. He is so gentle and trusting. "I love you," he says, and means it, as far as she can tell. So she succumbs for a minute, "I love you too," she says. But only for a minute, and to tell the truth, she is a bit abstracted even while she says it. For what does love mean? She feels like a college sophomore again. "Shut up," she tells her mind angrily. "Just live, for once!"

So there is Jack and he has come for dinner and she likes him and the kids like him. And now they all have to worry about liking him *too* much and maybe losing him. And can they take it? Well, she certainly can, Ruth tells herself. But not the kids. No, she doesn't want the kids to like him too much. If your dog is run over you're supposed to get another dog. But does this apply to men? "No," Ruth tells herself, a resounding "No." And besides, the kids do see their father. She cannot bear to see again the pain in their eyes, as it was when the ex-husband — even to herself she cannot refer to him by name — left.

"He's just a friend," Ruthie has cautioned the children, despite the fact that Jack has been coming around for a while. "Nothing special. Just a friend." And she prays that they — or is it herself she is praying for? — will not get involved. Nevertheless, Jack

148

does not seem to notice any of this. "Hi kids," he greets them cheerfully. "Hi," they answer, not looking up from what they are doing. "Hi Ruthie-Girl," he says, coming into the kitchen and putting his arms around her, kissing her as if he had a right. And Ruth straightens. "Hi," she says as coolly as possible. "Hey, easy in front of the children," she says. She tries to remove his arms, to continue with the cooking. But then part of her gives up and snuggles right in.

And now, so much later, it is cold in the kitchen, and her feet are cold, cold as the grave, she thinks. She tries to tuck them under her. A shiver goes through her, and through the room. Darkness comes in the windows, a faint bluish darkness as in the paintings of El Greco, when everyone is dead or dying, and people in museums and churches stand in front of these paintings and say "Oh what wonderful light!" But still it is the light of loneliness and suffering and death, and that is just the kind of bluish edgy night light coming into the kitchen, into her bones as she sits and stalls. She thinks of her warm bed upstairs, white and soft. Even with Jack in it, perhaps it is preferable to this moment when for once, Ruth sits still and thinks. And what comes up? Mortality, of course. "Forget it," she tells herself, as she starts to sink deeper and deeper. She gets up; her body is stiff and cold. And slowly, almost reluctantly, she goes back upstairs to him. He is lying there as she left him, half over onto the other side of the bed, one arm outstretched. And he is breathing heavily. He is asleep. Slowly, not to wake him, she edges into her side of the bed. She clings far over, careful not to touch his body. But even across the sheets he gives off heat. He is snoring, his mouth is open. She eases herself down into bed. She is starting to feel a bit better. She lies there straight as an effigy. Morning will come soon, she tells herself. Not too long now.

And Jack stirs slightly and reaches for her. He puts his large body around her. "Where have you been?" he mumbles. "I've been waiting for you." He half wakes up. "Come here," he says, pulling her closer. "I've been waiting so long for you." Ruthie's feet start to feel warmer, her whole body relaxes into a comfort and warmth, reluctantly given. But it is so simple and slow, when it happens. "I love you," Jack whispers, as his hands start to move on her. And it is so easy now to just lie there and take his comfort. You forget, when you get up close to someone, how difficult it has seemed to get there. And then you never want them to leave. So too with Ruthie, who is after all like any other woman, even awful Molly Bloom. "*Au fond*," as the French are fond of saying. Ruth, who has vowed to cope alone forever. Strong and practical and French. But her feet are so deliciously warm, as Jack is holding her. And now our Ruthie starts saying things to Jack as if this whole short story has never happened. "I love you," she whispers. "My darling. Yes." She says "I love you" again. And goofy things like that.

And she does, and he does too. And afterwards he sleeps. But she doesn't.

# The House of the Sleeping Drunkards

**Leon Rooke**

The old man was down on the floor crying, saying how hard life was. It had been hard before his accident, he said, when he had his legs — it had been God's own hell — but now it was harder. Now it was impossible.

He moaned and moaned.

Cissy Bains said, "Somebody give him a biscuit."

But we had eaten all the biscuits. We had consumed all the licker too. Not one drop was in any of the bottles.

"You'll have to git more," Cissy Bains said. "He can't git through the night without his biscuit."

"Can't," we said. "It's a blizzard out there and the car is broke down."

"Is there any lye?" the old man asked. "Ain't there any old sterno can about? Me and lye or sterno can git along just fine."

He moaned and moaned.

We were all moaning. We all needed a drink bad.

Cissy popped out of the door and a minute later we saw her crawling under the car. The snow was churning, all but hiding her and the car, but we saw she had a bucket with her and knew she meant draining antifreeze out of the radiator.

"It's too rusty," we told her when she came in. "There are certain depths to which we will not sink."

"Fine," she said, "that means more for me and him."

We gave the liquid in her bucket a good close look. It was near to black.

"That there rusty antifreeze will kill you," we said.

"Worse didn't," said Cissy.

"Let's git to it," the old man said.

We got busy and cooked up a new plate of biscuits.

"Make one of them a cheese biscuit," Cissy Bains said. "A sprinkle of cheese in that biscuit will really have him snapping his gums."

So we made a cheese biscuit and poured the antifreeze over it.

The old man was moaning and moaning. We were all moaning.

"Put it in a saucer," Cissy said. "He may be old and no account, but I won't have him treated like no dog."

"Yessir," the old man was saying, "it was God's own hell before I lost me my legs, but now it's got a heap-site blacker."

We gave him his biscuit.

"That there car block's going to crack in the cold," we said. "It ain't going to hold up through the night, not in this hard freeze. We are going to be stuck out here forever, without a good drink between us."

Cissy said, "Shoosh." She said, "Look on the brighter side. We got a whole night of drinking and rowdyism to look forward to this evening, and if we die it won't be absence of drink that killed us. Shove me over one of them biscuits."

So we shoved over the plate. The biscuits were right blackened and the smell took your nose right down to your stomach.

But the old man was moaning.

"I can't eat me this biscuit," he said. "It reminds me too much of my accident and how life is so horrible."

Then we remembered how the old man had been a garage attendant in his wild youth and how it was his accident had happened.

"Do as I aim to do," said Cissy Bains. "Just look up to the ceiling as you swallow it whole. That way the fumes git sooner inside your gullet where they can do the faster good."

But the old man was crying.

"If I hadn't been drinking that day," he said, "I never would of had me my accident. I'd have me my legs now and I'd be sitting up there at the table with the rest o' you."

We agreed with him on this, though Cissy Bains pointed out the trolley he was sitting on was the best money could buy.

"Drink is the ruination of us all," the old man said.

"Hey, now," we said, "now you have gone too far. You can't blame all our woes, or the whole of the world's woes, on good strong drink."

But the old man went on with his blubbering.

We were getting right concerned.

He scooted round and around on his trolley, smacking the floor with his fists and acting, Cissy said, exactly like an idiot.

"I'm never touching another drop," the old man said. "I have seen the light. Drink has condemned me to my everlasting hell."

Cissy Bains said, "What bedlam, a body can't hear herself think."

We each broke off a little nibble of biscuit and nibbled on that.

The old man's old hound dog had slunkered in out of the freezing cold. It had lapped out its great tongue and gulped down the old man's biscuit. Now it was down under the table twitching and coughing.

"Look at that dog," we said.

After a minute or two it stopped twitching and died.

"See!" the old man said. "There's your living proof of licker the killer, as I am here to tell you."

He dragged up the old hound in his arms and moaned over it.

We all moaned. It had been a good old dog, more like a brother.

So we dumped out our plate of rusty biscuits and told stories of this and that heroic deed the dog had performed over the full span of its perfect lifetime, and thus we passed that night without one drop of licker entering our gullets.

I tell you, mother, there was never a sorrier time spent by your fellow human beings than was that evening we spent that evening.

The old man was out on the gravesite among the pines, moaning over his dead dog.

We'd had to carry him out there in our arms and now we'd have to carry him back again.

We were wondering if it was worth it.

The old man was saying this old dog had been dearer to him than nearabouts any human being.

Cissy Bains said, "Let's leave him."

She said, "Where does that leave me?"

She said, "If he cares more about that old dog than he cares about me after all I have done for him then I don't hardly care if I keel over on this very spot."

She said, "With two bodies in that hole to fill it up wouldn't take near as much dirt."

We said, "Oh Cissy Bains, shut up!"

We left Cissy with him on the hillside and slunkered back to the house.

"God, I need me a drink," we said.

We went in and had one.

We picked us some collard greens out in the field and we cooked them flat and then we set down to table.

"Did that old dog ever have a name?" we asked.

"No, it never had no name."

We thought hard and deep on that turnabout.

"Where'd that old dog come from anyhow?" we asked.

"It just limped in one day."

"Then it ain't as though it was family, is it now?" we said.

"Naw. Naw it ain't. It ain't as though it was like a real brother."

We left a filling of greens for Cissy and the water they'd cooked in for the old man, for he would drink that, then we thought about licker again and maybe catching some shuteye.

It was gitting on towards dark.

We'd had us another full long day, mother, full of family woe.

# Naked Women
## Lowry Pei

The fight began on a Tuesday when my wife, Elaine, was rummaging around my workshop area in the basement, looking for a can-opener that could not possibly have been there, and found the pictures of my old girlfriends. The nude pictures, that is, the ones I had put inside the service manual for a VW Bug I hadn't owned in twenty years, which just shows that the can-opener story was not to be believed for a minute. I had almost forgotten they were there. There was a scream from the basement and then fascinated silence—I reconstructed this from the testimony of Naomi, who was only six at the time but had the observational and deductive powers of thirteen. When I got home from work that day Naomi said to me, in the tone of someone repeating a lesson, "Mommy says she has something she wants to show you in the basement."

"She does?" That failed to compute. "Is the washing machine broken?"

"No," Naomi said with a tiny smirk.

"Sweetie?" I called.

"I'm down here!" Elaine yelled from the basement with unnecessary volume. The pressure of her voice seemed to push open slightly the cat door I had installed in the door to the basement stairs.

"All right, I'm coming." I descended the steep, dangerous steps, thinking as usual as they creaked and wobbled under my weight that I would have to fix them soon. At the bottom, however, was something more risky than the stairs—Elaine holding up a five-by-seven color print of Michelle Strickland in the altogether, stretched on a large flat rock on a deserted beach in North Carolina. I'm sure Elaine didn't know where the beach was or, probably, that the picture was fifteen years old. In the photograph Michelle looked sort of like Manet's *Olympia* except she was doing nothing to hide what would conventionally be called her charms; it was equally obvious that Elaine was in a once-in-a-lifetime rage. "Where did you get that?" I said.

"It seems to me I ought to be asking that question, Tobias," she ground out. "You know very well where you've been hiding these."

"I went out with her a million years ago, before I even knew you existed," I said.

"Well, I don't want her in my house. Not without any clothes on."

"It's *our* house, Elaine. Besides, you never would have found them if you hadn't tried. You *could* just leave my privacy alone."

"With pleasure," she said dramatically but nonsensically, and ripped Michelle into four pieces.

"Damn it, Elaine—"

She reached behind her to my workbench, where the rest of the pictures lay in a pile, and grabbed up a tiny black-and-white shot of Marina Pratt, who happened to be the second girl I had ever made love to in my life. I remembered how daring we had felt when I had taken the picture, a modest one, really. I had only dared take her from the waist up. The trusting youthfulness of her small breasts and bony shoulders had made me feel a way I was sure I would never feel again. A glimpse of the picture, which I hadn't seen in several years, showed me how old I had become. Was that why I saved them?

"Skinny little thing," Elaine said, preparing the tear. Already I could see the delicate glossy surface of the image cracking beneath her trembling fingers.

"Don't do it," I said. "If you tear that there is going to be real trouble around here." That was my mistake; I should have made her think I didn't care, but I couldn't do it. She tore Marina in half. While she was watching the halves flutter to the floor of the basement, I grabbed the rest of the pictures and said, "GET OUT OF HERE! GO UPSTAIRS! OUT!" She was too startled to follow through on her obvious intention of grinding the pieces of the two photographs into pulp under her shoe. I made an effort to lower my voice. "You shouldn't have done that."

"*I* shouldn't," she echoed with a sneer. "We'll see who shouldn't have done what, Mr. Big Lover-Boy."

"For God's sake. I'm entitled to a past, aren't I?"

"If that's what you call it, fine. You can stay down here and masturbate, I don't care." She stomped gingerly up the stairs and slammed the basement door.

From upstairs I heard Naomi's unignorable voice: "Mommy, what's masserbate?"

Leaving Elaine to figure a way out of that, and knowing there was none, I picked up the two halves of Marina and the four pieces of Michelle, and fitted them back together. The tearing had left them permanently disfigured, making the past suddenly farther away than it had already been, but I taped the pieces as carefully as I could along the backs. Damn her. It wasn't as though I had luxuriated in the services of a harem, after all; I had had a not unusual number of girlfriends in the normal course of things before I married Elaine. Most of the pictures were of Michelle, because she had found that being pho-tographed excited her; besides her, there was that one precious and now half-destroyed picture of Marina, and two of a woman named Jessica who turned out to be impossible to get along with, but who had a wonderful figure nevertheless. What busi-ness was this of Elaine's, anyway?

It was obvious that nothing was going to be sacred anymore, and that I would have to do some serious hiding if I expected to keep these dangerous little mementos. After an examination of the basement I finally unscrewed the back of an old short-wave radio that had sat on a shelf serving no purpose for years, and stuck them inside. Elaine would never look there. Then I teetered my way up the steps, preparing a suitably impassive face.

Over dinner, Naomi was telling Elaine in some detail about the stupidity of her first-grade classmates who had to be shown how to read a book. I noticed that there wasn't a place set for me.

"If you're planning to have dinner, Tobias, you can serve yourself," Elaine said, interrupting Naomi's list of the mistakes she had heard that day.

"Toby," I said. "My name's Toby. Nobody has ever called me Tobias in my whole life."

Naomi looked interested. "Tobias," she muttered, as if testing it out.

"Toby. Don't you start, too."

"Toby, Toby, Tohh-by." She sounded like a tiny cheering section.

"It's 'Daddy' to you. Eat your broccoli."

"Tow, Bee, Tow, Bee."

I got a plate, but when I looked into the various pots it appeared that the reason Naomi hadn't eaten her broccoli was that she had been served mine. There was hardly enough dinner left to make dirtying a plate worthwhile.

"I think I'll go to Burger King," I said. "Anybody want to come?"

"I'm full," Naomi said. Elaine said nothing, fixing her water glass with a stare worthy of Edward G. Robinson.

It's about a mile to Burger King from our house, and it was a spring evening and the lilacs were in bloom, so I thought I'd walk. It would give me a chance to ponder the situation, and the walk back would settle the bacon cheeseburger which I would eat despite the certainty of indigestion.

This was not your average utility-grade snit. It surpassed even the famous attack of indignation that followed my leaving in the living room a plate with a blob of catsup on it, during a particularly precarious period in Elaine's self-realization. That was before I had realized how easy it was to commit male piggery; now avoiding it was a matter of course. Besides, Elaine had Naomi to worry about, who was female and could make more housework than two grown men any day.

It seemed to me that I had a perfect right to ex-girlfriends. If they bothered her, why did she go poking around looking for them? Except that she was always looking for something more to do, as if being a management consultant and the mother of a six-year-old prospect for College Quiz Bowl and a devourer of spy novels were not already enough. So she found those pictures, so what? I would probably have lost track of them if she hadn't. And just because Elaine had gone out with a succession of creeps—her own description—did that mean I had to regard my former lovers as scarcely worth the trouble of sneering at? But: nude pictures. I tried to imagine the tables turned. A strange idea; women didn't go for that kind of thing. Maybe *Playboy* imprinted certain images on the brains of little boys hanging around magazine racks at the age of nine, and after that it was all downhill. We grew up, wanted to sneak another look at a breast, and they grew up to read Doris Lessing. If this was God's sense of humor at work, I found it annoying, but the lilacs made it impossible to stay mad.

Maybe looking at a bunch of Younger Women made her realize she wasn't going to be Younger any more. But what was she complaining about? She could have been forty-four, like me. Try telling yourself that's not middle age. The more I pondered, the more the situation seemed beyond my control, just like the rest of my life; the only course of action was to have a double bacon cheese, with everything, and take the consequences.

I meandered back from Burger King even more slowly than I had gone there, in no hurry to get home under the circumstances, even though our skill at living together was such that a fight had never made a great deal of difference. So far, at any rate. Maybe this time would change things. I didn't like thinking that. But I also did not like being cast in the role of the family degenerate, especially since we had been jockeying for moral position ever since our marriage. Why should my whole backlog of points be erased for nothing? What about the incredibly slinky tax lawyer whose meaningful looks I had pointedly not noticed at the seminar on personal computer languages for business? What about the fact that I absolutely never made any remarks about Elaine's amazing flirtatiousness when drunk? Thinking of that irritated me anew—not that she flirted, but that she *wanted* me to make remarks. She actually had the nerve to get mad at me for not being jealous. I was almost sure she had never had an affair, because if she had, she would have made sure I found out. Unless she had just given up on the project of getting me satisfactorily enraged.

Well, perhaps she had finally found a way. If only I could take it seriously for more than five minutes at a time.

When I got home Naomi was watching "All in the Family" and Elaine was not in evidence.

"Toby," Naomi said, "do you get all the jokes on this show?"

"What is this, a quiz?"

"Well, do you?"

"I try not to," I said, sitting down next to her anyway. On the screen the usual shouting plunged on.

"Toby—"

"Call me 'Daddy,' okay? At least for a few more years."

"Is Mom all right?"

"Beats me. Are you?" I gave her what was meant to be an understanding paternal tell-me-everything look. Naomi crossed her eyes, stuck out her tongue, and pulled her braids around so they met under her nose.

"Beats me, too—Toby," she squealed. For a couple of minutes I tickled her mercilessly and she shrieked, and by the time that subsided, Archie Bunker and his insufferable relatives had called it a night.

"Now go to bed," I said, panting slightly.

"But I'm not tie-yurrd," she whined, on the verge, I could suddenly see, of actual tears.

"You are. Take my word for it. Go upstairs and put your nightgown on and brush your teeth, and I'll come up and tuck you in when I hear you get in bed."

"No."

164

"Naomi. It's been sort of a tough evening, so how about a little cooperation, okay? You're six years old, it's time for you to go to bed."

She got insulted every time I mentioned her age, and now — she really was tired — it made her cry. "Sometimes I just hate you," she wailed. I had to keep from laughing.

"Go on. You can hate me from upstairs."

Snuffling and for once acting her age, she stamped her feet all the way up. But to my surprise she did brush her teeth; after that she slammed her bedroom door at me and the house was, so to speak, at peace. I clicked off the TV and listened for any emanations from above that might tell me what Elaine was hatching now, but all I could hear was a passing car with its radio on some oldies station. "Tonight You Belong To Me" faded in and out abruptly but unmistakably, as if my high-school prom had just driven past, trailing memories. There comes a point in life when one is shamed by the predictability of one's own desires, and I had reached it. What was Marina Pratt doing now? Reluctantly, I knew the answer. Wherever she was, she was being forty-four.

With that dark thought in mind, I went upstairs. The door to our room was shut, and a dim light gleamed through the crack at the bottom. I peered cautiously in at Naomi; she was sleeping for all the world like a child. Or else she had gotten still better at pretending. I took some time brushing my teeth to give me and Elaine both a chance to prepare for the next scene.

But when I opened the bedroom door I found her lying asleep and naked, face down on top of the bedclothes, a *New Yorker* next to her and partly crumpled in one hand. She reminded me of Naomi; sleep took the edge off both of them and exposed the innocence that for some reason they both tried to keep a secret. I took the magazine away from her and straightened it out; she had been reading the book reviews, and I knew she'd want to finish them. The sound of crinkling paper woke her up; she turned over and looked up at me sleepily just as if we weren't in the middle of a fight, and I could see her remember to be mad.

"Hi," I said, starting to unbutton my shirt. She raised an eyebrow and tried to look stony. "Why don't you get under the covers?"

She sat up and reached to her right, and there on her night table — Elaine had always been a meticulous planner — was my camera. "I thought you might want to take my picture," she said, picking it up and holding it out at me. I didn't take it.

"I don't think there's enough light in here."

She started to cry; I could see that Naomi would look exactly the same when she cried as an adult. Usually Elaine tried to avoid anything that might cause wrinkles, but now she was beyond all that. "You creep," she said between sobs. "You've had those pictures down there all the TIME!" Convulsively she threw my camera down onto the bedroom floor, where it hit so hard it bounced. "What's the matter, aren't my knockers as good as theirs?"

"Elaine, you're being impossible," I said, picking up my dented Nikon and heading back out.

"Meee!" she yelled at me, red in the face, tears trembling on the curve of her jawline, ready to drop onto her shaking breasts. I closed the door on her and stood in the dark hallway taking deep breaths while her tears subsided. As my eyes adjusted, I could see Naomi standing in the door to her room.

"Toby, what are knockers?" she asked seriously.

I thought of saying Those things on doors, but I knew it wouldn't work. "Boobs," I said. "Now go to bed." It was too late to be any more understanding. I marched back down the stairs, poured myself a double Scotch, and lay down on the couch. There was no doubt about it; this was war.

I should have known better than to drink the Scotch; it knocked me out, as planned, but it also woke me up at 5:30 in the morning. Another effect of being forty-four. I lay there in the dark living room, no longer seething, and watched the light skating around on the ceiling when cars occasionally

166

passed. What a life, I kept thinking, amazed as usual by the peculiarity and disorderliness of feelings. The house was silent, as if no one were having a fight in it, or even, most wonderfully, as if no one inhabited it but me. That thought made me feel light, unburdened, off-duty—like myself—an old self, as far back as college or even before. I hadn't thought about myself disconnected from my various functions in life for a long time. Elaine did that better than me, and more often, and most of the time I admired her for it. She had managed to get her company to give her a computer terminal so she could stay at home and still tell other people how to run their businesses—that was something I would never have been able to pull off. But just then I didn't want to think about her or Naomi or my job or anything but the one unfinishable sentence, If I could do anything I wanted . . .

After a while I got up and returned to the basement, where all this had begun; I unscrewed the back of the short-wave and took out the pictures. Even if the old set could not bring me Radio Moscow any more, it would make a good place to keep a past that seemed no less distant. The tearing of Marina's picture had severed her torso with a diagonal slash which I experienced as a form of violence, an assault on tenderness. And then Michelle: I laid the five shots of her (one now patched together) on my workbench under the glare of the trouble light I used for fixing the car, and studied her delicious willingness. When I looked at her what seemed striking about sex was that it was such an innocent pursuit. An open secret: here we are together wanting what everybody wants and why the hell not? But somehow this simple world in which people got laid because they felt like it and had fun doing it was as fantastic as a Jules Verne book where people flew to the moon by firing off cannons to propel them.

As I moved slowly from picture to picture, I could feel my balls wambling around loosey-goosily in my pants, reminding me that a part of me—not that part that was Elaine's husband and Naomi's father—would always be horny and lonely and about twenty-four years old, walking around with a middle-aged body and an unsatisfied dong, in what was clearly no longer a world of unfolding possibilities. And novelty is the ultimate aphrodisiac — everybody knows that. We just don't talk about it much, because what would be the point?

No more Michelles, that was for sure. The thought was too depressing. I put the photographs back inside the radio and climbed the basement stairs. It was nearly five o'clock and outside the sky was already beginning to lighten. I wanted to go up to our bedroom, take off my clothes, and get in bed, but that didn't seem like a realistic plan. And presumably I would have to go to work; if people stopped analyzing the stock market every time they had a fight with their spouse, the financial structure of the U.S. would collapse in a week. Glumly I wandered through the dim downstairs. In the front hall I stopped at a picture I had originally picked out but hadn't actually looked at in some time — another naked woman. It was a print of a Carl Larsson painting, a young woman without clothes sitting at a desk, pencil in hand, perhaps writing a letter, a faint smile on her face. She seemed to be contemplating with satisfaction and even merriment what she had just put down. It had always been a pleasant picture but now I thought I knew exactly what he had meant. The question was, what would be in that letter — the one that couldn't even be written until I got undressed? I lay back down in the living room to think about that and promptly fell asleep.

The next thing I knew, Elaine was standing by the couch, not looking at me, but glaring more or less at the room in general. She seemed to be in the middle of a paragraph; the first words that registered were, "or have you just decided to quit going to work, too?"

"Too?" I said. "What is this 'too'? Come off it."

She looked down at me, disgusted. "Don't talk to me like that," she said, and left.

I looked down at my watch; it was seven-forty-five, which meant that I would almost certainly be late for the office. As

I trudged upstairs to shave and put on a tie, I could only hope that this fight was as much of a strain on her as it was on me.

When I got home she confronted me in the kitchen as I was pouring myself a drink. "I want to talk to you upstairs," she said, in a tone that suggested no alternatives.

"Do you mind if I get something to eat first?"

"Yes."

Naomi, who was watching the local news on the kitchen TV with the volume turned up high, gave us both a baleful look over her shoulder. I felt unreasonably guilty as I followed Elaine out of the kitchen.

"All right," she said, when we were in the bedroom with the door closed, "which one of them are you going out with? Or is it all three? It's probably not all three, because nobody wears their hair like that skinny nineteen-year-old anymore, and any-way nobody her age would be interested in you. That leaves the other two. Now—"

"Elaine," I said, realizing this could go on for some time, "I told you. Those are old pictures. Very old. I went out with Michelle Strickland fifteen years ago, when I was twenty-nine, and the other one was even before that."

"Oh yeah?" Elaine looked ready to tear out her hair. She panted a couple of times, through clenched teeth. "I can't believe you can just stand there and lie right to my face," she said.

"I'm not lying, Elaine. I know you think I am, but you're wrong, so why don't you just grow up?"

I was still holding my drink in my hand, and with one irresistible slap she propelled hand and drink upwards so that the whole thing splashed in my face. "You bastard! You really have some nerve."

Now I was finally as mad as she was. I put down the glass on my dresser, took off my glasses, wiped my face, and thought about exactly what to say. Elaine looked a little worried already, as if she hadn't meant to go that far. It occurred to me that for some reason she almost wanted me to be having an affair. Was that what she was up to?

"You're absolutely right," I said. "I've been plunging Michelle Strickland every chance I've gotten for years."

Elaine leaned forward, her eyes widening. We must have looked like an umpire and a manager arguing over a called third strike. "Is she good in bed?"

"She's wonderful."

"Well, I've got news for you. I've been having an affair with Joe Milnik for a year and a half."

"What? You've been screwing a guy from my car pool? How the hell did you manage to keep it a secret?"

"You were too busy with Michelle to notice."

"Why that little runt—"

"He's not as little as you might think."

Joe Milnik? She must be out of her mind. He was even less fascinating than me. What was she, desperate? But I needed something to tell her. "Well, you know when I went to that seminar on computer languages at the Sheraton Tara? I met this lady tax lawyer who was six feet tall and platinum blond. We started sending each other hot notes on the computers and ended up taking a room for the afternoon instead of pushing buttons."

She looked completely unfazed. "You know why you got transferred out of Chicago? Because I was seeing Waldron Cooper and his wife found out."

"You were messing around with one of the senior partners? What do you want to do, ruin us?" Waldron Cooper! A martinet like that, screwing my wife, giving me fishy looks in the corridor every day—so that was why! Suddenly I got the idea that I had lost my grip years ago without even realizing it. Senility would be next. I made one more effort. "Well, when I used to go to the day care center on Saturdays to clean up, I made it with Jolette on the playroom floor, every single time." Jolette had been the day-care teacher of the three-to-five-year-olds; she was twenty-five at the most, and I knew plenty of fathers who had the hots for her.

That got to Elaine; the blood rushed to her face. I could almost see the wheels turning furiously. "When you went to

Seattle for a week," she said in a deadly undertone, "I called the TV repairman and when he got done he put a tape of a porno movie on the Betamax to show that it worked and then we made it right there in the living room and he came back every day that week and we did every single thing that was in the movie." She stuck out her jaw belligerently, trembling a little, and we stared at each other for several breaths. I was dazed, and I couldn't top what I had just heard. I was the first to look away, and there in the doorway stood Naomi, with nothing on — framed, as in a photograph. The sight of her froze me and Elaine both. How much had she heard?

"Daddy, what did you make with Jolette?" she said in a tiny voice.

One sentence, I thought — even one word, the word "love" right now, would change my entire life, call in the lawyers, send this household flying apart. "Nothing, honey," I said. "I didn't do anything but clean up the playroom. I just made that up."

She looked both of us over, and for a moment no one moved.

"Could I see?" she said.

"See what?" But I knew of course.

"Those pictures."

"Have you been listening the whole time? You know you're not supposed to spy on us."

She lowered her head slightly, but kept staring at me from under her level brows.

"Those pictures aren't for you. They aren't for little girls. You wouldn't like them."

"I would too."

"Sweetie—" Elaine said, but then seemed to get stuck. "What are you doing with your clothes off?"

"Who's Joe Milnik?" Naomi said to her. See how you like it, I thought.

"Oh, nobody. He's a friend of Daddy's. I hardly know him."

With dignity, clothes or no clothes, Naomi turned and went back in her room and closed the door. Elaine and I breathed out, unable to look at each other. "Well," she said.

"I've got Scotch all over my shirt, thanks to you."

"Are those pictures really fifteen years old?"

"Yes, damn it."

"I'm sorry I messed up your camera," she said, but I could tell she wasn't. "I'll get it fixed, okay?"

"You do whatever you want."

"I want —" But she didn't go on. A divorce? No. That hadn't been what she started to say. We had not gotten to the edge.

"You want what?" I said, but she only looked at me in the terrible solidarity of marriage.

Naomi reappeared in the doorway, decently dressed in a T-shirt and a pair of shorts. "I'll go to the Burger King with you this time," she announced.

"Tell me," I said to Elaine. "Tell me what you want."

"You're getting bacon cheese," Naomi told me, "and you're getting plain cheese," she told Elaine, "and I'm getting a hot dog and I get to help you eat yours."

"Who said we're going anywhere? And how do you know we want any help?" I said to her. But Naomi had already turned her back and started down the stairs.

# Sounding Underwater
## Chris Spain

The first thing we thought was that anyone fishing with dynamite *ought* to die of diseases they had no immunities for. Then we thought about those living trophy fish, swimming smart-ass uncaught by us, and there was nothing we could do to save ourselves. They had to die. If someone had told us then that we would have to kill ourselves to kill those fish, we would have jumped gladly into a grave.

Jump into a grave is what we did. Punky stayed. Frank and I crawled from it, having seen it close up. It was the last thing Frank saw. His eyes were sandblasted to the nerve. I was looking, but looking the other way. My eardrums though, they were sheet-on-a-line shotgunned-in-the-breeze. The last thing I heard was I heard myself say, "We are going to depth-charge the bastards, war at sea."

What I think I am not hearing now is wood on wood. If the tree falls in the forest with only a deaf man to hear, who is to say? I watch Frank lift the paddle, drip water on water, and then lay it at his feet. He holds the gunnels with both hands, not moving until the canoe stops on the water. He is listening for it to sound the same on all sides. The lake gives the sky a good look at itself. Frank reaches for the casting rod I fixed for him and flies a lure. When it has the distance he wants, he drops it like a duck shot both barrels. It splashes, blurring the sky. I wait for Frank to bring it in. He doesn't. He is casting deep, going for redwoods, going for General Grant on the bottom.

It turned out we had plenty of dynamite. Frank had packed it in a Saltine can full of sand. The sand was my idea. I said if we did not pack it in something we would not get any kind of concussion. What happened was the wires got tangled and I grabbed a fistful and yanked. The copper must have touched. Punky was in front of me. He took most of what there was to take. A metal piece that was Saltine can stuck in his chest. He was dripping all over. Frank stumbled for the shore with his hands out in front of him, as if he were playing murder in the dark in the light.

The redwoods might have been a last-ditch effort to save us. But it was only after the taking us to see the redwoods that we could put a name on what we were after. We saw General Grant, Abraham Lincoln and Auto Log, and we were fine until the ranger showed us General Sherman, the biggest and oldest living thing. He said it was a thousand years older than Jesus Christ; that it would live a thousand years longer than we would. That it would live a thousand years longer than we would insulted us more than the smart-ass uncaught fish insulted us. When the ranger turned his back we unpocketed our pocket-knives and we were on that tree like lumberjacks.

It was the redwoods on the bottom that had us up before the sun, hoping we would surprise them stupid-hungry so that for one second they would forget how old and wise they were and we could jerk them from the lake. When the man who was our father took us to the hatchery, and we actually saw them, we completely lost our minds. Past any good for breeding, they looked like logs rolling in the water. The hatchery guy said they were his living trophy fish. His. It made us crazy. We could not sleep. We called them redwoods. We called them dead. In the morning we did not even care to throw a line in the lake. And when we did and a little perch latched on, we stomped him with no pity just because he occupied our hook.

We had a cabin on the lake then, we still do. The porch of that cabin is where I am sitting now. I think all the leaves that will fall have fallen, and I am seeing how close things are that

176

I remembered far away. Far away is how I remembered every-thing here, but I don't know if I would go by me if I were you. This is someone speaking who could not tell his brother what blue looks like. It makes me think hearing must have some-thing more to do with than just hearing, because it seems to me that more than that is gone. Frank says it smells the same. What is different to me I do not know. All I know is that it is bigger than no wood on wood, no water on water. In the almost dark, Frank's life vest reflects the last orange light in the sky.

It was in no light at all that we fished that summer. We waited until they closed our door, counted until we couldn't, and dropped into the dark. Our rods and tackle were on the porch. "So we can get an early start," we told them. We walked through the woods and, fishing pole first, rolled under the bottom strand of barbed wire surrounding the hatchery. The moisture on the grass, what we called frog piss, brushed our faces. We went straight for where the hatchery guy kept the redwoods, his liv-ing trophy fish. Frank had us convinced they would hit so hard they would drag us in. Punky belted himself to me just in case. But it was as if we were throwing rocks at a puddle. We tried everything on the hook, we tried spoons and came back with a fly. We casted ourselves silly in the dark but we never got a nibble the whole summer long, not one bite.

We called Punky Punky because he was that small. Small enough to slide through the gap beneath the door of the tin shed where they kept the avalanche dynamite. Dynamite they used in winter to bring down snow in the canyon.

It is dark now and I am worrying about Frank falling in. What he said before I pushed him away from shore was, "Point me for the middle, I am going after General Grant." I asked Frank how he would find his way on the lake, and he said that he could tell by listening to the wind on the trees. When he got it so it sounded the same on all sides, he would know he was in the middle. I am waiting for him to light a match. Then I will bang an oar on the dock so he can hear his way back.

By the time we were ready to depth-charge the bastards there was light enough to see. It was the light that the man who was our father said on North Atlantic convoy they called the see-who-made-it-through-the-night light. Frank wanted to wait for another night when it was still dark. But I could taste the slaughter already, I could see the beauty of it. The redwoods were awake, log-rolling to the surface, eating breakfast off the water. I said, "Enjoy your last meal, Kraut bastards."

I am forgetting how to talk. This is what Frank tells me. He says soon no one will understand. At first he said I sounded as if I were underwater. Now he says I sound as if both of us are underwater. He does not actually say, he writes. He wants me to take lessons. He says there are schools for that. Schools that keep you from forgetting. I say to him that as long as he understands.

By the August of that summer we were in a blue fishing funk. That they would go uncaught was unbearable to us. It made us so weak and skinny in the mirror that we could not look at ourselves. We stopped eating and the woman who was our mother thought we had discovered some evil something that was taking our appetites away. They began to leave our door open. We had to count until we couldn't twice or three times before we could drop into the dark. In the mornings we could barely climb from our beds. We only had strength to lie inside, not talking, staring at a television with sorrowful come-home-empty-handed faces.

The dynamite-raft was a life preserver we ripped from a tree where it was kept to save drowning people drowning in the Swimming Only. We had fixed a wire sling in the middle of it, like a hammock, and we hung the Saltine can there. We did "odds or evens" to see who would push it out on the pond. Punky lost. But in the end Frank and I could not keep ourselves out of the water. Punky was belly-deep in the pond when the wires got tangled. I turned and saw they were tangled, and I yanked.

I see a flame on the lake. It burns straight up. I walk out on the dock. The dock is wooden and floats on fifty-five gallon

oil drums. It gives beneath my feet and I feel as if this is Look
Out, and I am on a maybe-it-will-maybe-it-won't branch. Punky,
who almost weighed nothing, always won at Look Out. The
winner was the one who climbed the highest and saw the
farthest. To keep going you had to trust the branch, or not care.
When the branch broke everyone on the ground looking up
would say, "Look out!"

I pound the oar on the dock until my arms ache. I do not
see Frank until the canoe bumps the dock. I look in the bottom of the boat to see if he caught General Grant, but there
is nothing there except the casting rod. I follow the blue forty-
pound test from the rod to the red and white Mepps which
is hooked into Frank's lip and hanging on his chin.

Frank has told me he is forgetting also. He wonders to me
if there is a school that could keep him from forgetting what
blue looks like. I have tried to tell him what blue looks like but,
finally, I have not known, and I have told him that for myself
seeing has been no help.

It was a program about the Amazon. Something about how
the last frontier was soon going to be gone. We saw big tree-
crunching machines drag chains across the forest, knocking
down all the wood. We saw fires that were so big the smoke
from them made rain clouds. We saw Indians dying from diseases they had no immunities for, and we did not care; then
we saw them fishing with dynamite.

The fish were sledgehammered off their feet.

We walk through the woods through the dark, Frank and I.

Knocked dumber than fence posts.

Frank holds my arm.

They breached like blown-up submarines.

I think he thinks I am keeping him from falling.

It was a log-jam on the pond.

At the barbed wire, we roll under the rusted bottom strand.

I looked down, feeling in my heart triumphant as the U-boat
blaster, who was my father, looking down at the oil slick, the
life vests, and the spilled breakfasts of the men below.

The grass is dead and the frog piss frozen.

I said, "Deep-sixed is what you been."

•

With no paper, and me forgetting how to talk, we are the same as silent.

When I realized I had not heard what I said, I turned and saw Punky dripping all over and Frank stumbling with his hands out in front of him.

Ice is running on the water.

Our living trophy fish went rotten in the August sun. A dump truck hauled them away.

We slide down the dirt bank to the edge of the pond. I tell Frank what it looks like, but he shakes his head. I tell him there is no paper, but he shakes his head again. I show him where to write on my hand. What he writes on my hand is that he can no longer understand me. It leaves me Look Out high on a maybe-it-will-maybe-it-won't, holding onto nothing, feeling as if I could fall out of the biggest tree.

To save myself, I hit him on the face, knocking him backward through the sheeted pond. Standing in the shallow he unhinges his jaw and I think maybe I will hear, but I only see that I am seeing to the bottom of the deepest to where I have never seen before. I wade to him and I say, "Hit me here, hit me here, hit me here." He cannot understand but he understands enough. I move closer, saying, "Harder, harder, harder." My legs break at the knees and I am falling.

When the see-who-made-it-through-the-night-light comes, we are still here. I am in my blind brother's arms, watching him cry blind brother tears. The pond is quiet beyond no sound. I look up at the big empty and the nowhere and it blurs on me. What I am thinking is that it didn't matter, that there is never anything we can do to save ourselves, that all of us always are dying of diseases we have no immunities for.

# Beulah, Hazel, Lillian, Ruth
**Ann Darby**

I'll tell you that I didn't much care what the interior of this place was like. It was broom-clean and that was good enough for me. All I wanted was for it to be some place different. I thought this as the woman who managed the property walked me through the rooms. As I sized up the rooms and the woman sized up me, I thought I didn't care that I'd owe this place to a Mrs. something with a *d* who died one day. And the things that she had left—the chairs, harp- and oval-backed, the odd-sized table, the negative shadows on the wall where Mrs. D-something must have hung things—these made no difference to me.

"We're not planning to paint," the manager said. "If that's what you're wondering."

"No," I said. "I wasn't wondering."

"The mister used good stuff the last time he did it," she said. "High-quality, durable stuff."

"I wouldn't want it painted," I said. "I wouldn't change a thing."

"Oh," she said. "Well. Good for you," she said. "Most young women would. Most of them would change everything."

I cannot say I'm one of those who can see the young face in the old. To me the manager was just her face, and her face was just that powdery skin. And her skin was only old.

"You understand, this place is just for one," she said. "Of course, I won't say anything about guests. Guests are your own business."

They say we age by cooking. Every day the very heat of our bodies cooks us. All day long, all over us, our skin is broiling away.

"Look, it's a good place," she said. "Solid. Built to last," and she struck the wall with the soft of her fist. "Everything's in working order," she said. "Look."

And she walked me into the kitchen, where she turned one faucet and then the other on full, and from there to the bath, where she did the same, to the sink and to the shower. She even flushed the toilet for me, and then she walked me to the bedroom where she opened all the closets so I could see just how big and empty they were.

I can't keep them straight, the old ladies at this address.

Beulah, Hazel, Lillian, Ruth.

I can't put the names with faces.

I can almost put them with hands, the ones they put in mine when they told me their christened names. But even at that I fail.

I know the ladies instead by what they've done. There's the manager woman, who manages, and Cookies, who brought me a small plate of same. There's the grass lady, who stops me on the walk to say how brown the grass is turning. And there's the lady who does nothing but leans. Or that's all I see her doing, leaning against where we get our mail.

"Is it the first yet?" she asks when I pass her. "Is it the first?"

"It's not right to talk about the dead," the manager woman said.

"No," I said, "it's not."

She had come to my door with a bag for me, and I'd thanked her and asked her to stay.

"And not in what used to be their own homes," she said. "Not with their things still there."

I held the bag, while she walked through my rooms, touching things as she went, not that I had much for touching.

"No, you shouldn't," she said. "But I'll say this: Esther got as much as she deserved."

She put her hands on the harp back of the chair, on the table. They were the hands I put with Ruth, but I couldn't be sure. She moved them as if she were touching for dust.

"Esther had husbands up to almost the last," she said. "Imagine. Esther married twice after most people retire."

"Twice," I said.

"And they both died simple deaths on her," she said.

I put the bag on the table and went to the kitchen for tea. "How many husbands before she retired?" I asked from the kitchen.

"Esther said three," she said. "But I never believed her. I think seven. Or ten."

Carrying unmatched cups and no saucers, I returned to Mrs. D-whatever's, to Mrs. Esther D-whatever-it-was's, odd-sized table, and I sat in the oval-backed chair. The manager woman sat, too, but forward in her chair, as if it were easier to reach her tea with her feet flat on the floor.

"Look," she said.

What I looked at were the negative shadows on the wall, the rectangles (some bigger, some smaller, some higher, some lower) where the blue-green of the wall was a truer blue-green.

"I think those were their photo-portraits," she said. "I think she hung all those old dead husbands there in plain sight."

"So many?" I asked.

"Gave her cancer," the woman said. "Right there where all the young women get cancer today."

She put her cup down and sat back in her chair, her feet dangling above the floor.

"I don't for a minute think Esther had a better life than mine," the manager woman said. "Not for a minute do I think Esther had a better life. She had more but not better."

"I'm sure," I said.

"This place was full of things when Esther lived here," she said.

"I don't need much," I said.

185

"Everybody needs," she said. "Who do you think you are?" She prodded the bag as if that were what I needed. "Aren't you even going to look?"

I emptied the bag into my lap and found a cloth like linen, with lace at the corners that was going brown. I spread the cloth out over my knees and said the appropriate thing.

"Yes, it is beautiful," she said. "That's my handiwork. When I had eyes, I could tat like that."

I put the cloth on the table and the diamonds of lace, pinwheels and petal shapes, hung toward the floor.

"Esther wouldn't have had time for tatting," the manager woman said. "Too busy with husbands."

I asked about *her* husband as we drank our tea.

She said, "He was gone before he was gone," and she told me all about him and his long death.

She told me about their family and their life, and I thought as I listened that the manager woman had virtues that even I could see.

"I almost couldn't touch him at the end," she said. "What with the sputum and the smell."

She told me she had moved everything from their room. She had not wanted to dress or to do her daily things in the room where he was lying.

"In all my life," she said, "I'd never touched anything near-to or dead.

"I almost wouldn't," she said.

"I wanted him to do it alone," she said to me. "I didn't know what I'd do if he made that sound. I didn't know what I'd do if I had to go in to him," she said. "I'd sit in the front room with the lights out, and I'd watch everybody's doings. I could see Beulah with her TV on, and I could see the lights switching on and off in Hazel's place. And Lillian, I could see her making her slow way, from chair to couch and couch to chair."

She put her tea back on the table.

"I felt that I could see the goings-on in every room, as I sat in my parlor chair not getting up to the sounds he made.

"And then I'd hear *them*," the manager woman said, "Esther and her latest. His big feet and her bitty ones. I'd watch them come into view at my window, Esther in her new new clothes and him with that bald head held up as if it were wealth.

"I'd sit in my chair and watch Esther and him open their door and go into that place with all their fine things and the twenty dead husbands hanging on the wall. I'd sit and watch them do their animal doings in the night.

"That was a terrible thing, wasn't it?" she said.

I must have said no.

"It *was* terrible," she said and sat forward in her chair so her feet touched the carpet. "I judge myself by it.

"You're young," she said to me, "and you don't know. You're so young you would never think of anything like that, would you?"

She put her hand on my knee then, the hand I put with Beulah or Hazel, Lillian or Ruth. She put her hand there.

"You'd never do such a thing," she said, and with her hand resting on my knee, I felt that, all over, down to the deepest bottom of me, I was cooking in my own skin.

# As Long As You Can Remember Those Things
**Judith Wolff**

Hester stands by the observation window in the lobby of the town swimming pool, watching her seven-year-old daughter balk before the water as she has balked at nearly everything since she was born. This is Annie's fourth lesson; she hasn't actually been in the pool yet. The lobby is crowded with other mothers and children too small to swim. The children press against Hester, trying to get a view of the pool and of their brothers and sisters. A small hand clutches her leg, reaches up her thigh. Someone jostles her arm and the book she is holding onto — a novel about a husband and wife who are kidnapped and given hallucinogenic drugs — drops out of her hand. She bends to pick the book up, feels blood rush into her head. It is too hot in here. Other mothers speak loudly with one another about illnesses, fights with husbands, Halloween costumes. They all share the same regional accent and Hester feels out of place even though this has been her town, too, for nine years. She crosses her arms over her chest, holding herself in.

On the other side of the glass the children are already in the water, clinging to the sides of the pool, kicking up furious green waves. The girls wear brightly colored swimming caps with plastic flowers on the tops or fishes swimming in rows. Annie's bathing cap is plain white. When Hester gave it to Annie she looked at it with disgust, pulled it over her head and then ran after the dog, waving her arms.

Now, Annie stands by the five yard mark hugging herself, bare feet turned in, watching the fat swimming instructor with a look of terror and awe on her face. The instructor, a masculine woman in her mid-twenties, leans over the water shouting "Kick! Kick! I wanna see you guys kick!" When she turns around and points at Annie, Hester feels the shock as if she were pointing at her. "You!" the instructor yells. "Get in the water, pronto!" Annie continues to stare at the woman, shaking her head. Then the instructor lunges, hoists Annie up in her arms, throws her. There is a splash. "Did you see that?" Hester hears. "Eileen just threw a kid in." Hester is surprised to hear the instructor's name; that she even has a name. For the past month Annie has referred to her only as "that lady," and has been working out her fear of the woman by talking about killing her. Sometimes Hester wonders if *she* is Annie's intended victim: the stories are so pointed, so direct. Hester watches the place in the water where her daughter has disappeared. She holds her breath, waiting. The swimming instructor picks up a long silver rescue pole, puts the pole down, poises to dive.

Then the plain white swimming cap comes up and Annie is moving in the water, flailing her arms, like a drowning spider, Hester thinks. When she reaches the end of the pool the women in the lobby clap and shout, "Atta girl," they say. "Way to go, kid." "Look at that, will ya?" Their voices are painful to Hester's ears. She walks away from the window and sits down on a bench near the front door where the air is cooler. She takes a deep breath, opens her book, tries to find her place. After the swimming lesson, they must pick Josephine up at the art center, where she spends every Tuesday and Thursday afternoon smearing paint and clay into her hair. As soon as the car pulls up Josephine will be running down to meet them, waving her arms frantically—as if, Hester thinks, she doesn't believe her own mother can recognize her without help. After the art center, they'll stop at the grocery store for pumpkins, but Stephen has demanded that they wait until he gets home to supervise the carving, and God only knows what time that will be. Annie will pick the biggest pumpkin she can find, not caring if it has black spots. Josephine will want to stay for hours, choosing the smallest, the roundest, the pumpkin that most wants a face.

Hester will grab the nearest two for Phoebe and Daniel and then there will be one pumpkin for each child. And then supper. Hamburgers? Meat loaf? Chicken? It doesn't really matter what Hester cooks, because the kids eat everything and Stephen will say it's fine, but then he'll just pick at his food. Then there will be unpleasantness, as there is every single night. After the children have been excused from the table, Hester will wash the dishes as loudly as she can in response to his gloominess, and then she'll start thinking about something else. When she looks up again she'll be alone in the kitchen. Why should this night be different from any other?

When Hester looks up again, Annie is shuffling across the lobby, sneakers flapping loosely on her feet. She sees her mother but pretends not to. She walks over to the candy machine and stands in front of it, pushing buttons. She feigns nonchalance, even pounding her small fists against the machine as if she'd put money in and been cheated. The impatience of the gesture reminds Hester of Stephen. Of the four children, Annie looks most like her father. She has his hair, his paleness, his freckles. She has his way of walking into a room. Phoebe, Daniel and Josephine are more like Hester—unsure of themselves, unsure of their place in the world. Hester stands and stretches her arms over her head. "Come on," she says, and waits for Annie to balk. She shakes her head at the outstretched hand. "No money," she says. "Supper in two hours.

"Come on," she repeats, and walks out of the lobby into the cold air. It is already getting dark out. The sky is deep purple and Hester feels suddenly, horribly sad. She doesn't get used to this early darkness until winter is almost over, and here it's only Halloween. She breathes in the cold air, the smell of decaying leaves, and realizes that what she feels is homesick. But home is just a mile away, up the hill and around to the right. They can almost see the house from here; how absurd to feel this overwhelming longing. She takes Annie's hand as they cross the street.

"Smell the air," she says. "Breathe in deep."

"I can't," Annie says. "My nose is stuffed up."

When they are in the car Annie tells her she peed in the pool. "I couldn't help it," she says. "How was I supposed to know she was going to throw me in? I hate that lady," she says, and thrusts out her lower jaw.

At Cypress Street Hester turns left and drifts through the intersection, waving at the policeman directing traffic. The policeman turns to watch her; for an instant their eyes meet and Hester feels a surge of pleasure. "You shouldn't hate anyone," she says after a moment, then snaps on the radio.

Paul Benzequin is arguing with a woman from South Boston about the bussing issue. The woman is enraged about something another caller has said. "I'll put it to you like this, Paul," she says. "I live in this area for a reason, and I don't want my children bussed out to some place in Dorchester.

"And I'll tell you something else, Mr. Benzequin: I don't want them colored kids coming into our schools. They have their own, and if they aren't good enough that's not my problem—" Paul Benzequin interrupts the woman to tell her he finds her attitude offensive. He tells her she needs to examine her conscience and morals. He keeps talking. He thanks her for calling. He cuts her off the air.

"She had no right to touch me," Annie says.

"*Shhh*," Hester says. "I'm listening." There is something so annoying, so self-righteous about Paul Benzequin that she has to keep listening to him. He is strident, intolerant; she toys with the idea of calling him up and asking why he bothers to have a radio show if he can't stand listening to other opinions. It doesn't make sense.

"I'm going to get a gun and blow her brains out," Annie says.

"Oh, you are, are you. Where are you going to get a gun?"

"Adam Rand's father has a gun."

"Adam Rand's father," Hester says, "isn't going to give you anything of the sort."

"Yes, he will," says Annie. "Edward loves me."

"And since when have you started calling him Edward?" Hester wants to know. She doesn't approve of children calling adults by their first names. This is not something she would have even thought of doing as a child. For the first two years they were married, she called Stephen's father Doctor, and not once did he suggest she call him something else.

"Since yesterday," Annie says. "I played the piano for him and he said, please call me Edward."

"You're lying," Hester says. "And furthermore, you have a father. Why do you want another one?"

Annie unwraps her towel from around her neck and drapes it over her head. The image reminds Hester of a bowl of rising dough. When Annie speaks, her voice is muffled.

"What?" Hester says. "What are you saying?"

"I said I swam, Mummy. Didn't you see me swim?"

"I'm sorry." Hester says. "I wasn't watching." Listening to the silence that follows, a sick feeling rising in her stomach, she thinks, these are the moments you can't take back. "Of course I was watching," she hurries on to say. "Didn't you hear us clapping for you?"

For once, Annie keeps her thoughts to herself. But as the car pulls up in front of the art center she stands and climbs over into the backseat. Hester feels her kicking around on the floor.

Josephine gets into the car and slides into her mother's arms, her chest heaving with grief. "What is it?" Hester says. "What?" She presses her cheek against the top of Josephine's head, breathing in smells of glue, finger paint, peanut butter. For a moment she is overcome with nostalgia for her own childhood. Sometimes when the little girls are asleep, she stands over their beds, watching them. Sometimes she imagines she smells the ocean in their hair. "What?" she says again. "Tell me."

"You're late," Josephine mutters between gasps. "You're so late, Mummy."

"Josephine, my dear," Hester says. She pushes up her coat sleeve, taps the face of her watch. "Look at this. See the minute hand? It says exactly five-o-clock. I'm not a minute early, not a minute late." The child blinks at the watch, then breaks into fresh sobs. Hester pulls her onto her lap and pats the heaving back. Josephine has always cried — too much and too often. She's always grieving for one reason or another. "Listen," Hester says. "What's our number?"

Between gasps, Josephine manages to mutter, "RE4-3645."

"And where do we live?"

"On Hewitt Road."

"There," Hester says. "You know everything you need to know. As long as you can remember those things, there's always a way to get home. See?"

Josephine nods against her breast, smears her streaming nose against her coat. "Nobody's going to leave you," Hester whispers. "I promise. You won't get left behind." She lifts Josephine off her lap and settles her on the seat beside her. "Put your seat belt on," she says. "And tell me what you did in art class today."

"It's a secret," Josephine whispers loudly. "I made presents for everybody, even Daddy."

"Wasn't that thoughtful of you," Hester says. She pulls away from the curb, turns the radio back up. Paul Benzequin is still orating. His voice rises in irritation. He is appalled, he tells them all, with the narrow-mindedness of the people of Boston. Never has he heard such bigotry in one afternoon.

"Amen," Hester says.

"Amen," Josephine repeats, and sniffles.

"What kind of present did you make?" Annie asks from the back. Her face appears in the rear-view mirror. Hester watches shadows drift across it, smiles at her daughter's reflection.

Josephine tries to turn in her seat. "Can I get in back?"

"No."

"What present did you make?" Annie repeats. "Is it crayons again? Because if it's crayons again I don't want any. Last time you gave me and Daddy all the ugly colors."

Josephine's chin begins to tremble again. "Look at the trick-or-treaters," Hester suggests quickly, pointing at two tiny ghosts hurrying across the street. "Did you see that, Annie?"

"I'm not talking to you anymore," Annie says.

"Did you see the trick or treaters, Jo-Jo?"

"I wish we could go trick or treating," Josephine says.

"People who go trick or treating get poisoned and die," Annie announces, and the tone of her voice sounds startlingly like Stephen's. "When we go to school tomorrow," she continues, "nobody will be there. They will all have gone trick or treating and everyone will be dead."

Then they are home. The little girls run across the lawn and up onto the front porch, but Hester stands by the car, looking at the house. When they bought it she loved its symmetry, its regularly shaped rooms and open spaces. She had never been in a house so large, and for months after they bought it she would walk through its rooms, half-expecting someone to appear and tell her she would have to leave. But the house is an embarrassment now. The front lawn is overgrown with weeds. The dark wooden fence leans in toward the house. The front porch sags in the middle. Yellow shutters hang from the windows at crazy angles. The house seems to be collapsing in on itself. Stepping across the lawn, Hester bends to pick up a couple of bricks the kids have pulled out of the front walk. She sets the bricks on the porch next to a rusting tricycle which has been sitting there for two years, through rain and snow. Since they've owned the house, Hester has painted each room at least once, each time a clean, hopeful white. She has hung wallpaper which later peeled and was never fixed, she has organized drawers, cupboards, hung hooks for coats and towels, shoveled snow, seeded a lawn which grows everything except grass; she has tried to hold chaos at bay, but the house defies her; Stephen defies her. He refuses to see that the house is shabby; that like the children it needs his attention. As Hester unlocks the front door and follows the girls inside, she prepares herself, as she does every day, to see the house as a stranger might, someone who could look past the deterioration and appreciate the open space.

"Uh oh," Annie says. "Ginger shitted on the floor."

"Uh oh," Josephine repeats. "Bad dog. Bad, bad dog."

The girls leap over the piles of shit and race into the kitchen. Hester stands in the front hall, listening to the sounds upstairs. She doesn't take off her coat. She walks to the foot of the stairs and looks up. She hears footsteps, somebody running across her bedroom floor. The linen closet door opens and squeals shut. "Daniel?"

No answer.

"Daniel? Come downstairs and clean up this mess, please." Nothing.

Hester reaches the first landing and pauses, the bannister cool and smooth under her hand. "Stephen?"

"Whoever you are," she shouts, "get out of my linen closet." Then her son appears above her. She starts to shake with relief. Then, anger.

"Hi!" Daniel says, smiling a sickly, insincere smile.

"What have you been up to in my bedroom?"

Daniel shrugs, tilts his head to one side. "I wasn't in your bedroom," he says, grinning now, and showing his teeth. "Must have been somebody else."

"You're lying," Hester tells him. "Now get down here and clean up the mess."

She feels him hesitate. He doesn't say yes, and he doesn't say no, but she feels his annoyance, then she's charging up the stairs after him, taking his curls in both hands and banging his head against the wall. "You'll do what I tell you to do," she hisses. "Don't ever argue with me again. You do what I tell you to do, buddy boy." She realizes that she's hurting him, bangs his head harder and harder, the sick feeling rising in her stomach, thinking that when Stephen comes home she'll tell him things have to change. Something has to be done about Annie's violent streak, Josephine's nightmares, Daniel's lying. He is their father and he has to take some responsibility for raising them. She needs time to herself; time with him. She needs to feel something other than this rage. Her life cannot continue to be consumed by these details. There must be something larger. There must be.

Her hands come away from Daniel's head and hover strangely in the air. He pushes her, ducks under her, runs down the hall. She hears a door slam, hears him kick something across his room, and suddenly the house is silent. Downstairs, the little girls have stopped talking. Hester hears a stair creak, realizes they are crouched on the first landing, watching her.

"Go to your room," she says. "Everybody go to your room."

Hester walks into her bedroom and turns on the bedside lamp. Beside the lamp is a drinking glass filled with daisies. Her bed has been made, the blankets tucked tightly in, the way she taught her children to do it. The air smells of furniture polish. The carpet has been vacuumed. As she stands there Hester looks at the tracks Daniel made in the carpet when running out of the room. She places her foot over one of his prints and marvels at how much smaller his feet are than hers, how tiny he is. She can remember being that small, even smaller. She can remember being so small that when she ran her legs took over her body and it seemed she would never be able to stop. Just where are they afraid she's going to? she wonders, plumping up a pillow and tossing it back down. She sits down on the bed and folds her hands in her lap, obediently, the way she was taught to. Just where do they think she's leaving for? I'm here, she thinks. I've been here all along.

# Interview with
# Ann Beattie

**G.E. Murray**

$A$*nn Beattie's first novel,* Chilly Scenes of Winter, *and* Distortions, *her first collection of short stories, were published together by Doubleday in 1976 to enthusiastic reviews. "This is a significant literary debut. We had better take due note of it," the* Chicago Tribune *reported. Another critic called Ms. Beattie's two books "a feast of top grade fiction."*

*A frequent contributor to* The New Yorker, *Ms. Beattie also has published stories in the* Atlantic Monthly, Transatlantic Review *and* Virginia Quarterly Review.

*The following interview took place at the* fiction international/ *St. Lawrence University Writers' Conference in Saranac Lake, New York. Ms. Beattie had just returned to her cabin after teaching a fiction seminar. It was late on an unseasonably cool afternoon, June 11, 1977.*

**G.E. MURRAY:** Let's start with one of those inevitable and practical questions. Your publisher released your first novel and first story collection simultaneously. That's a curious rite of publication.

**ANN BEATTIE:** It was Doubleday's decision. The reason behind it, I'm sure, was to attract attention, which it did. It's certainly true that first books aren't greeted with open arms in most places. So perhaps the publisher felt this would create an advantage.

**G.E.M.:** I believe in a review John Updike referred to you as "best of the generation . . . "

**A.B.:** No. (Pause) That was the *Village Voice*. (Laughter)

**G.E.M.:** I don't mean for you to pontificate, but your growing reputation in a variety of circles seems to put you in a position to address the nature of change in contemporary fiction.

**A.B.:** I really don't read with categories in mind. That sort of thinking makes me more aware of what I'm doing in my own "artistic" process, and I don't want to know about that. As much as possible, I need to be in the dark about what I'm doing, because to me writing is mysterious. If I cracked the mystery, then it would all end. I feel the same about other writers, although I could probably lump people into groups if you held my hand over a fire.

**G.E.M.:** Who do you read?

**A.B.:** Contemporary?

**G.E.M.:** Yes.

**A.B.:** One of my favorites is Stanley G. Crawford, who wrote an amazing book, called *Log of the SS. The Mrs. Unguentine.* Other favorites include Anne Tyler, Joy Williams, Richard Yates, Donald Barthelme, Don DeLillo, Mary Lee Settle, John Updike, Steven Millhauser. I also read a lot of people in small magazines.

**G.E.M.:** I heard a rumor that you were something less than an academic whiz-kid in high school, and in fact, you graduated low in your class. Now you're teaching at Harvard. . . .

**A.B.:** Yes, I see the irony (Laughter). In retrospect, it was probably a combination of boredom, mediocre academic programs and teachers, a lack of interest and understanding . . .

**G.E.M.:** At what point did it change? When did you turn to writing?

**A.B.:** I think I would have been a writer if I had been a waitress. School didn't determine it. At least that's a romantic notion of mine. I guess I became interested in literature in college, more so than high school, but I wasn't interested in anything in high school. Still, I don't think academic pursuits correspond to being a writer. I hope that taking part in the academic world doesn't have anything to do with the creative process.

**G.E.M.:** When did you begin to write seriously?

**A.B.:** I started writing seriously, which to me means more than a couple stories a year, in 1971. I must have written 15 or so stories that year. I was in graduate school, and I was miserable. So I pushed my desk against the wall and started writing instead of reading criticism about writing all day.

**G.E.M.:** You publish frequently, not regularly, in *The New Yorker*, where you first established your reputation. That's a tough market. How did you arrive there?

**A.B.:** I came in over the transom. No agent or friend, except my manila envelope. It's unusual, I know.

**G.E.M.:** Do you adhere to any writing schedule . . . a certain number of hours per day, days per week?

**A.B.:** No, I've gone six months without writing anything. I doubt any schedule would help me. I do think of writing as being mysterious, so I can't conceive of being mysterious from, say, 9:00 a.m. to noon. When I do write, it's almost always late at night. That's not as odd as it seems. I just don't key-up until late in the day. That's when I'm most energetic.

**G.E.M.:** Have you developed any habits related to your writing? For example, John Barth is a notorious coffee drinker at the typewriter, while Joyce Carol Oates is reportedly without addiction to anything but the trance of her work.

**A.B.:** At first, I thought I had none. Then people would ask, "Don't you do this or that?" So I began to realize I did have certain peculiar habits. I have to have a particular typewriter, a certain brand of correction paper . . . I only edit with a fine-line black pen.

**G.E.M.:** You couldn't write here, out in the woods?

**A.B.:** Oh, no! I couldn't even write a letter home from here. Also, being around writers — and this is a problem I found in teaching writing — I find I lose interest in my writing. It's enough to be around writers, to have proof positive that there truly is a world of writing. In that atmosphere, I never feel the need to sit down and write another story.

**G.E.M.:** There's the ongoing debate as to whether or not teaching inhibits or inspires practicing writers . . . You've taught at the University of Virginia, and now you're going to Harvard . . .

**A.B.:** Yes, and I don't really care for it. It's not that I dislike teaching. I don't. What it is, is I get into it too much. When I teach a course in literature, such as I did at Virginia, I somehow can make the separation between literature as I teach it and as I write it. But inevitably, because I'm a classroom personality identified as a writer, it becomes more difficult when I "teach" writing. I just find it hard to write when I see so much writing. When I see it in a book, that doesn't seem to affect me. But when I see 20 bad student stories in a week, I think, "Oh, there's too much bad writing in the world already." And then I don't do my work either. So I try to avoid teaching it . . . but here I am at a writers' conference . . .

**G.E.M.:** What starts a story for you? Image, plot, character, a phrase?

**A.B.:** Most often I get some kind of physical feeling. Sometimes I'll be elated, other times depressed. Another thing that helps me start a story is my husband's insistence that I write stories. In my story "Dwarf House," I had the first line kicking around in my head. What made me suddenly know that the line, *"Are you happy?" MacDonald says. "Because if you're happy I'll leave you alone,"* was being spoken by a man to his dwarf brother, I couldn't tell you. But suddenly it started to jell. But that's not usually the case. Occasionally, a character's name gets things going. I don't ever start to write because of ideas.

**G.E.M.:** Let me address several general aspects of your fiction, which I've read and reviewed. That of course, doesn't suggest I know anything about it.

**A.B.:** I probably know less than you do, I assure you.

**G.E.M.:** For some time I've had this feeling that you specialize in minute choices. By that I mean, that by the time a story is over, some small choice has made a major turn in direction for one of your characters. This seems to be a structural thread running through your work, whether stories like "Dwarf House" or "Hale Hardy and the Amazing Animal Woman," or the novel.

**A.B.:** There is nothing I develop consciously. I've been absolutely shocked in classrooms where I've heard my stories discussed. Sometimes I've been so enlightened, I've taken notes. But now I've gotten to the point where indeed I'm informed, but want to forget about that enlightenment immediately. A while ago, for example, my editor at *The New Yorker* wrote to say he thought a story I'd written was good, but he wanted some changes. He mentioned that I often used scenes in restaurants to mark time . . . and I was horrified to be told that. I just don't want to get hung up by knowing too much about what I'm doing.

**G.E.M.:** It seems there are two major adversary elements in your work, namely, faith and despair. . . .

**A.B.:** Yes, I think so. But it's not intentional. I agree with you. Yet I wouldn't have been able to name those elements unless you just did.

**G.E.M.:** Much has been made of the thematic drift of your novel, which moves from the dreamy understructure of the social '60s to—what?—the hedonistic '70s in America? Is this important to your novel?

**A.B.:** Actually, I resist and resent being categorized as a spokesperson for the '60s. That seems to me to miss the point of the book. I have a certain attitude in the novel, just as Salinger has an attitude in *Catcher in the Rye.* Some people see Holden Caulfield only as a mixed-up, pitiful person, but that isn't entirely Salinger's attitude. He has a very distant and ironic perspective on Holden. Yet people often miss that. And I feel the same about my book. I'm not trying to make a statement about what it was like in the '60s, or how people felt coming through to the '70s. That's just a detail of consciousness, like Ban deodorant or racquet ball may be a detail of consciousness. People were looking for the novel I didn't write. You can do that, I suppose, but it seems a reductive approach to the book. What I wanted was an ironic perspective on my main character, Charles. I didn't mean for him to be the long-suffering, misplaced bureaucrat who survived the protest on Washington. He, the character, may think that's important. But I don't. It's his attitude. Not mine.

**G.E.M.:** You're talking about developing a great deal of

distance from your characters?

**A.B.:** Exactly. It depends on how close to home they hit. Sometimes it's necessary to draw away completely.

**G.E.M.:** Are you fond of any of the major characters in *Chilly Scenes of Winter*?

**A.B.:** All of them.

**G.E.M.:** Here's one for the academicians out there. Some critics have taken delight in citing echoes of *The Great Gatsby*, correlating Charles and his remote lover, Laura, with Jay Gatsby and Daisy Buchanan and even envisioning Charles's ne'er-do-well friend Sam with Gatsby's narrator, Nick. Any truth to the echoes?

**A.B.:** I think that's interesting, and it's certainly possible. I realize the allusions are there. I mean, *Gatsby* is referred to. One character even says, "What do you think this is, *The Great Gatsby*?" The spirit of what Fitzgerald was getting at was something I wanted to restate. I do see some similarities between the 1920's and 1960's—that whole idea of being in a frantic state and still seeing real-life possibilities. That was deliberate. So there are echoes there, but not that strongly. It's not a rehash of Gatsby by any means.

**G.E.M.:** Is *Chilly Scenes of Winter* a book about disillusionment?

**A.B.:** I guess so. It's safe to consider that an underlying attitude of mine. At least as a strain of my subconsciousness.

**G.E.M.:** Two of your stories in *Distortions*—"Snakes' Shoes" and "It's Just Another Day in Big Bear City, California"—are two of the finest stories I've read in recent memory. . . .

**A.B.:** I didn't think "Snakes' Shoes" amounted to much, so I tossed it in the pantry, where garbage piled up. Later my husband asked what happened to the story about the two people who sit on a rock at Hall's pond. He dug it out, patched it together, and got it off to *The New Yorker*, where it eventually appeared. Sometimes I don't have a clear perspective on my work.

**G.E.M.:** Do you find yourself leaning on editors for perspective?

**A.B.:** I think most writers can accurately perceive their extremes, and know when something is either excellent or awful. But most work falls somewhere in between. I realize, for instance, that "Hale Hardy" has structural faults. But it has enough redeeming graces for me to consider it good. There are times, though, when you have to call out for help and advice. I listen to three people: Roger Angell, my editor at *The New Yorker*, my husband, and J. D. O'Hara, whom I met at the University of Connecticut, and who publishes a lot of reviews of contemporary fiction.

**G.E.M.:** I know many people who are busy stealing time from this and that endeavor in order to find enough minutes and hours to write a novel. How long did *Chilly Scenes* take you?

**A.B.:** I'm embarrassed to say. Actually, I worked on the novel no longer than it took me to write all the drafts of a long story called "Colorado." But you should know I never intended to write a novel. *Chilly Scenes* started as a story. Eventually, it got to be about 50 pages and I was still interested in it, so my husband convinced me to continue. He even picked up my teaching duties for me so I could work full time. Some days I worked 18-20 hours. Other days only 1-2 hours. It wasn't constantly manic. My husband also suggested I think in terms of "chapters." So I did, saying just a few more "chapters" and I'll have a novel. Soon enough ... I had a novel.

**G.E.M.:** Can you discuss what you're working on now?

**A.B.:** After *Chilly Scenes* I spent a long time on another novel, but I wasn't happy with it. What happened was I had a couple of minor characters in it who suddenly became interesting about page 300. They just took me over. And the quality of writing improved, and I became more involved, all the while holding myself in check saying, "dammit, finish the novel you started." And I did. But now I know what I have to do ... scrap the hundreds of pages and write about those two characters from scratch. I'm not eager to do that, but that's what'll happen. I really wish I knew how to write novels. I wish someone had 10 rules we could follow.

**G.E.M.:** Do you use your dreams in your work?

**A.B.:** I rarely retain my dreams. But other people's dreams have appeared in my work.

**G.E.M.:** I don't mean this in a negative way, but today we find the housewife in Hackensack and the mechanic in Maine aspiring to the conditions of the fiction writer . . . What advice, if any, would you offer to people with some inkling of talent?

**A.B.:** Lie low and hope it works out. It's always difficult to deal with moderate talent — and that goes for both student and instructor. It's a hard thing. With my students, I write specific comments on their manuscripts. Perhaps that helps some people. There are some things that are easy to talk about — some technical things — especially to novices, such as don't put word counts and "North American Serial Rights" on manuscripts you send out. Certain writers' magazines recommend this, but it only earmarks you as an amateur. As for more substantial sources, I'd recommend reading, say, the sensible things about writing that Flannery O'Connor has to say in *Mystery and Manners*.

**G.E.M.:** Anything else in the way of advice?

**A.B.:** Well, I would also recommend not being afraid of your imagination. Sometimes people take that advice as an endorsement to become Kafka or Barthelme, and that's not what they want to be or can be. It's not my point, either. I'm simply saying that it's a natural instinct in writing and life to restrict our imagination. We backtrack before we get anywhere. Instead, I believe in going full-steam, freeing imagination, then cut back as you will. Otherwise, we end up with box stories, all the same. Explore and develop imagination fully. Don't go with what you think people want to read. Write what fictions you feel ought to be read.

**G.E.M.:** It's become a popular pastime to lament the current state of fictional art. Is this a concern to you?

**A.B.:** I worry about it more for other people, especially those who may have good work but aren't getting it published. Let's face it, good fiction markets are drying up quickly. Many publishers are reading only agented material. Had that been the case with me, I'd never have been published. I just sent into the slush pile. I didn't go to any writers' programs. I didn't know any agents or have any publishing contacts.

**G.E.M.:** Perhaps the practicalities of publishing fiction today are beginning to influence the actual writing of fiction. . . .

**A.B.:** I agree. The trends and themes are often gloomy. A lot in the confessional mode—which is not to say all confessional work is bad. But there's an overwhelming amount of I'm-Sad-to-be-a-Housewife stuff around. It's very flat and predictable, even though it is in vogue. There will always be trendy work. Who knows what will survive?

**G.E.M.:** The survival of fiction is sometimes cast in competitive terms with cinematic arts. Do you see literature, notably fiction, in a catch-up position with film?

**A.B.:** In my cynicism, I usually say film is way ahead of literature. Right now, this may not be so true. A decade ago, film was clearly leading. But there's a new undercurrent. Take, for instance, Robert Altman's film "Three Women," which is to me a failure because Altman was too literary. His films rely on things that are often found in novels—fictional structures—but they don't seem successful to me because he deals with ideas the way a writer does, not the way a movie maker should. I think Altman has read too much. I think you can be more subtle about allusions in writing than you can when presenting them visually in a film. You can hide them in a book or story easier. Writers seem to better understand the necessity of transforming something from the visual to the written. It's not so much a problem for novelists as for some movie makers.

**G.E.M.:** I think, too, the fictional forms are gaining in depth and variety in terms of film. The classic case was nineteenth-century painting versus the advent of photograpy. People didn't just pack up their paints. Painting moved in entirely new directions. I see a latter day parallel in the relationship between fiction and film. Perhaps another way to say it is that today's fiction is more refractive, less reflective.

**A.B.:** Yes, I know from my viewpoint, fiction is becoming increasingly dark, deeper, subtle, and more mysterious than ever before.

# Interview with
# Richard Stern

**G.E. Murray and Mara Anne Tapp**

$F$irst winner of the Carl Sandburg fiction award for his novel Natural Shocks, *Richard Stern is a key figure in Chicago writing circles and an integral voice in American fiction. He is a faculty member at the University of Chicago, where he has taught literature and creative writing since 1955.*

*Stern's novel and story collections include* Golk *(1960);* Europe, or Up and Down with Baggish and Schreiber *(1961);* Teeth, Dying and Other Matters *(1964);* Stitch *(1965);* 1968 A Short Novel, An Urban Idyll, Five Stories and Two Trade Notes *(1970);* The Books in Fred Hampton's Apartment *(1973);* Other Men's Daughters *(1973); and* Nature Shocks *(1978).*

*For nearly two decades, Stern's fiction has received significant critical attention. In commenting on Stern's first novel, Saul Bellow said, "Golk is fantastic, funny, bitter, intelligent without weariness . . . pure—that is to say, necessary." Of* Other Men's Daughters, *Philip Roth noted. "Stern's accomplishment (here, as in all his work) is to locate precisely the comedy and the pains of a particularly contemporary phenomenon without exaggeration, animus, or operatic theology." George P. Elliott has called Stern "a real artist of the short story." In praising Stern's latest and prizewinning* Natural Shocks, *Peter Prescott, in* Newsweek, *concluded that "Stern is a remarkably deft and witty writer. His novel is wound so tight as to have a springy texture . . . Stern offers a kind of fond satire; he likes his creatures too well to carry them to the point of caricature. His theme—the retreat from human feeling and a reawakening to it—is as grand as any that fiction can accommodate."*

*We conducted this interview in Stern's office at the University of Chicago on May 31, 1979. Stern turned his telephone upside down in its cradle to avoid interruption, and we began talking.*

**G.E. Murray:** By now, discussions about the death of the novel are old and boring. But what attitudes, either social or intellectual, gave rise to the rumor of the demise or death, if you will, of the novel?

**Richard Stern:** I would say that it's the enormous extension of non-fictional stories and the expertise with which techniques, most of them developed in the novel, have been used by sociologists, reporters, case-history writers, anthropologists like Oscar Lewis, and tape-recorder anthologists such as Studs Terkel. Enormous amounts of story material went into non-fictional guises and put all kinds of pressure on the novel. I usually compare it to what happened to nineteenth century painting as it related to the advent of photography. I think there are other things involved in this. For example, the tremendous twentieth century concern with the type of mentality which goes into construction. It's almost the displacement of construction by what Valery in the poem *Pomegranates* calls "secret architecture," that is not: "the art that conceals art," but the story within the story. This is related to the prurient interest in personality and gossip.

At the beginning of the century, we had the great museums and scholarly assemblages. Then we had the technology of collection which enabled individuals to collect the great works of the world in the form of reproductions, records, inexpensive editions. These imaginary, or rather real, personal museums generate in sensitive people the desire to know what these things have in common, what lies behind them, what kind of mentality is there. Can the traditional novel satisfy this kind of mentality? Sometimes not. So we have the development of the "Joycettes," those who, in various ways, try to express the ways human beings have had their experience *written about*.

So it is a serious concern but, to someone like myself, it is not something which puts me out of business. I maintain there is a genuine interest in actualization of external events, the representation of ever-finer degrees of consciousness. I do not think consciousness has been exhausted at all. I disagree with

216

my friend, John Barth, and my acquaintance, Robbe-Grillet, about disinterest in psychology. That, to me, is most of the ball game.

**Mara Anne Tapp:** You've been writing fiction for almost three decades. In what ways have you seen fiction move during that time?

**RS:** There has been an enormous amount of good, skillful work. Some of that work responds to the extraordinary experience available to writers all over the world. This bewildering amount of material has created new forms of summary, parody, mockery, reduction. These are creative stages for mimetic types like Thomas Pynchon, whose biggest difficulty is finding a form to contain his great trapeze acts.

**GEM:** Pynchon is almost exhaustive. . . .

**RS:** And yet the concept of a book is very difficult for Pynchon, and one feels that his peculiar trance-like gift overruns the forms which he finds for it. He comes up with fancy twine, sensational parallels which do not draw me on as I am drawn on by powerful story writers, tracers of consciousness or — if I can neologize — resplendors of character such as Saul Bellow.

**GEM:** It seems to me and many others that there is more competent fiction being written today than possibly ever before in this country. But, I think even important writers, such as Donald Barthelme and Stanley Elkin, sometimes fail to hit a substantial vein. They're incredibly clever writers, but often the net effect is something that's rather trivial. Character, for instance, hasn't been portrayed to a high level of satisfaction. It seems to me that *you* are more concerned with consciousness, with the psychology of characterization.

**RS:** With the way a chaotic world is organized for the moment of the novel, in the particular character or group of characters, my concern is the creation of an orderly world in the old-fashioned mimetic way of Homer, Tolstoy, and Bellow.

**MAT:** If you were to summarize your views about writing in the last two decades, would you say that a good writer attempts to synthesize and create an order out of a lot of disorder?

**RS:** Well, to some degree this always has been the case. But nobody can be an epic writer today. Pynchon has tried to put it all in and, just now, Barth in *Letters*. But there has been no Thomas Aquinas to supply the blueprints, and nothing commands common assent, certainly not the "history is fiction is life is dream" of the Pynchons-Barths.

We have a group of marvelously gifted people backed up by a wide audience, some of it expert, who, as you say, create and receive brilliant fragments. There is also terrific concern with language, as with techniques of fiction. This is related to the belief that realities are as much created by the words and conventions which represent them, as by anything else *out there*. In physics, we had and have the great debate between the Planck-Einstein people and those who follow Mach, Bohr, and Heisenberg.

**MAT:** In your last two books — *Other Men's Daughters* and *Natural Shocks* — you have many characters, all of whom are very developed and complex. Those books also are filled with other books and letters and ideas and encounters. The readers who come to those books need to do a lot of work in order to understand the characters better. In other words, if I'm reading along and I find out that Cynthia Rider is reading *The Pure and The Impure*, I may want to go back over that book. How much do you expect a reader to do? Do you think about that at all when you are writing?

**RS:** Not very much, no. I think the Colette citations in the book are full enough to give you what is needed. I do think those novels of mine are different from each other. I hope the books are different from each other. *Other Men's Daughters* is the old type of French novel. There really is an intrigue, or a double-intrigue: two stories, a story of gain, a little romance story, and a story of deprivation and loss. It's a smaller book, but it's more exhaustive. The plot is more conspicuous. *Natural Shocks* works somewhat like an earlier novel of mine, *In Any Case*. It was a spy novel, and every time it appears to close in, I open it. I open it because it's related to my theme of treason and betrayal. I can't reconstruct the thinking which went on behind and during the composition, but I remember every time I had the possibility of closing off a relationship, I unscrewed it so that it opened up and betrayed itself. Now, with *Natural Shocks*, you have a book about a man who has had enormous worldly experience of the sort I've been talking about. He's a reporter, he's been here and there, he's interviewed left and right. He's also intelligent — or is supposed to be. Yet, as he says to another character in the book, his great contribution has been his mental filing cabinet, his internal Dewey decimal system. Now, the book could well have concentrated on the central episode, which is the reporter Wursup's encounter with a fatally ill young girl. That business about illness is the center of the book. But, again, the impulse which I remember clearly was not to close off the book with romance. I tried to keep inventing characters and situations to the last page. I throw in two new characters in the very last paragraphs. If you read *Natural Shocks* as you read *Other Men's Daughters*, it will be *coitus interruptus*. You'll say, "Come on! Come to something! Let's see what we have here." Still I think the book is its own form of amorousness, and some good readers have preferred it to the more popular book. I suppose the impulse to write it as I did has to do with the notion that since you can't write an epic, you can suggest one by covering lots of ground and plowing it with a strong temperament and intelligence. But you can't summarize it. You can't have an orderly process of ingestion, digestion, nourishment and defecation. It's not there. So, instead, I think there is a thematic sign in the book, namely, a man who has seen everything. You can make him "Everyone." Now the only thing "Everyone" has in common is cessation. Death. That is, no more experience. So Wursup *studies* it as if he's going to another war. And then, pop, pop, pop, pop, here and there, people start dying around him. How does he react? That's the rough form of the book. The last scene — I didn't know *the meaning* of it — came auto-

219

matically to me. He's where the book started, on the roof, staring in the dark at the city lights wiping out the starlight. His ex-wife's apartment is dark, empty. Maybe somebody else is moving in, maybe they're there already—just out for the night—or maybe they're dead. This is as much as Wursup, anyway, can say. And as it's the book's end, it's meant to have resonance. It's not a great epic conclusion, but that's half the point.

**GEM:** If it is possible, talk about the kind of changes that you've gone through since you published your first novel, *Golk*, to *Natural Shocks*. I mean, what kind of writer was the man in the late 50's who wrote *Golk* versus the man who a year or two or three years ago was writing *Natural Shocks*?

**RS:** That's a difficult and interesting question, and it's one actually I don't think I've ever asked myself or answered. Let me say an obvious answer would be a kind of Borges answer. This man, the man represented in the different books, is of a single consciousness.

I do remember that *Golk* was the book for which I said, "I am going to break through short story size and go on to write a longer work." At any rate, it was written quite quickly. I was a more furious person then, I believe. Mockery was one of my components, and a kind of benign contempt, or a contemptuous benignity. I can't remember *Golk* very well.

It's related, I guess, to the one I just described, because it's a way of containing a lot of the world in miniature. The miniatures are the scenes of the "You're on Camera" program. But there was more security in my personal system then.

*Other Men's Daughters*, which I suppose has some of the old-fashioned qualities of beautifulness, was written at a time of personal disruption, when for a year, I didn't get a full sleep at night. I'm a kind of classic "burgher." I work at the office, I'm anonymous and quiet. But I was threatened more then than at any other time. In between, who knows? I guess I was being that "burgher."

My changes often came when I was off somewhere traveling, or living for a year abroad, or experiencing in fantasy some of those things I did not experience in actuality. I think I've always been curious. I've been a reader. I have no gift of languages, but I've always tried to learn and read in different languages. I've tried to make contact with people who are considered the most interesting of their time, trying to learn from them and see what they're about. My books may exhibit some of this curiosity. I don't know how I have changed — perhaps other people can tell me a bit — but I don't yet feel old. I do see at age fifty that one is not going to go on forever. I also see that things are much more difficult to do really well.

**MAT:** Do you think it's harder to write the longer you write, or is there one book that was the most difficult?

**RS:** Every book has been difficult. Some stories, including a couple I've just written, have been fairly easy to write. But I have hundreds of pages with some of the best writing I've done sitting around in agony waiting for a home. Because one has less time, perhaps, one wants to get a lot in and make it exceptionally beautiful. It may be that this is a self-defeating presumption, an excess of self-consciousness . . . as if one can determine where one's constructions will be in the public streets of literature.

The best thing to do is go on and work from day to day and have the greatest pleasure in life which, I've discovered, is just sitting and thinking, or letting the typewriter think. *Finding one's mind.* One is so lucky to have either time, or the absence of agonizing problems, bad debts, bad teeth, sick children, whatever.

**GEM:** Talking about the rare private times that writers or any type of people run into today, it seems to me that if we can characterize American fiction in the 1970's, it's been one of the writer as celebrity as opposed to the writer as writer. I'm thinking of presences such as Truman Capote, Norman Mailer, and Erica Jong.

**RS:** Well, there is tremendous hunger for inside stories. Irreligious people need celebrities, and there are some writers who can serve along with actors and beauties.

221

But the secret history of literature is much more fascinating, and its gossip columns are intellectual history.

**MAT:** What about less celebrated but deserving young fiction writers? I'm thinking especially of Barry Hannah, whom you have praised.

**RS:** When a new writer comes along, you feel the rhythms and speech and a new way of looking at things that is thrilling, and so last year I discovered, along with several hundred people, Barry Hannah's short stories, *Airships*, with great joy. His book is an event. It was not nominated for the National Book Award — but it was deserving of that kind of recognition.

**MAT:** Besides Barry Hannah, who do you enjoy reading?

**RS:** Well, two friends, certainly — Saul Bellow and Philip Roth.

Bellow may be a somewhat greater writer in the old European or Western tradition, perhaps a richer talent. But Roth is a very fine writer, in ways an underrated writer, though very popular. And there are others. I'm looking forward very much to John Barth's *Letters*. I hope that it will be for him what parts of *Chimera* and much of *The Sotweed Factor* were. I'm also fond of Grace Paley — a wonderful writer of the Barry Hannah school; that is, original rhythms and conception. Her characters are defined as nobody else's.

**GEM:** What about Joyce Carol Oates?

**RS:** Although Joyce Carol Oates has terrific skill and is able to do many things, I have never finished an Oates book. I can admire the skill, I get involved a bit, and then I say, "Jesus, why are you taking so long to do X and Y?" Now, I probably haven't read a fifth of what she's written ... I don't know who has. She writes constantly.

**GEM:** Do you see poetry lending anything to fiction, or fiction lending anything to poetry, these days?

**RS:** I think that artists — except those who are closed off and obsessive, and have a demanding story controlling their consciousness — are affected by anything, particularly anything verbal. It may be graffiti on an underpass, a new law, or the

Cronkite news report. But surely poetic rhythms, formulations, and mentalities are more likely to influence a fiction writer. God knows what composes any consciousness! I am not systematically influenced by poetry, but I know there are passages in my books which come out of stanzas of Rimbaud. There are certain poems in my life, like Baudelaire's *Le Voyage*, which are so deep in me that they must become part of my books. I read Dante at a crucial time and Eliot's *Wasteland* in my teens. Mind-dominating texts.

**GEM:** Let me shift gears on you for a while. In some ways, your work reminds me of John Gardner — not in terms of technique or intention, but I think in terms of scope. Both of you are reaching to encompass whole worlds. Gardner's *Moral Fiction* is clearly one of his more controversial books of recent times. At one point in that book, Gardner cites what he calls our national penchant for tawdry writing and suggests strongly that the lack of first-rate literature may eventually lead to a sick society. Can you comment?

**RS:** I think that the finest art, and the finest moments in oneself, come from a layer which overrides any judicial, moral, or other humane structure. It may come from the wildest part of the nature, and if it has social application, it is of a complexity beyond what John Gardner describes in *Moral Fiction*. It is an emblem, an outlet for the troubled. It becomes a visible and beautiful and releasing expression of a time. It takes its place in the richest human tradition, the mental tradition, which is connected with language and the history of this richest of art forms — prose fiction. Its social application has to do with the refreshment of language — so that language does not become a dike against original expression — and secondly, with a representation of behavior so that behavior doesn't become calcified. Thus, in a sense it's social lubricant, social watchfulness. But above all, you can call it personality — the creation of a form which will allow other human beings the sense of a powerful new personality, the writer behind his writings.

That is the highest kind of morality. That is why a writer

223

so wicked in some ways as Celine can be in my sense a deeply moral writer. *Mein Kampf*, had it been written by a man of literary genius, despite the frightful opinions expressed therein, could conceivably be as morally valuable as *The Divine Comedy*. My guess about *Moral Fiction*—I do not know John Gardner and I don't know his works nearly as well as I should—is that that book is a way of wrestling with his own nature which is, possibly, more chaotic than most. He probably comes from a tradition which needs to think itself morally sound.

**MAT:** The question of morality interests me in terms of Wursup, your main character in *Natural Shocks*. I'm not saying that you shouldn't have been concerned, or that you were, but here's a man who is in an emotionless profession and goes through this great revelation that you've spoken about earlier and really tries to come to terms with his feelings. Wouldn't you say he becomes a better person? Doesn't he gain a kind of moral consciousness?

**RS:** I think so. I wasn't conscious of making a moral trajectory the center of the book by any means, but since a book of this sort is almost always an education for the writer, if for nobody else, it probably rubs off on the leading character.

**GEM:** By virtue of your position at the University of Chicago, you are occasionally referred to as an academic novelist. It seems to me that whether you sell insurance or automobiles or teach literature, a novelist is a novelist is a novelist. Is there such a thing as an academic novelist?

**RS:** I do think so, yes. . . . Just as you could say the dominant profession in Shakespeare's day was the theater, and you could see the theater emerging as metaphor in the work of poets, and you can see in a particular sonnet of Shakespeare's (III) that he was disturbed at being a professional actor. I think you can say that there is something about some of the leading writers of our time which is powerfully involved with the kind of learning which is associated with universities. Now, for instance, *Giles Goat Boy* by Barth began when Barth heard a lecture of Leslie Fiedler's. Its very theme is the university. It may not be the most successful book by John Barth, but that's something explicit. Borges, in his work, reflects a student of literature, whether he's in the university or not (though Borges worked for years in universities). The heroes of Bellow's books are frequently university teachers. Whether the setting is the academy, as it is in *Other Men's Daughters*, or not, is not crucial. There is one thing about the academy, however: if you *believe*—complicated word—the texts that you teach, then you should somehow live in relationship to them. You have a greater obligation. Literature is an interesting mentor and, therefore, an interesting literary situation in itself. It can be said that *The Odyssey*, written by a close student of *The Iliad*, is the first academic novel.

**GEM:** What are some of the disadvantages of being a professor at a major, internationally known university in terms of being a writer?

**RS:** Bourgeoisification. The ease at which your students, a captive audience, can laugh at things or get moved by them and, therefore, the easy purchase of attention which may slip into your writing life. You have to discipline yourself that it does not. You have to be damned careful that you don't try and buy your way in as easily as you can in a class. I don't say teaching is easy. In fact, right now, I'm finding some of the difficulty and some of the routine quite painful. That's true in any job the writer might have. So I have to "teach Beckett" Monday, have to prepare, read, think. Usually, that's enriching. But, if you're working on something very different it can constitute an interference.

**GEM:** You were part of literary history in the making back in the late 1950's, when there was a great brouhaha over the *Chicago Review* trying to publish some of the Beat writers, especially parts of William Burroughs' now classic novel, *Naked Lunch*. As I recall the story, certain *Review* editors eventually resigned over the matter and started another magazine, but not before the university, a Chicago newspaper, and the post office got involved. You were a faculty adviser to the *Review* then. How do you recall the circumstances of that event?

225

**RS:** It was really a literary story that eventually involved the late Mayor Daley, the Chicago City Council, the Catholic Church, President Kimpton of the University of Chicago, and others.

I think it was about 1958-59. There was an editor at *Chicago Review* — a very difficult guy, hoping to make mileage with his difficulties, but he was also the guy who had latched on to Allen Ginsberg and other emerging Beat writers. His name was Irving Rosenthal.

**GEM:** I thought Paul Carroll was involved?

**RS:** And then Paul Carroll got into it. Well, the *Review* had been in trouble because they had printed 9,000 extra copies as a way of selling it across the United States. The *Review* was in debt, so a Faculty Committee was put in charge of looking over the damn thing. That's how I got into it. When Rosenthal was editor, some staff members began complaining that some manuscripts which were sent in weren't even logged. There were no votes taken on the manuscripts. They were only going to print this one group of writers. Then Jack Mabley published a column in the *Chicago American* asking that the *Review* be censored. So, I, Ned Rosenheim, and the other members of the Faculty Committee were called into President Kimpton's office. I had not met him before. We talked about the problem, and were advised to kill the issue. I said we'd be the laughingstock of the world if we did that. You can't censor literature. You have to print everything that's been accepted. What you do is institute procedures, you know, have votes taken on manuscripts, and so on. The main thing is you can't go on acting or even looking like Nazis. If so, we'd all resign, etc. So Kimpton immediately said we were right, then called me into his office and said, "You know what my concern is? This University has been saved by Mayor Daley and the City Councilmen. Daley has driven measures through a Catholic City Council to preserve this neighborhood, so the University won't move — he knows it's one of four or five things which count in Chicago." Meanwhile, some of the priests in the church were telling some of the people on the City Council, "Look, this is a matter of faith and morals. This is an obscene publication. The Church can take a stand on this." Daley was afraid that he might lose his Council vote. Cardinal Stritch had died about this time and there was a power fight in the Church. One of the factions was led by a man who was a priest with Back-of-the-Yards. He issued a publication criticizing the University. He didn't care about the *Chicago Review*, but about the University squeezing blacks out of this neighborhood into his. He had a problem on his hands with this, so, he attacked the University with whatever came to hand. Namely, obscenity in the *Review*. This put more pressure on influential members of the City Council. That was part of the complexity. What finally happened was the students took over the whole business. There was an election, and Rosenthal and Carroll quit the *Review* and started *Big Table*. They also took their side of the story to the press, to John Ciardi, who printed an account of it. I answered in a letter. There were distorted accounts in many of the papers—especially in San Francisco. I tried to answer every one. The best accounts are in the *Chicago Maroon*, which printed all sides of the issue for weeks, and it's absolutely fascinating. I have various letters, too. It's a remarkable story which covers church, state, religion, literature, and so on. I should add that I appeared in the first benefit for *Big Table* and published in *Big Table* because somehow literature climbed over the political and religious barricades.

**GEM:** It's a story that people are going to be talking about for years to come, I'm sure.

**RS:** They could. I thought it had been forgotten. Allen Ginsberg thinks—naturally—it was one of the most important events in American literature. I was so close to it that I never saw it that way. And don't now, by any means.

**MAT:** You've been interviewed a lot.

**RS:** More in South America than I've ever been in my life.

**MAT:** The interview is becoming a fairly common literary vehicle. How do you feel about it?

**RS:** Well, I've done a few myself and I've commented on it.

It is a modern sort of thing and it's an interesting form. It's dramatic, it puts you on the line. It also enables you to exhibit changes of mind and it documents you. I feel it's certainly important . . . primary documents in literary mentality. My God, look at the writers-at-work series in *The Paris Review*.

**MAT:** So, you see it as illustrative, informative for people to get to know how writers work, how writers feel, how writers think.

**RS:** It's an occasion for a writer to generalize. I don't know— maybe there's some harm involved. The kind of harm I've talked about in *Natural Shocks*, in which you tend to be fixed by a portrait. I have seen this happen, and I have been involved with it in a minor way.

**MAT:** And also the depersonalization that you talk about in *Natural Shocks*.

**RS:** Yes, right. God knows, it's fascinating. You know, minds which squeeze topics together and work on each other and then record them. You might go back to Plato's *Dialogues* if, to any degree, they were representative of different views expressed by different human beings. So, in that sense, the interview belongs to one of the richest traditions of Western literature.

# Interview with
# Grace Paley
**Maya Friedler**

$T$*he following was recorded on May 30, 1981, for* PUBLIC REPORT, *sponsored by The Women's Forum and funded by a grant from the Illinois Humanities Council.* PUBLIC REPORT, *broadcast on WBEZ (91.5 FM, Chicago), presents dialogues with prominent persons in politics, arts, and letters. Maya Friedler is moderator and co-producer.*

**MAYA FRIEDLER:** Grace Paley is the author of some of the most direct and wonderful short stories in American literature. Susan Sontag says, "Grace Paley makes me weep and laugh and admire. She is that rare kind of writer: a natural with a voice like no one else's . . . funny, sad, lean, modest, energetic and acute." Her two books are *Enormous Changes At The Last Minute* and *The Little Disturbances of Man.*

Grace, you're being honored at a dinner for the benefit of Women For Peace. They are not only honoring you as a writer but as a political activist. . . . All those parts in your life—political activist, feminist, writer—how do they relate to one another? What takes priority? Or do they all mess you up?

**GRACE PALEY:** It's not that they "mess me up" . . . but in a sense they do. I mean I see my life as a *life*, and not as a careerist or as an activist. All of these things *are pulls*. Sometimes I write and sometimes I'm a family woman. I've raised kids, and that was very important to me, too. And political work has always been very important. So, whatever is the most important at the time pushes the other two aside. But, basically, the writing is really about all of that . . . it's about family life, it's about a personal life of politics, so to speak, and it's about

231

how people live—especially how women live.

**MF:** About how people live . . . what do you think the major issues are?

**GP:** For me, really, the major issue is a question of the life or death of this earth and of life on it. But it's all connected. The life of women is particularly connected to the life of whether we survive or not. In a sense we are really being run into the ground by a horde of men. That's really what it amounts to. There's a strong political explanation for this, and an economic one. There are multi-national corporations and imperialism and all that, but it really is the same idea of the world that has kept women in a second place—in ninth place!—in some centuries . . . after men's horses and things like that. So I see that interconnection. I think the violence in the streets and a growing militarism is related. The Family Act—the Right to Life Amendment—is part of the same oppression. And it's always been going on . . . certainly for fifty years . . . really, hundreds of years—this idea of dominating bird, beast, and female.

**MF:** The political passion you have—while it is reflected in the writing and I feel it—really is never stated. It doesn't ever seem to be a diatribe. It never seems to reveal itself in the terms you're suggesting now because the writing doesn't seem to be particularly political. It's about people and their emotions and their relationships. And they are funny. Really, I don't remember a story of yours where you have placed women in that same kind of "ninth place" or "second to men's horses."

**GP:** Now we're sort of used to the idea of writing about women, but when I first began to write about women and children, people really weren't. That came after that long period of heavy masculine writing which followed the Second World War . . . so that I'm not speaking for myself or by myself alone. Lots of other women really felt that their lives were not interesting. And I certainly felt like that. I mean I felt that I was a writer and what was I going to write about? These ladies in these kitchens and these kids? Who'd be interested in that stuff? And, then, at a certain point, I just *had* to write out of feeling for the life of the women around me. And then I thought, well, maybe it's trivial, maybe it's nothing; but that's what I have to do, I thought, and it's what I *will* do. So nobody'll read it . . . what can I do? So that's a political *imperative*, in a way.

The reason I'm interested in the political life of this world is that I'm interested in the people. The politics and literature come from the same impetus, really. It isn't that it's the same thing, but it comes from the same concern: how ordinary life can be lived in our cities. Countrysides, too.

**MF:** You talk about interest in the people, and we haven't mentioned your role as a teacher at Sarah Lawrence. . . . I understand one of the assignments you gave is to "write in the first person as if you were a person that you were in conflict with, or someone in a situation that you really don't understand." Do you still give that assignment? Would you give it to yourself?

**GP:** I really don't remember that *exactly*, but I do give that assignment . . . a little differently in the sense that it says: "Write a story from the point of view of a person with whom you are in conflict." But if you're in conflict with that person, you *know* that person. So I would really put a sub-heading on that (or a sub-something-or-other) and say just what we write about is *what we don't know about what we know.* You're in conflict with a person *but* you know that person somewhat.

There are many reasons for that. One of them is the question of tension. When you're dealing with something you don't quite "know," or when you take this other voice — you're making a "pull." You're pulling towards another head. And that pull towards what you *don't* know . . . well, that's the story itself. The story is that stretching . . . that *act* of stretching.

**MF:** How far will you stretch? Are there some people whom you simply won't write about? Some who will not be part of your literature, to whom you cannot possibly imagine giving voice?

**GP:** There are people in all kinds of countries that I don't know — and I don't have time *not* to know what I *don't* know about them. So I probably wouldn't. . . . But I did write a story about a visit to China which dealt with just that problem. It was about taking pictures, about photographing, and it really was about dealing with another people. There's no telling what you can do in your life, if you live long enough.

**MF:** About "giving voice"—and as an extension of that question—I hear your voice so clearly in so many of your stories . . . obviously, they can't all be you. But they all have such direct personal voices, as if they really are the people talking. . . . I think of your story, the one with the three black men and the little girl. Now, those voices are very vivid and real. They are not you. How did you find those clear and true voices?

**GP:** Well, that was, of course, a terribly hard story to write. But I was very close to one of those guys. He was an old friend and we had done a lot of political work and tenant organizing . . . .That's what interested me when I was young. He was a good friend of mine and he was the one who told me the story. He told me the story of the killing of this little girl about four times. I mean, he would grab me—sort of—by the wrists and just stop me on Macdougal Street or on Sixth Avenue, or wherever, and just tell me the story again and again. So that I had to tell it for *him*. I had to tell that story for this guy, Bill, who is dead now. . . . And so, he was what I knew and the story I told was what I had to go after—to *stretch*—for what I didn't know about that. But it began with him . . . .The other people were invented because I didn't really know them. But I did know fourteen/fifteen-year-old kids. I did know runaways. I know the park. But it was hard.

I think it's something for students—or anybody, really—to think about. Everybody is a *storyteller*. We all tell stories all the time. . . . Every storyteller is a story HEARER first. So students who don't listen will never be storytellers. They just won't.

I wrote a lot of poetry in the beginning of almost all my life. But I couldn't write stories, really, until I really heard—LISTENED—to enough other voices . . . until I began to pay great attention to other voices and tried to make that *stretch* to other voices. Then I really found my own. Until I was in my

30's, I would try to write a story and I couldn't do it.

**MF:** You remind me of the conversation with your father in the stories. He is such a shining, brilliant man . . . but he questions you about craft and technique and one of the questions was about plot and your feelings about that. Do you want to develop that feeling about plot and beginning and end?

**GP:** Well, I think that that story in which I say that I'm opposed to plot because it takes away the open destiny of life and literature has been interpreted that I'm against plot. But you can't be against plot. Plot is something that happens, whether you DO it or not. Plot is only the movement of a thread through time. It's what happens after something else happens. You can't stop plot like you can't stop time.

**MF:** Let's talk about time. In the first story in *Enormous Changes* called "Wants," you deal with a whole lifetime in three pages. Is that ability, that perspective, that voice of yours similar to what other women would do in dealing with time? . . . . Now, Virginia Woolf would say that there is such a thing as a woman's voice. . . . I wonder if that surfaces itself, particularly in dealing with time? Men like Borges and Marquez come to mind, and they have such different global concepts. Yours seems to be a lifetime — or a moment. Can we talk about that?

**GP:** I think the people you mentioned were South Americans who are really involved in an historical investigation apart from anything else . . . which is all mixed up with history and myth and different cultures coming together in South America. They're really doing something else. . . . But when you ask about women and time, or women's voices or anything like that, I know that people do feel that women have a particular voice, maybe . . . or a style or a language. Certainly I think that women's language is often different than men's. . . . In the next twenty years I don't know what women's voices will be like. Virginia Woolf wrote at a time when she was, first of all, an extraordinary writer. She lived among critics and writers. Second of all, she was pretty well thought of by lots of men and she was an original, too. In the sense, say, that Gertrude Stein was an original. And yet, all these people were strong influences on others that came after. Gertrude Stein influenced a lot of male writers. So, you have to pay a lot of attention as a scholar, and think about it a lot and be crazy about having an opinion if you want to argue that matter. I have none of those feelings.

**MF:** What about influences? Can you think of influences from your past — from your writing and other people's writing?

**GP:** That's another thing that interests me. . . . People talk a lot about who influenced you. Well, as a kid, I was a big reader, like a lot of us. We read a lot: all the nice books and the good books and all the rotten books, too . . . all the trash that we could.

But we don't talk enough about the other influences that are really enormous literary influences. And that's the influence of your family's language, the way people speak in your house, the languages they speak, the language of your street and of your time. Where you are. Where's your longitude and latitude and what's spoken around you? In that way, people from different countries can sometimes sound alike. Not because they're under the same literary influences but because they've the same parents . . . or the same KIND of parents.

Some have said that sometimes I'm a little like the Russian writers. . . . The fact is that I did read a lot. But I loved *Dubliners,* too, and I think it had a strong influence on me. I read all the Russian writers, and they all spoke to me in some way. Which of them was most important is really hard to know. The writer herself can say one thing and the rest of the world can say, "Ho-ho! THAT'S what YOU think!" I'm just right in the middle of my own time, that's all.

**MF:** I seem to hear, or think of, Chekhov quite a bit with your stories. There's a kind of acceptance without despair, despite all the hardships that your people seem to go through.

**GP:** That's sort of the influence of my family as much as Chekhov. It's not that my family was not despairing. As a matter of fact, very often I would say to my Aunt Mira, "What is it? What happened? How are you today? How are you?" And she'd say, "Ah-h-h, read Dostoevsky."

**MF:** I would like a go back to the lessons for a young writer and students. One of the comments you made is that it's possible to write about anything, but the slightest story ought to contain the facts of money and blood. Do you want to elaborate on that?

**GP:** I guess I mean something very simple. It really means family, or the blood of ordinary life. . . . As for money, it's just that everybody makes a living. And that's one of the things that students forget entirely. . . . I mean it's not that they have to say what they do at their job . . . it's just that they never go to work. The story takes place between eight in the morning and eight the next morning with nobody ever leaving the room! And those are the things that our life in this world and in this society and in every other society is really made up of. . . . It's made up of our relationships—our family relationships are of the utmost importance, and when they don't exist they're equally important —and how we live, how we make a living. The money in our lives: how we either have it or we don't. . . . If people live without working, that is very important. It's called "Class." And that really is another way of saying that you really DO write about classes, whether you know it or not.

**MF:** You always seem to be writing about real people, too. There is that ring of truth. . . . I noticed in an old book that you had six lies that writers had to avoid. The first is the lie of injustice to characters; the second is the lie of writing to an editor's taste or a teacher's; the third is writing to your best friend's taste; the fourth, the lie of the approximate word; the fifth, the lie of unnecessary adjectives . . . the sixth one—the lie of the brilliant sentence—you love the most. Personally, I do think that most of the sentences are unforgettable in your work and I have a feeling that you really did love them.

**GP:** Yes, but I really didn't love *them* the most.

**MF:** What happens in your preparation for your stories? Do you keep journals? What happens in this writing process? What feeds it, what's the research, what's the process that goes on for you?

**GP:** It's hard to say. I think I try to write pages. I try to keep notebooks, but I lose them. So I don't. I just keep pages which I put into files. So I have a lot of pages and sometimes I keep going with them. . . . But I never have a time when I can't write. I used to—when I was much younger—but I never have it now because I have all these pages that I've been working on and I simply go through them.

Since the head—the skull—is the main form for all this, you're really thinking about something all the time. You're really thinking about the same thing and one of those pages simply takes hold at some point. . . . You add a sentence to this one, to that one. Actually, you've been thinking about it a long time. And, finally, one of the stories takes hold.

**MF:** Then you don't go through periods such as Tillie Olsen in her book, *SILENCES*—her fifteen-year period of silence?

**GP:** No. I've written hardly at all this year. I did a lot of writing last year, but not this. . . . My silences are somewhat different. First, I didn't write most of my stories until my mid-thirties . . . . I mean, she's quite right in her book, in her various silences. I have just been doing a lot of other work and I feel very desperate about it. But I'm not blocked in any way. If I sat down—if I went to my typewriter tomorrow—I'd have four or five stories I could be working on. I've simply not been able to do that. It's not just "busy-ness." It's a flow.

**MF:** Does that take us back to the beginning of our conversation? The other things you're doing?

**GP:** It does. It brings us back to Women For Peace. . . . I certainly feel a powerful sisterhood with them. . . . I feel a terrible urgency. . . . I have a pretty new grandchild—about sixteen months old—and my heart turns over; it scares me when I look at her. I just don't know what this world has in store for her. It certainly seems to me that if people don't act, these kids aren't going to get to kindergarten, let alone junior high school. So I would say that, up until this year, I suffered a good deal of despair, despite my stories. And if I feel any better about it, it's because I see a lot of young people beginning to move here and in Europe. So there is a little hope. But it just seems that the horror of the arms race is not being attended to. It's seen but people really are afraid; they think if they don't talk about it — if they don't say a word — everything will be all right . . . .There's such fear of the human being, of the life of the mind. But that can be reversed. If we have time.

**MF:** As it's been said: "Grace Paley is in a class by herself. She has a way of capturing more than the human voice: more important, the heart."

# Interview with Gordon Lish
## Patricia Lear

$W$*hen he is teaching, Gordon Lish says he feels most himself. I watched him lecture in his fabled writers' workshop in New York City and he seemed to me to be possessed by the urgency of one who is constantly amazed. His spontaneity is the kind usually reserved for small children. We've got to listen! Feelings flow through him as if he were simply their conduit for six hours nonstop. There is no formula, no code. He discovers it as he goes along, and from moment to moment it is all new. His teaching is the result of a clear gift.*

*I attended two of the workshops in New York City in April 1987, and taped an interview in his office at Alfred A. Knopf where he is a senior editor. He also edits the new journal* The Quarterly *and is the author of two novels,* Dear Mr. Capote, Peru, *and a story collection,* What I Know So Far. *Teaching is a role he has never spoken to, and although he agreed to the interview, when the interview was complete and the tapes in transcript form, he read them and felt that he did not, and can not, and should not, speak to what goes on in the classroom. Having been present for what he does, and having read the creditable transcript of a creditable interview, I must admit that for him to reduce it to words is to reduce it, and that Gordon Lish the teacher is not made for the textbook, but rather for experience.*

**PATRICIA LEAR:** I was afraid to meet you. I was afraid to interview you.

**GORDON LISH:** I can't imagine why. I'm a very mild fellow. (laughter)

**PL:** Well, from what people have said about you. Many, many stories circulate. And last night, I was amazed at the love

243

you put out. That's what struck me first. The intensity that you want this to work and the caring about these people, the writers in the room. I didn't expect that. I thought it would be the kind of thing where your students had to "earn" you. An uphill battle.

**GL:** Well, I expect that, not unlike any extraordinary event, if I may characterize what goes on in that room as an extraordinary event, those who are not present for it are inclined to develop rather inaccurate notions of what goes on. One has to be there. Much of the report that has centered on my private workshops is terrifically wide of the mark and not infrequently, I suppose, informed by a degree of presumption that arises out of displeasure. Displeasure because something's going on and one's not there for it, so it really can't be worth being there for. I don't think there's any way to quite capture the arc and character of one of those workshops without being present.

**PL:** Or you. Gordon Lish. I read a lot about you. Amy Hempel has told me about you. In my life all of a sudden you seem to be everywhere and you're not at all what I expected. I didn't even know when I walked into the workshop last night that that was you and I've seen pictures of you. You're that different.

**GL:** Perhaps I've put on weight. Yes, that's probably it. (laughter)

**PL:** But what I saw was a very open man, even somewhat vulnerable in his openness. Very genuine and real.

**GL:** You're very kind. But it may all be the teacher's device. One doesn't know. It may all be an act. I don't know what I do when I'm teaching. I really become, I think, transported in a kind of way and can't claim to be that person when I'm outside of a classroom setting. In a classroom setting, I have no fear and no hesitation and no doubt.

**PL:** So, at cocktail parties, you're not like that?

**GL:** No. Not at all.

**PL:** Have you always taught?

**GL:** I've taught since 1960. I was fired out of school-teaching. In, I guess it was, 1962, 1963, in California, and received the event with great ill will. I wanted to teach. I held teaching to be the highest calling.

**PL:** Was it high school or college?

**GL:** High school and junior college. I had gone from having the most lauding reports from my supervisors, to being cashiered for what I think eventually reduced itself to a case of rate-busting.

**PL:** Rape? Rate?

**GL:** Rate-busting is an expression that had favor with, ah, really disfavor, with trade unionists some years ago. Someone came along and turned out more widgets per hour than you were turning out—you went to your foreman and you delivered a complaint about rate-busting. Everybody had to turn out so many widgets—so if you were teaching, and then stayed on after school to keep teaching, you'd be likely to inspire a certain disapproval among your colleagues. So that what originally was a novelty, and much admired, and spoken of with enthusiasm by the administrators in that school district, after about three years, wasn't viewed with such pleasure by them at all. There was a lot of pressure on them to get rid of me. That in combination with my connections with people like Ken Kesey and Neal Cassady sent me packing in due course.

**PL:** Were they in the same place?

**GL:** Well, no. I was in a small town in California and they were in another small town in California, but we were loud enough to be heard. Kesey was a participant in my magazine, *Genesis West*, and we were all three great good pals.

**PL:** Were you writing then?

**GL:** No. I had abandoned writing some years before on the well-founded judgment that I would never be first-rate and that if you couldn't be first-rate, don't do it. I've since come to the view that everyone can be first-rate given an utter investment of will. But I had no will at that time. I would look across the way at writers like Stanley Elkin and Grace Paley and Edward Loomis and James Purdy and be convinced that what was present in their programs was something that would always be

245

denied me. And so was only too delighted to give up the task. I had, in my early twenties, even in my late teens I think it may have been, had two books accepted for publication here in New York. Both were really the kind of obvious undertakings of someone who has been in a nuthouse; you want quickly to report on the experience; partly, I think, to claim some points for yourself as having had the experience and partly to . . .

**PL:** Had you had that experience?

**GL:** Yes. Twice. And partly, too, I think, to punish those persons you feel were responsible for it. So I had written two such novels. Both of them were wretched but not unremarkably wretched. Both were taken for publication and I therefore withdrew them. Not out of any kind of high standard that suddenly occurred to me, but rather because I was fearful of disgracing my family. I withdrew both books—in one case, in galleys; paid back the money and that was that. Soon after, I took up the short story as an occupation. But that lasted not very long.

**PL:** You were around twenty-five now?

**GL:** Twenty-three, twenty-four, twenty-five, twenty-six; in there, I guess. I had a story that went out to the *Partisan Review*, a story whose title I will never forget. It was "Gasserpod, Gasserpod," which was a child's corruption of the word gastropod, I think it was. The *Partisan Review* held the story for an exceptionally long time. It may have been as long as two years, never responding to my letters. There must have been somewhere along the way that they gave me to believe that they were really, in fact, in possession of the story. Then, at the end of about three years, I got a letter from them rejecting the story. (great laughter) I felt so keenly wounded by that experience I did not try to write fiction again, of a kind that I would put my name to. I had, in fact, written fiction all through the years that I was at *Esquire*. I would write under other names.

**PL:** Was that for any reason?

**GL:** To put chicken and peas on the table. I had four kids and *Esquire*'s wages to me were of such . . .

**PL:** They didn't want you moonlighting?

**GL:** They didn't really know about this, but I don't think they would have interfered. I've always been someone who worked around the clock. I never deprived *Esquire* of any of my energies. I would arrive for work at seven in the morning and work until at least eight at night. In fact, we not infrequently were there until twelve midnight. It was a highly keen bunch of folks. We were all quite enthusiastic about it. No few of us still remember it as the best time of our lives, when we were engaged on the *Esquire* that was Harold Hayes' *Esquire*. It's become many different *Esquire*s since.

**PL:** You were fired?

**GL:** By Clay Felker.

**PL:** No, no; before that. Out of California. How did you end up at *Esquire*?

**GL:** Well, I was fired out of school-teaching, and was told I should go teach in university and I'd say that isn't what I want to do; that what I wanted to teach was high school, and I wanted to teach in the school my kids were going to be going to, and I wanted to live in the town I was living in then. And I sort of refused to take a university job. But I was around a lot of university people, and was working on a book on English syntax. I had a contract for two books on English grammar. I was putting out a literary magazine called *Genesis West*. It was being printed at a plant just south of San Francisco, and the man who headed up that plant said that he was printing a lot of material from an outfit called, I think it was, Sullivan Associates. And he thought this man, Sullivan, Maurice W. Sullivan, was the smartest man in the world. A man with two PHDs, three MAs, all that stuff, and he was much interested in the syntax of the language. The fellow thought I ought to get in touch with this Sullivan, that he and I would have common concerns and might hit it off, and I did. It was through Sullivan that I met a man who had been sort of Sullivan's teacher, or associate, and who headed up an outfit called the Behavioral Research Laboratories. At all events, BRL offered me a place

247

to work and called me the Director of Linguistic Studies.

**PL:** What is Behavioral Research Laboratories?

**GL:** A high-sounding name for a rather straightforward affair. It was a clutch of behavioral psychologists and me, who is not a behavioral psychologist, putting together the means to teach people more efficiently, more effectively, than anybody could teach them in the absence of such means—from telling time and tying shoelaces to taking apart a rather abstruse sentence in English. So that's what I was doing there. And it was in that period that I went from teaching to developing teaching mechanisms and I began to do some work for the government, and put together, for the Office of Economic Opportunity, something called *A Man's Work*, and then another something called *Why Work?* And these things gave me some fame as someone who knew how teaching could be done, how learning could take place. And that all was abruptly set aside when I left California and took the *Esquire* job. I took the *Esquire* job, thinking that I would not last very long at it because it meant being in New York, which I'd left many years earlier. I used to be a radio actor here and I'd left because I thought New York had become uninhabitable.

**PL:** Were you brought in as fiction editor?

**GL:** Brought in as fiction editor, took over from Rust Hills, had to process manuscripts at a terrific clip.

**PL:** How do you do that?

**GL:** You just do it. Well, I don't want to tell anybody how I do it. Let them assume I don't read, okay, I don't read. I just take them out of their envelopes, and put them in other envelopes. Well, say I'm a reliable looker, not a reader, but a reliable looker. And I find what I'm looking for. I cannot go easy to my bed at night knowing that the day's work has not been surmounted. So that I simply will stay at it and stay at it and stay at it, looking and looking until the day's looking is done.

**PL:** You have four fulltime jobs. You're editing this new magazine, *The Quarterly*—

**GL:** Yes.

**PL:** —you're teaching, an editor here at Knopf's and . . .

**GL:** And I write.

**PL:** How do you shift gears?

**GL:** I'm not so sure that that's really required because these activities tend to be continuous with one another. Certainly my editing and my teaching seem to me to draw on the same impulse. The only occasion requiring me to reset myself is when I come to the page as a writer. And that's because there's a certain arrogance in teaching and editing. However much one doesn't want to be, one is forced to make judgments of a kind that tend to objectify questions. Whereas the kinds of judgments one makes as a writer oughtn't to be all that objective. And I'm very inclined to be rather too clinical as a writer, rather too knowing in my approach to the text; rather too observing and too conscious of what the values are; what the structure is; how it might be made another. I know too much, is what I'm trying to say, and I'm inclined to believe it's desirable not to know so much. I'm inclined to become too clever on the page so that I end up speaking only to a certain form of attention in myself rather than to my whole heart. My short stories tend to be too intricate, too shrewd.

**PL:** That's it. I've read your stories and I expected you to be very different than you are.

**GL:** Yes. They tend to be very self-reflexive and . . .

**PL:** To me, you're not like your work.

**GL:** But, contrastedly, my novels, the ones, the two that I've signed my name to, I've written fifteen, twenty books under other names, when I was at *Esquire*, and made large sums of money from doing so; novels and non-fiction. The two novels I put my name to, and the one I'm working on now, represent rather different versions of myself. Come out of a deeper place in me. They are still as fraudulent because they arise out of some kind of exercise I do with myself. So they're also fraudulent; I'm of the opinion that in uncovering ourselves we simply set aside one fraudulence for another. But at the moment that we reveal the new layer beneath, I'm sure we're earnestly convinced that we've touched bone, revealed something authentic. But there is nothing authentic. It's just theater. Us the audience for ourselves or God the audience.

**PL:** Could you go over last night, what you were saying about the role of art and its importance? In your class you set such standards; you speak of art in a way that I've never heard.

**GL:** Art is a way to manage our death. I think we die more easily, or less horribly, to the extent that we have done our work. The crudest being is competent to summon for himself some kind of magic for managing his mortality. A bean, a pebble, he's got a magic pebble in his pocket. Even if it's only the pressure of his grasp on the hand of a friend that is sitting at his bedside. We all of us, I think, require magic to manage life. That's what art is—magic. What I try to do is to relieve my students of the notion that they can't stick out; to convince them that everything that is required for sticking out is present in them.

**PL:** So you screen them for will.

**GL:**Absolutely.

**PL:**How do they apply?

**GL:**No formal process. It's often by recommendation. Somebody else, they know someone . . .

**PL:** What if someone is reading this and says, Oh I want to do this workshop? I get it. They have to find their own way!

**GL:** They have to find a way. They have to come find me. (laughter) I'll give you an example of what will happen. Someone will call me up, say, "Gee, I read about your workshop, and I'd like to know if it would be possible to get in it." And I say, "Well, let's talk about that." And at the end of the conversation, I'll say, "Well, now I think it would be wise to sum up these remarks in a letter to me." So then they say, "Oh. Oh. You want a letter." And I say, "Yes, yes, I want a letter," and they'll say, "Well, where are you?" and I'll say, "Alfred Knopf," and they'll say, "Well, what's the address there?" "The address?" I say. "You want the address?"

**PL:** Just figure it out.

**GL:** Figure it out. Because, you see, it's not for whimsy, nor for caprice, that I take this position. I know that if they don't have the kind of resolve to persevere in the face of *that* small task, how in the world will they *ever ever ever* stand up to . . .

**PL:** To what happens next.

**GL:** To what happens next, exactly.

**PL:** Do you look at manuscripts at all?

**GL:** Oh, sure. But I don't take any of the writing that is put to me as a sample of ability quite as seriously as I do the person himself.

**PL:** When you talk about the lengths people go to, to be admitted, and then what they have to deal with in their lives to get here—you've had people move here, and take apartments . . .

**GL:** It's an enormous, enormous investment. I just had a fellow who wanted to move here for the term from Paris.

**PL:** Have you grown over the years?

**GL:** Every time I teach a class I am instructed by what is put on the table as much as is anybody in the class. Every time anybody else comes away with a deal of knowing, I come away with a deal of knowing, too. I have no hesitation to talk about other aspects of my life, but I've never really talked about my teaching. I used to let people record it because I would feel that (1) there ought to be a record and (2) if persons who were legitimate participants could not be present for a certain class, the tape could then be sent to them or be available to them. And I stopped doing that . . .

**PL:** But why?

**GL:** Because even the tape, out of the context of the class, seemed an eerie and inaccurate object.

# Interview with John Cheever
## John Callaway

J ohn Cheever — *long regarded by critics as an American Chekhov — earned many distinguished awards and prizes during his lifetime. He was the author of six story collections, four novels, and one novella.* The Stories of John Cheever *won the Pulitzer Prize, the National Book Critics Circle Award, and an American Book Award. He received the Howells Medal of the American Academy of Art and Letters for his novel* The Wapshot Scandal, *an O'Henry Award for his story "The Country Husband," and the National Book Award for his novel* The Wapshot Chronicle. *He also was presented the National Medal for Literature for his "distinguished and continuing contribution to American letters." His other novels and novella include* Bullet Park, Falconer, *and* Oh What a Paradise It Seems. *He died in 1982.*

*The following interview was aired nationally October 15, 1981, and was presented by the Public Broadcasting Service, and was a production of WTTW/Chicago.*

**Interviewer:** (on location in Quincy) John Cheever probably is not a household word in America. In an age of television, few writers are. But some of his critics regard him, because of his short stories and books like *The Wapshot Scandal* and *Bullet Park* and *Falconer*, as one of our greatest, if not our greatest, living writer, continuing the American literary tradition of James Fenimore Cooper, Herman Melville, Edgar Allan Poe. And so it may well be that when the images on the tube have faded to black, his work will live on and on.

John Cheever grew up on this block in Quincy in a big old Victorian structure that stood where this house now stands. He was born to a traditional New England family. They prized the virtues of practicality, reticence, privacy. It was almost a storybook childhood. But there's a darker side to John Cheever's memories. When he was thirteen years old, his father, who was a self-made businessman, lost all of his money. One night John heard his father engaged in a loud and violent argument with the local banker. And the next day, the Cheevers had to move. The house was torn down. And young John Cheever was never told why.

**Cheever:** After, shall we say, after thirteen, a great deal — a great many violent blows were dealt me or were dealt my family.

**Interviewer:** Your father went into bankruptcy?

**Cheever:** My father went into bankruptcy. My parents separated. My mother went into business. A great deal went wrong.

**Interviewer:** You came from a seafaring family — if you go back a couple of generations.

**Cheever:** I came from a family of seafaring men, yes. My grandfather sailed to China and Ceylon from Newburyport. And my great-grandfather, Benjamin Hale Cheever, was a well-known ship's master. My father simply sailed cat boats.

**Interviewer:** And what kind of business was he in?

**Cheever:** My father had a shoe factory in Lynn. Once a year I was taken and held up in the air, and there was a cord you pulled. And that was the twelve o'clock whistle. Everybody then took their sandwiches out of their paper bags. And that was my participation in the shoe industry.

**Interviewer:** Was the breakup of their marriage because of the economic circumstances that they faced? That was what — 1928, 1929, around in there?

**Cheever:** That I think contributed a great deal to it. Of course, well, it robbed him of his power. She opened a gift shop to support the family. And it made her immensely happy to find out that she could make money of her own. That she could purchase an automobile, for example, without consulting anyone, was for her an intoxicating experience. My sympathies all lay with him. And I worried terribly about what would happen to him. I was afraid that he would commit suicide. And presently the situation seemed to be insoluble. And I simply left.

**Interviewer:** Had your grandfather committed suicide?

**Cheever:** It is rumored that my grandfather had committed suicide. Well, I was drinking with my father one stormy—it was a northeaster. We were in one of the old houses in which we lived. And we had both drunk at least a pint of whiskey. And I thought, Well, under the circumstances I can ask about my grandfather. And I said, "Dad, would you tell me something about your father?" And he said, "No."

**Interviewer:** It's interesting. You've been quoted as saying that one of the aspects of your writing is that you can say things in your writing you cannot say to your sons.

**Cheever:** Yes, that's quite true. Well, I think of literature as an extremely intimate means of communication, involving sentiments, passions, regrets, and memories that simply don't belong in the spectrum of conversation.

**Interviewer:** It was later, wasn't it, that you came to understand your mother's pride in running her own gift shop and buying her own materials?

**Cheever:** It wasn't until I was in my late sixties that I finally understood this. My wife's poetry is being published this fall. And the joy that she has in having her own name on a book, rather than to find her husband's name on a book, has thrown a great deal of light on the pleasure my mother took in being able to buy a car of her own.

**Interviewer:** I mean, to be simplistic about it, this is partially what we talk about when we talk about liberation, is it not?

**Cheever:** It seems to me the only thing we talk about.

**Interviewer:** And so you were in your sixties when that caught up emotionally.

**Cheever:** When I finally understood my mother, yes. Well, she did damage my father. And my father's well-being was very much my concern.

**Interviewer:** When did he die?

**Cheever:** He died during the Second World War, sometime

257

in the forties.

**Interviewer:** Do you remember when you started to read the masters? The good stuff?

**Cheever:** Oh, I expect I was in my early adolescence. I remember the excitement of reading nineteenth century Russian novels when I was still in secondary school, which would have been when I was fifteen. The Garnett translations of Dostoevski were just coming out and that was very exciting.

**Interviewer:** But you wanted to write, didn't you, before you started that?

**Cheever:** I wanted to write. I think I decided to be a writer when I was about eleven. And these were in the days of absolute parental authority. I went to my parents and said, "I would like to be a writer." And they said, "Well, we will think that matter over." And they went into conference. And several days later they said, "We have decided that you may become a writer if that's what you intend. So long as you are not concerned either with fame or wealth." And I said, "I'm not concerned in any way with fame or wealth." And they said, "Very well, then. You may plan on becoming a writer."

**Interviewer:** And you even said many, many years later that you weren't a money player.

**Cheever:** I know very few writers who are, as a matter of fact, money players.

**Interviewer:** Doesn't go together, does it?

**Cheever:** It does from time to time, but very infrequently. Most of us have been offered, for example, opportunities in film and various other means of communication, that would be infinitely more profitable and secure than writing what we want to pursue. And almost all of the men I know would say, "No, thank you. It's nice of you to inform me, but no, thanks."

**Interviewer:** It's not the money per se that's the problem, is it? It's that it would distract you from what it is you need to do.

**Cheever:** It would rob us of that independence, which of course is imperative to literature. You must make your own decisions.

**Interviewer:** What is it in your life, that made you want to be a writer and to know that at the age of eleven?

**Cheever:** I think—I can't be counted on for the truth this late in my life, I think it was—I like to think it was—the fact that I found life immensely exciting. And the only way I had of comprehending it was in the form of storytelling.

**Interviewer:** What time do you write?

**Cheever:** I work in the mornings, which is by far the best time for me. And it seems to me that most of the serious writers I know work in the morning. The legend of the writer who began work at midnight, usually quite drunk, very often debauched, I think is an exploded legend. One works when one is most in command of one's intelligence and one's strength.

**Interviewer:** You did not get through Thayer Academy. What happened when you were sixteen?

**Cheever:** I was expelled. I was expelled presumably for smoking.

**Interviewer:** What do you mean, "presumably"?

**Cheever:** I believe I was expelled because I was an intractable student. I questioned teachers. Thayer Academy was a preparatory school. I was being prepared for Harvard. There wasn't any point in my remaining a student if I had no intention of going on to Harvard. I had no intention of going on to Harvard. The headmaster, Stacy Southworth, was an extremely understanding and a vastly intelligent man, and felt that he was simply wasting his time arguing with me. I chain-smoked out behind the tennis court, and so he expelled me. However, I did receive an honorary degree from Harvard. So it all worked out.

**Interviewer:** Have you ever gone back to Thayer?

**Cheever:** No. No, I've never been back to Thayer. I've been asked to go back for baccalaureates, but that's it.

**Interviewer:** Then did you go to New York or did you join your brother in Boston?

**Cheever:** I joined my brother in Boston, and we both then went abroad, and spent some time in Germany. We returned.

And then I left my brother in Boston and went on to New York.

**Interviewer:** And you lived on Hudson Street.

**Cheever:** I lived on lower Hudson Street, yes.

**Interviewer:** Did you by any chance live at 323 Hudson Street?

**Cheever:** It sounds very familiar.

**Interviewer:** The reason I ask is there is a guard in *Falconer* who says—late in the novel, "Well, I'm going home to 323 Hudson Street."

**Cheever:** Really?

**Interviewer:** Yes. He says, "I'm going home to 323 Hudson Street and drink some Southern Comfort." He's gonna drink a bottle of Southern Comfort, and if that isn't enough, he's gonna drink another bottle of Southern Comfort, and if that isn't enough, he's gonna drink another bottle of it.

**Cheever:** Well. That is a curious trick of memory. I expect it was 323 Hudson. I didn't know that.

**Interviewer:** What was life like there?

**Cheever:** On Hudson Street? It wasn't nearly as bad as one would have anticipated. This was during the Depression. There was a longshoremen's strike. I lived on the fourth floor which was the cheapest floor. Rooms were two dollars on the fourth floor. You went down to the third floor, the rooms were three dollars or two dollars and fifty cents, something like that. And it was full mostly of unemployed longshoremen. And with my accent, my gray flannel suit, and my blue button-down shirts, I was something of a curiosity. And they couldn't have been more helpful.

**Interviewer:** In what way?

**Cheever:** They wanted me to take some sort of an extension course. They wanted me to get into the government. They thought I could take an exam for post office work. They couldn't have been nicer. The thought of being locked up in the attic of a Hudson Street rooming house with a bunch of unemployed longshoremen does not in any way anticipate or describe their kindness, their wit, or their pleasantness.

260

**Interviewer:** And so here you started to write short stories?

**Cheever:** Yes. Yes.

**Interviewer:** Was it hard? Did it come easily? How was that experience?

**Cheever:** It's always been a great pleasure. And any pleasure, of course, is a matter of mixed ease and difficulty. It's always been an enormous pleasure.

**Interviewer:** When did you meet the woman you were to marry?

**Cheever:** I wasn't to meet her until, oh I believe, the year before the war.

**Interviewer:** 1940. How did you meet her?

**Cheever:** I met her on a rainy afternoon in an elevator. I can't remember the address—one of the buildings on Fifth Avenue. I'd spent a very pleasant summer working as a boatman and water skiing, which had just come in. And I saw a woman in the elevator. And I thought, "That's more or less what I would like." And went up and then she got off the elevator at the same floor. And she went into my literary agent's office. And I asked who she was. And I was told she was Mary Winternitz. And I asked her for a date. And presently married her.

**Interviewer:** You said about your marriage to Mary, "In forty years there's scarcely been a week in which we haven't planned to get a divorce." Why is that?

**Cheever:** I suppose it's because we're both uncommonly contrary people. However, considering the vast discussions of divorce that have gone on within the containment of our marriage, I'm enormously indebted to my wife for having shown me the melancholy as well as the pleasures of a marriage. Had it not been for her, I would never have known about certain degrees of loneliness and rejection. And also had it not been for her, I would never have known about many aspects of happiness—of sustained happiness. It has been, of course, the longest relationship I will ever have.

**Interviewer:** What is it you learned about loneliness that you learned through marriage? The other—melancholy, joy, all the rest of it. What about loneliness?

**Cheever:** Through feeling that one had failed as a husband, I expect, is probably one of the loneliest sensations I know.

**Interviewer:** Did you ever feel you weren't worthy of the —

**Cheever:** "Worthy" is not the word I would settle on. No, it's simply a question of not having made any money. That, in itself, is quite enough to go on.

**Interviewer:** You've never had a lot — I mean, I don't know what your condition now is, but you know what it is to be broke, don't you?

**Cheever:** Yes. I do, yes. I've been broke quite recently.

**Interviewer:** A lot of people think — well, John Cheever, *The New Yorker* — all those stories. All these books, the best seller list here and there. You were broke. I read something where you were broke as late as 1977.

**Cheever:** I think that was true, yes. I was broke when I was writing *Falconer*. I didn't have enough money to finish the book. And there was a question of a film option. They were going to pay twenty thousand on a film option. And I said, "Fine but you can't . . . " I had published one chapter in *Playboy*, that was it. And somebody wanted to option it for film for twenty (thousand). As soon as they found out I was stone-broke, they cut the option to ten. Ten would not have solved my problems. Ten would not have paid my debts. And I told them what they could do with ten and hung up, leaving myself with nothing. However, another studio, having heard that studio A was willing to put out twenty — they hadn't heard about the split yet, and they hadn't heard that I was broke — offered forty. So it all ended very happily, and I was able to finish the book, pay the debts, and, I don't know, buy another dog.

**Interviewer:** Okay. We're talking about ten, twenty, forty thousand dollars. And in the past three years we've read of advances of eight hundred thousand, a million-five; two and a third million.

**Cheever:** Well, there are paperback sales. But these paperback sales have nothing to do with the work I do, nor have they ever. This is to assume that the cloak and suit business, for example, is one simple business. To assume that publishing is one simple operation is a great mistake. One doesn't mind at all, for example, that a book like *Scruples* sells millions of copies. It satisfies a group of perfectly responsible citizens. And if one is number one or number two or number three on the best-seller list, you're usually cheek-by-jowl with a book that is basically banal and vulgar. It doesn't make any difference. The company you keep makes no difference. It's a question of being recognized by those people you enjoy.

**Interviewer:** (on location at Sing Sing) John Cheever came here to teach at Sing Sing prison — notorious Sing Sing on the Hudson River, in Ossining, New York, not far from where he lives. Cheever taught English composition to the prisoners for two years. He stopped when he had a heart attack, his second. But the experience here provided the context for his most celebrated novel, *Falconer*, published in 1977.

*Falconer* is about a college professor who's doing time for a crime of passion — the murder of his brother, but it's as much about the incarceration of the soul as the imprisonment of the body.

**Interviewer:** I felt that *Falconer* was a — not a departure from what you'd done in the past, but that it went beyond. That it was a —

**Cheever:** I'm glad you felt that way. A growth or extension, yes.

**Interviewer:** But even more than a growth. Growth isn't quite the right word. It was almost a leap of experience. John Leonard said — and I don't know quite what he meant. I have to get him on here some day and ask him — he said, the book, it seemed to him, was almost willed more than imagined. I felt that it was a huge leap from where you'd been, but totally tied to where you'd come from.

**Cheever:** Oh, I'm so pleased you felt that way. Of course, all the work has dealt with the mystery of confinement. And

*Falconer* brought confinement up to confinement in a jail. I was very pleased with the book. Leonard, I think, gave it one of the few bad reviews it received. But what sort of reception the book would have, the publisher didn't know, and the printing was quite small. Saul Bellow came out for the book very early, which made a tremendous difference. And then almost all the reviews at an international level—you know, Germany, Japan— were highly enthusiastic. The only country where the book has not been published, so far as I know, is Soviet Russia.

**Interviewer:** May be wise of them.

**Cheever:** Oh, it did very well in the underground I've been told.

**Interviewer:** I don't mean to tie the two directly, because I know there was more to it than your experience at Sing Sing. But how did you come to teach at Sing Sing?

**Cheever:** I had received something like five offers of good visiting professorships in the space of a month. And had thought quite seriously and quite mistakenly of myself as a teacher— perhaps I should show up at Yale or Princeton or Harvard. And then at a party someone said, "If you're thinking of teaching, Sing Sing has two thousand inmates and six instructors operating on a straight academic year." So I went down to the warden and said, "Well, look, you're short of teachers. I'd like to teach composition." And he said, "I don't think you do. Why don't you get out of here?" And I said, "Well, you damn well will take me as a teacher or I'll make a stink about this." So he took me on as a teacher.

**Interviewer:** You had to insist. I love it. So what happened?

**Cheever:** I taught there for two years.

**Interviewer:** How do you teach in a prison? What kind of a setting was it? Did they bring people into a hall?

**Cheever:** Everything in Sing Sing is relatively squalid. The first class—I think there were close to forty men came in to see what it was. And I told them it would be a course in writing—a course that would involve writing letters, for example. A course in telling stories. A course, if possible, in making sense of one's life by putting down one's experiences on a piece of paper. And there were enough people who were interested, who stayed with me, to make the course extremely interesting for me and, I think, for them. None of them published. However, a good many of them on parole would write me saying—that very often on parole, they are susceptible to every sort of temptation; that is, every criminal will try to get a man on parole, you know, for drugs or for any number of offenses. And by putting down what they did, who they met, and what they said in the course of a day, they were able to hold onto themselves in a degree that they hadn't enjoyed before.

**Interviewer:** I can't think of a group of people who might more need and want to make sense of their lives than somebody who's in confinement.

**Cheever:** Well, this seems, in many instances, to have worked with them. Keeping a journal, which is something I would insist on in any student, is something that several of them did. And by simply waking up in the morning and putting down, if necessary, the weather, the address of the house where they happen to be, and then carry on through the day, they were able to avoid immediately going into drug pushing or anything else of that sort.

**Interviewer:** How long have you kept journals?

**Cheever:** I have journals from the age of, I believe, twenty-two.

**Interviewer:** How do you use them?

**Cheever:** I use them infrequently these days, but there are aspects of—there is a freshness of experience that one loses. And I can find it if I go back into the journals. It's the excitement of a smell or a sound or of meeting someone who strikes one as being accomplished and exciting.

**Interviewer:** When you were teaching at Sing Sing, did you feel in any way that a prisoner was teaching prisoners? Did you feel any sense of confinement in your life?

**Cheever:** I felt a sameness there. But this, I believe, is simply my fondness for anything that strikes me as being heretical; that is, if the cons and I were lined up against a guard, well, I was all with the cons. It was very simply that. I don't take the stuffier aspects of organized society ceremoniously.

**Interviewer:** Yet you take the ceremony seriously enough to go to church?

**Cheever:** If I think it of first importance, of course. Well, then I do take ceremony seriously. But there is, I think in all of us, a glee, a good deal of pleasure in seeing a stuffed shirt exposed.

**Interviewer:** But when I talk about you as a prisoner communicating to prisoners, weren't you coming, by that time in your life, to terms with your own addictions or your own confinements?

**Cheever:** I shouldn't say so. No.

**Interviewer:** You weren't? Did you do that later?

**Cheever:** No. It wasn't until I'd left that teaching. I had a heart attack when I was teaching at Sing Sing. Which is why I stopped teaching. And it was as a result of the heart attack that I stopped drinking—which had been a great problem.

**Interviewer:** But then you started again, didn't you?

**Cheever:** Yes. I drank for another year. And then I had another heart attack and stopped for good.

**Interviewer:** How did you stop?

**Cheever:** Oh, I went to a rehabilitation clinic and I joined Alcoholics Anonymous.

**Interviewer:** Why did you stop?

**Cheever:** I would have killed myself otherwise. Also the brain damage was—the damage to my—because of the basic loss of dignity. I believe very strongly in the dignity of men and women. And this was a totally ignoble position.

**Interviewer:** Did it make a difference in your life? It seems to me it's made a difference in your writing.

**Cheever:** Well, yes. It made what I consider to be a splendid difference. There are people who consider me, now that I'm sober, to be much more of a boor than I ever was falling down. But they seem to be few.

266

**Interviewer:** In *Falconer*, one of the characters says, "I'm kind of excited about what's on the other side." He's ready to die, and he says, "I'm ready to die. And I'm looking forward to what's on the other side." Did you have any sense of that when you were dealing with this? People I know who've been alcoholic, and gone all the way to the bottom, have really faced their Maker, in effect, and said, "I don't want to quit yet. I gotta keep going." Did you have anything like that at all?

**Cheever:** No, I think not. I was certainly at the bottom. I was at totally self-destructive bottom. But with no commitment to see my Maker. What we are concerned with, of course, is living as intelligently as we can in the world in which we find ourselves.

**Interviewer:** Do you believe in a Hereafter?

**Cheever:** I've never asked myself that question. It seems to me quite incidental. I am concerned with making as much as I possibly can of the world in which I find myself. And I use the word "find." It's not a world into which I've strayed or a world in which I've entered. It's a world in which I was placed. And to make sense of it, to appreciate it, it seems to me, is a totally absorbing task.

**Interviewer:** The themes that you have written about—and I may be misusing the word "theme"—but I see in your writing a lot of light and sky and a lot of wonderful rain. Am I mistaken in that these are major strains somehow that come through your work?

**Cheever:** No. Light is of the greatest importance to me. And it seems to increase in its importance as I grow older. I dislike spending any time in dark cities these days. And the light of the sky, I seem to associate with virtue or with hopefulness. Rain—love the sound of rain. I come, as I say, from a seafaring family. I don't think my father ever planted a vegetable. I think he regarded people who planted things with absolute scorn. I do have a vegetable garden. And I seem to respond to the rain with the enthusiasm of an agricultural citizen. But I love light. And I do love the sound of the rain.

**Interviewer:** Isn't that beautiful country where you live?

**Cheever:** Yes, it is.

**Interviewer:** I'll never forget the first time I discovered that. I think that's where I want to go sometime.

**Cheever:** The Hudson Valley is one of the most beautiful places in the world.

**Interviewer:** I remember I came across from Long Island. I was going to Garrison, New York, and I discovered, not forty-five miles from New York City, the lushest densest forest. It was in the middle of July. And it had rained. And it was just lush and thick and primitive.

**Cheever:** As a matter of fact, much of it is Precambrian, very early. Laurel and rhododendron are Precambrian, and it's very very strong in the Hudson Valley.

**Interviewer:** I miss that very much.

**Cheever:** Well, it's there waiting for you to come back.

**Interviewer:** Somebody said, "Well, you're gonna talk with John Cheever. He must be reading these articles in the *New York Times Magazine* about how the suburbs ain't what they used to be. And ask him how he feels about that." And I said, "Well, I don't know if that really has anything to do, frankly, with what his work is." You're looked at as a suburban writer. But I don't see you as a suburban writer. I look at you as a writer — as far as I'm concerned — who could have been coming out of Tallahassee, Florida.

**Cheever:** Oh, I'm very pleased you feel that way. But I do understand being categorized. People categorize everything. It's simply a way of getting a handle on it or comprehending it. Well, I've been criticized — I've been confined by my knowledge of — You know, it doesn't matter.

**Interviewer:** But as a citizen — forget about your role as a writer — as a citizen, do you get that sense of profound change in the suburbs?

**Cheever:** The suburbs, as I understand them, have always been an improvisation. It was a way of life that started about fifty years ago when rentals in the city, when raising children in the city, became an impossibility—when schooling children in the city became an impossibility. It still is an improvisational way of life. It still is an invention. It doesn't cling to tradition.

**Interviewer:** One of the things I like about what you've done, and I talk about it a lot, is that young reporters will complain to me that, "Oh, my God, I got stuck with the zoning thing in the suburbs." I say to them, and I know I sound pious as hell, "You'll find the whole story, the whole human condition, can come out of that zoning hearing—greed, ambition, love, death, it's all there." And everybody says, "Get me back to city hall and Mayor Byrne! Don't stick me out in the suburbs." But isn't it all there?

**Cheever:** I think it is, yes. It seems to me there's more vitality, more change, in the suburbs than you find in urban life.

**Interviewer:** Talk to us, if you would, share with us—I think an English teacher I had called it the process of transmutation. You have this rich experience. It's used creatively in fiction. And yet it is not to be confused with crypto-autobiography. How does it work? What is and what isn't? Three-twenty-three Hudson Street? That's a fact. That relates to a factual part of your life.

**Cheever:** That was a memory. The process of writing is an employment of an area of memory that is marvelous and that is not yet understood. When one tells a story, one tells it to no particular reader. The marvelous thing about writing and storytelling is that the book-buying public is one public that completely escapes any computer analysis. No one knows who the intelligent, who the mature reader is. And yet they are there, and they are there by millions. And they would much sooner read a good book than sit through a bad television show or a bad movie or get stoned in a bad disco.

So it's operating in an area of memory that I know really very little about, that is disciplined to tell a story to someone whom I don't know. And yet if it is successful, whoever it is—it could be someone in Israel, or someone in Japan—will write me a letter and say, "Oh, but that story was just what I wanted to read on that particular rainy afternoon." And this, of course, is the enormous pleasure of writing. And I, as a reader, of course, recognize the same thing. Certainly to read a book that strikes me as a clarification—a book that makes me feel that life is full of promise—that not only the present, not only the moment, but also the past is bewilderingly beautiful—is a terrific experience. And of course, when you realize that most American fiction is translated into eight or ten languages, you realize that the audience is international.

**Interviewer:** Do you agree with John Gardner that the writer has to be connected up to a moral vision?

**Cheever:** Well, that's an interesting question. But literature is basically an account of aspiration or hopefulness. I have described it as our only coherent and consistent, continuous, history of man's struggle to be illustrious. We have a literature of the decadents. But it is pretty much confined to the end of Rome and to nineteenth century France. Very little of our great literature is self-consciously decadent. Most of it is a question involving, in one way or another, human greatness or the possibility of human greatness and dignity. Most of it involves the mystery, of course, of love and death.

**Interviewer:** At the end of *Falconer*, Farragut gets out. And he gets out through death. He could be picked up two minutes later, but he's really free in a new sense, isn't he? Isn't he self-possessed, almost?

**Cheever:** Yes. He's quite free as far as I'm concerned. Of course, you don't know what happens to him after that. But I felt that was none of my damn business. I knew that he was out. And it closes on the word "rejoice"—Rejoice, which I very much enjoy reading in the various translations. Except in the Japanese, which I can't pronounce.

**Interviewer:** When you came to terms then with your addictions, because you were also—weren't you popping pills with the drinking?

**Cheever:** I was, yes. Certainly.

**Interviewer:** When you came to terms with that, and after this book, if I said to you, "Let's get on a plane this afternoon and let's go back to Boston and let's go back to Symphony Hall," would you be comfortable with that?

**Cheever:** I think not. I think Symphony Hall is a part of the world that I can avoid for the rest of my natural life without any great loss. I was in Boston last week. I walked from the Public Garden to the museum and back again. My son, Ben, ran in the Marathon last week.

**Interviewer:** Ben—who's an editor at *Reader's Digest*?

**Cheever:** Right. Did the Boston Marathon in two hours and forty-six minutes. Which is very good time. And I don't see any reason to worry about Boston. It is a part of the world in which I came of age in a very troubled way. And there are still memories there that disconcert me. Also, the sense of the past in Boston is very strong. There are a great many Cheevers buried on Copp's Hill. My father took me up and showed me the Cheever graveyards. What I do remember about the family, and about Boston, is that Ezekiel Cheever established the first school in Massachusetts, the first school in the New World. And that on his death it was said, "Here lies Ezekiel Cheever. The welfare of the Commonwealth was always upon his conscience, and he abominated periwigs."

**Interviewer:** How do you feel about what you're doing—what you've been doing with public television?

**Cheever:** It was not I who did the adaptations. They were done without me. I did an original which is yet to be produced. Public television came to me and said, "Would you do three stories?" And I said, "No."

**Interviewer:** What do you think about what was done with them?

**Cheever:** I don't enjoy adaptations of any sort. Prose is meant to go where a camera cannot penetrate. One is writing in an altogether different voice than camera work. A prime example of something that cannot be photographed is *The Great Gatsby*, which I think has been made into at least three or four films.

You simply cannot photograph a good novel because the novelist intended that you shouldn't be able to photograph it. If he had wanted to write a screenplay, he would have.

**Interviewer:** You can do a nice job with a limited piece of writing. You take *The Day of the Jackal*, which is a kind of nice story. It's not literature, but it's a nice action thing. And it's kind of flat. It doesn't have much depth. And it really works nicely. And it's—movies are kind of surfacey.

**Cheever:** Yes. There was a dreadful novel called *Poldark*, or something like that, which made a marvelous television series. If it's really very very bad, then you can do anything with it. You have your principal characters. You have changes of scenery and so forth. Then you can just run with the ball. But if you really get a good book like *Gatsby*—or it seems to me that most of the work of any of my colleagues—John Updike's works simply will not photograph, nor will Saul Bellow's. You can't do anything with Saul's work.

**Interviewer:** What do you read?

**Cheever:** I read most contemporary serious novels. I very much enjoyed this year Tom Wolfe's book, *The Right Stuff*. I very much enjoyed Barbara Tuchman's *A Distant Mirror*—was it—the fourteenth century? Oh, there was a new history of the American Revolution by Page Smith which I very much enjoyed, and I've read most of the novels that claim to be serious.

**Interviewer:** Do you read mysteries or anything like that, ever?

**Cheever:** I'm extremely fond of mysteries, yes. And I think Le Carré is first-rate. Although I do feel that he's never done anything quite as good as *The Spy Who Came In From the Cold*. I've read all of Le Carré.

**Interviewer:** Do you have demands made on you by aspiring writers—"Please read my manuscript"?

**Cheever:** Yes. My mailbox is full of manuscripts. And I spend a great deal of time taking them to the post office and mailing them back. I cannot read, of course, unsolicited manuscripts. I've been on various grants committees. One is, of course, at my age, asked to judge manuscripts for prizes. And the obligatory reading one does can be overwhelming. It isn't that one lacks the time. It is that one lacks the discernment. There is an hour, two-fifteen, sometimes three-thirty, when one is no longer discerning about the value of a manuscript. And it's absurd to go on reading.

**Interviewer:** What would you say to the person who considers him or herself a short story writer, but who looks around and says, "My God, Updike, or Cheever, or the great writers have got *The New Yorker* sewed up for the next ten or fifteen years! I'll never be able to break in there! And there's not much left, except the *Atlantic*, and it just seems hopeless." Would you say, "Keep writing," or what?

**Cheever:** I would say, number one, that was a display of damn foolishness. Anyone who reached that conclusion, I don't think, would have the intelligence to be a writer. Updike and I, of course, have no corner on any market. To the contrary, we're both extremely hospitable, and we'd do everything we possibly could if we thought a good writer was coming along.

**Interviewer:** But the markets aren't there, are they?

**Cheever:** The markets are not there. But the success of my collection, I think, does imply that there is a market for a short story, for a good short story.

**Interviewer:** When did you first write for *The New Yorker*?

**Cheever:** I think my first story in *The New Yorker* came out when I was twenty-one or twenty-three.

**Interviewer:** So that would have been in the 1933-1934 area?
**Cheever:** Yes.

**Interviewer:** Harold Ross had had the magazine what, six, seven years?

**Cheever:** Yes. It was very much his magazine.

**Interviewer:** Did you have much of an association with him or did you just send it in through the mail?

**Cheever:** The first story of mine was sent to *The New Yorker* by Malcolm Cowley. It was sent to Katharine White, who was Ross's associate and partner. I did see Ross. I didn't know Ross intimately. But I lunched with him, you know, a few times a year. Ross was an eccentric. He used to clean his ears a lot. He used to tuck his shirt tails inside of his underwear so that a broad band of underwear, showing something like green dice, could be seen. He used to use strong language at lunch—I think principally because he knew it would make me jump, as it did. And he was, as far as I could see, a genius. He used to say, "Goddamnit, why do you write those gloomy stories?" And he would buy a story, and hold it for three years, four years, and then he would run it. And it would be an enormous success. This used to bewilder him. But he continued to do it.

**Interviewer:** Now do they still do that? Will they take a story—?

**Cheever:** I think not, no. No writer would put up with that anymore. We were quite patient. Also we were economically absolutely dependent on Ross. Ross held a story of mine called "Pot of Gold" for four years. And then when it ran, it was an enormous success. It was much more successful than a series of funny jokes, which he thought readers wanted. And he would say, "Goddamnit, why the hell are them gloomy stories successful?"

**Interviewer:** I love that magazine, and yet there's a side of me that says—well, they, with their standards about how they handle language which seems rough, they could have never published *Falconer*.

**Cheever:** It doesn't seem to me to make much difference one way or another. My editor there did read *Falconer*. And wrote a very, very understanding note saying, "You do understand of course that we can't publish this, but you also understand how enthusiastic I am about the book."

**Interviewer:** Is that okay that *The New Yorker*'s prudish that way? Should we hope that one day somebody else will come in and say, "We want Norman Mailer's toughest stuff, and we want *Falconer*"?

**Cheever:** I think not, no. Magazines, very like people, are confined within their own characteristics. And you cannot be a universal magazine, any more than you can be a universal man. You have ways of walking and talking and tastes in clothes and food and sex and so forth. Universality, it seems to me, escapes all of us.

**Interviewer:** Are awards important to you?

**Cheever:** Awards, as far as I'm concerned, mean the esteem and very often the affection of strangers. And the esteem and the affection of strangers is something I very much enjoy.

**Interviewer:** How much mail do you get?

**Cheever:** It depends entirely on the amount of publicity. For example, if you've been on a television show, and it is understood that you answer your own mail, I will sometimes get one hundred letters a week. I very much enjoy my fan mail.

**Interviewer:** What do people say to you?

**Cheever:** They are usually extremely discreet. They realize that they cannot involve you in a lengthy conversation. They very often say that they've enjoyed a story, or they have enjoyed a paragraph in a story. They've enjoyed a novel. I have received very few unfriendly letters. I did receive a letter from a woman who had bought *Falconer* and thought it was disgusting and tried to burn it. She went into some length about how she had tried to burn the complete book, and it would not ignite. And then she had tried to burn the book by taking off the jacket. And it was only by tearing the book in little pieces was she able to ignite it. And then she bought the collection two years later and wrote a letter saying, "I am terribly sorry. I am the woman who burned *Falconer*—and please accept my apologies."

**Interviewer:** That's wonderful. Do you read your critics?

**Cheever:** It was very nice. Yes, with pleasure.

**Interviewer:** Even when they—

**Cheever:** Well, the assumption, of course, is that one is far from perfect. Their intent is to express their vision of what literature should be. And if this happens to be sympathetic, I'm very anxious to see where they think I've failed.

**Interviewer:** Have you ever learned from a critic?

**Cheever:** Yes, I should say I have. If I've disappointed a man whose judgment I esteem, I certainly will go back over my work and see how I could possibly have improved.

**Interviewer:** How do you feel about this controversy over the National Book Awards, and that they've gone commercial?

**Cheever:** I haven't informed myself on the matter at all because it seemed to me that if you mix commercialism with publishing, of course you're totally lost. The wonderful thing about writing, and the wonderful thing about reading and publishing, is that it is not angled for the maximum profit. It has absolutely nothing to do with merchandising, or very little. People write books because they feel they have something to say. People buy books because they feel that something may be within the book that they want to hear, or that will help them live more happily or more usefully, or more beautifully. And publishers work as an intermediary between the reader and the writer. And commercialism has no place in this — or very little.

**Interviewer:** Talking about commercialism, how did you get involved with the Rolex ads? I saw your — it's a wonderful ad. It's a lovely ad — in *The New Yorker,* in April.

**Cheever:** They asked me if I wanted a gold watch. And I said I certainly did. And then I said, "Well, what do I have to do?" And they said, "All you have to do is to go in town and be sketched." So I said, "Great." So I went into town, to an advertising agency in New York, and somebody drew a picture of me, and I got a gold watch.

**Interviewer:** How do you feel about your daughter, Susan, turning novelist?

**Cheever:** Oh, I'm very happy about Susie's career. I'm very happy about her success. I'm happy about it in that she's not felt that being the daughter of a writer is something she ought to be ashamed of. I'm very happy that she hasn't taken up a career, for example, as an opera singer. I'm very glad that she's not taking a couple of years off waiting on tables at Aspen to find herself. She knows damn well who she is. She knows damn well what she wants to do. I'm very gratified and pleased with the whole thing. And the book has been very successful.

**Interviewer:** *Looking for Work.*

**Cheever:** *Looking for Work.* Yes.

**Interviewer:** What did you think of it?

**Cheever:** I thought it was—well, I was delighted, of course, to find out that it was not, as far as I was concerned, a crypto-autobiography. Her father is described as a man who rides with a Myopia Hunt, a North Shore Hunt, and parts his white hair in the middle. This is, I think, not a photographic description of what her father is like.

**Interviewer:** What do you think of your wife's poetry?

**Cheever:** I think my wife's poetry is first-rate and I'm delighted that her book is being published.

**Interviewer:** What does she write about? What can we anticipate?

**Cheever:** Oh, she writes about men, women, children, dogs, landscapes. She writes about her children. There are poems to all three children. Oh, she writes about the Hudson Valley, which she very much enjoys. She writes not at all, as far as I can figure out, about her husband.

**Interviewer:** Do you read her material as an editor, or do you just read it as her—?

**Cheever:** I read it as a colleague. I read it as a man who knows her. I don't read it as a husband.

**Interviewer:** Is there still as much give and take in that marriage as there was earlier? Is there a different sense of it now?

**Cheever:** No. No, the elasticity is in no way diminished.

**Interviewer:** Do you have any advice for anybody about marriage—love?

**Cheever:** My sons from time to time come to me for advice. And what I convey to them, I think, is that I am perhaps more bewildered than they. But it is not a sorrowful bewilderment. It's rather an exciting sense of confusion.

**Interviewer:** I haven't asked you about politics, and I won't. But a lot of us feel a sense of political gloom, and a lot of problems that don't seem to be easy to resolve. Could you sum up—how you feel about this civilization, where we are?

**Cheever:** I think civilization where we are is not in any way a melancholy situation. And as far as the political gloom goes, the president of Bulgaria is an acquaintance of mine. And when I returned to Bulgaria last summer, I said how pleasant it was to be back in his great country. And he said, "Isn't it a great country? I've been president for twenty-three years." And whenever anybody objects to the confusion of the American presidential election, I always think of my Bulgarian friend and his simplified twenty-three-year presidency.

**Interviewer:** Thank you.

# Biographical Notes

## About the editors:

**Anne Brashler** has published poetry and fiction in fifty-plus publications, including *The Ohio Review*, *New Letters*, *The Literary Review*, and *Confrontation*. She has also served as Writer-in-Residence for the Illinois Arts Council. *Getting Jesus in the Mood* is her story collection. She has a book of poetry, *Talking Poems*, and is currently completing her novel.

**Melissa Pritchard**'s fiction has appeared in numerous magazines, including *The Kenyon Review*, *Epoch*, *The Ontario Review*, and *Story Magazine*. Her story, "A Private Landscape," was included in *Prize Stories: The O'Henry Awards*. Pritchard's *Spirit Seizures* won the Flannery O'Connor Award for Short Fiction, and the Carl Sandburg Literary Arts Award, in addition to an honorary citation from the PEN/Nelson Algren Award for several of the stories. She has completed a novel, *Phoenix*, and is at work on a second story collection.

**Diane Williams** is a frequent contributor to many magazines including *Conjunctions*, *The Quarterly*, *The Ohio Review*, *Epoch*, and *Agni*. Her collection of stories, *This Is About the Body, the Mind, the Soul, the World, Time, and Fate*, appeared in January 1990, published by Grove Weidenfeld.

## About the authors:

**Ann Beattie**'s new novel, *Picturing Will*, is out from Random House. She currently lives in Charlottesville, Virginia.

**Janet Burroway**'s novels include *Raw Silk* and *Opening Night*. She is now at work on her seventh novel, *Cutting Stone,* and a third edition of her textbook, *Writing Fiction*. She is a professor of English Literature at Florida State University.

**John D. Callaway**, senior correspondent for Chicago's public television station, is currently the host of WTTW's Emmy-award-winning "Chicago Tonight with John Callaway." He has received more than sixty broadcast journalism awards, including seven Emmys, and the George Foster Peabody Award.

**Daniel Curley** had a long and wonderful career as a writer and as editor of *Ascent*. His latest book, *Mummy*, was published by Houghton Mifflin. His short story collections include *Living With Snakes* and *Love in the Winter*.

**Ann Darby**'s stories have appeared in *Northwest Review* and *Blue Light, Red Light*, as well as in *StoryQuarterly*. She teaches composition at Columbia University, where she received the Bennett Cerf Prize for Fiction in 1985. She was coeditor for fiction for *Columbia*, Volume 14.

**Stephen Dixon** is the author of seven collections of stories. His most recent story collection, *Love and Will*, appeared last fall (British American Publishing). Of his four novels, the most recent, *Garbage*, was published in 1988 by Cane Hill Press. Dixon teaches at Johns Hopkins University.

**Maya Friedler** produced and moderated weekly public affairs forums with a women's perspective, through WBEZ, a National Public Radio station. She has served as Chair of the Piven Theatre Workshop, the Roslyn Group for Arts and Letters, and the Loop YWCA Board of Directors. She is a founding member of the Jane Addams conference, and Chair of the Chicago Board of Directors.

**Thomas Grimes**'s novel, *A Stone of the Heart*, was published by Four Walls Eight Windows in 1989. Grimes, currently working on a novel entitled *Love and Death in the American Novel*, is teaching at the Iowa Workshop through 1991.

**Glyn Hughes**, born in Cheshire, England in 1935, has written poetry, novels, radio and television plays, and journalism. His novel, *Where I Used to Play on the Green*, received both the Guardian Prize for Fiction and the David Higham Prize for Fiction in 1982. Since that time he has completed two more novels, part of a trilogy entitled *Hawthorn Goddess*, and *The Rape of the Rose*.

**Patricia Lear** has published interviews with Mary Robison, Amy Hempel, Gordon Lish, Ann Beattie, Mona Simpson, James Purdy, and Mark Richard. Her fiction will appear in *The Quarterly*, and she has a collection of short stories scheduled for publication with Alfred A. Knopf.

**Gordon Lish** has published three novels and two collections of short stories. His most recent work of fiction is *Extravaganza*, a novel published by G.P. Putnam's Sons. He is also the editor of *The Quarterly* and an editor at Alfred A. Knopf. He teaches fiction writing in Manhattan.

**Yannick Murphy**'s collection of short stories, *Stories in Another Language*, was published in 1987 by Alfred A. Knopf. Her recent work has appeared in *The Quarterly* and *Conjunctions*.

**G.E. Murray** is a poetry editor for *Chicago* magazine and *The Chicago Tribune*. He has published poetry and criticism in over eighty magazines. His poems, *Repairs*, published by the University of Missouri Press, won the Devins Award for 1980.

**Lowri Pei** is Director of Writing at Simmons College in Boston and author of the novel *Family Resemblances*. His story, "The Cold Room," appeared in *The Best American Short Stories*, 1984.

**Donna Poydinecz** lives in New York City and is writing a screen play.

**Leon Rooke** has published over two hundred stories in a variety of North American magazines. His latest novel is *A Good Baby*, 1989.

**Chris Spain** is running and writing in Palo Alto, California.

**Kathleen Spivack**'s collection of stories, *The Honeymoon*, was published by Graywolf Press. She has also published four volumes of poetry. Her most recent book of poetry, *The Beds We Lie In*, was a Pulitzer Prize nominee. Her work has appeared in more than three hundred magazines and anthologies world-wide. Spivack also directs the Advanced Writing Workshop in Cambridge, Massachusetts.

**Linda Svendsen**'s collecton of stories is to be published by Farrar, Straus & Giroux. Her work has appeared in *The New Generation* (Doubleday), *Best Canadian Stories, 1987,* and *The Contemporary Atlantic, Short Stories: The Best of the Decade.*

**Mara Anne Tapp** is a former editor of *Chicago Review.*

**Art Winslow** is associate literary editor for *The Nation.*

**Judith Wolff** is in law school at Boston University. She wishes she had more time to write.